Anita Desai's *In Custody*

A Critical Appraisal

Neeru Tandon

ATLANTIC

PUBLISHERS & DISTRIBUTORS (P) LTD

Published by

ATLANTIC

PUBLISHERS & DISTRIBUTORS (P) LTD

7/22, Ansari Road, Darya Ganj,
New Delhi-110002
Phones : +91-11-40775252, 23273880, 23275880, 23280451
Fax : +91-11-23285873
Web : www.atlanticbooks.com
E-mail : orders@atlanticbooks.com

Branch Office
5, Nallathambi Street, Wallajah Road,
Chennai-600002
Phones : +91-44-64611085, 32413319
E-mail : chennai@atlanticbooks.com

Printed in India at Glorious Printers, A-13, D.S.I.D.C., Jhilmil Industrial Area, Delhi-110095

Preface

> Creation is only the projection into form of that which already exists.
>
> —*Srimad Bhagavatam*

When Booker Prize winner novelist Kiran Desai dedicated her book *The Inheritance of Loss* to her mother Anita Desai saying that "the debt I owe to my mother is so profound that I feel the book is hers as much as mine", she in a remarkable act of literary filial devotion began the task of turning her mother into almost a joint Booker winner. Once again the world started thinking and talking about Anita Desai and her fictional world. Anita Desai who wrote primarily about the functioning of the human psyche in a subtle and inimitable style is known for the symbolic, sensitive and psychological fiction.

Senior Desai's novels being nominated for the Booker Prize three times further consolidated her international acceptance and reputation, showcasing her immense dexterity in handling complex interrelationships and probing deep into the psyche of her characters. The painstakingly perfected chiseling is perhaps the secret of her four decades long success. As a child, Desai used to speak German at home and Hindi, Bengali or Urdu outside, while learning English in school. Also shortlisted for the Booker, her 1984 novel, *In Custody* is a profound commentary on the many meanings and colours of language as it unfolds through life and art.

In Custody is woven around the life of Deven, a mild-mannered professor who seems to interview Nur, the greatest living Urdu poet of the generation. The old Nur seems to suggest the fall from glory of Urdu, the mellifluous language of great poets, and thus the history of a language emerges as the subtext of the novel. Desai's courageous attempt to render one language through another—in that case, Urdu through English—becomes a metaphor of inter-cultural translations:

> Indeed in this novel as in others, she also tries to translate, from an Indian language into English without falling into the dangerous trap of reducing serious characters into caricatures or stereotypes.

In Custody presents Desai's ironic story about literary traditions and academic illusions. Nur, an Urdu poet, is in the grip of tough situation, and Deven, a professor of Hindi, realizes that the beloved poet is not the magical genius of his imagination.

In Custody was turned into a beautiful—albeit too colourful for Desai's liking—film by Ismail Merchant in 1993. The Film *Muhafiz* won the 1994 President of India Gold Medal for Best Picture, and stars the noted actors Shashi Kapoor, Shabana Azmi and Om Puri.

In this critical re-appraisal of the novel I have tried to focus on factors like expectation and experience, fantasy and actuality, illusion and reality, poetry and the poet, art and life, etc. in a very simple way. I have also discussed the problem of alienation of an educated young college teacher from his own roots and culture along with existentialism, irony, problem of love and marriage, language controversy, imagery, nature portrayal, etc. Various other textual issues are discussed in the form of subjective and objective question-answers. The emphasis throughout has been on clarification and evaluation while the treatment is comprehensive and elaborate. It in no way precludes a study of the original text which is essential for a proper and genuine understanding. The book will be useful to students, teachers and researchers of English literature, especially Indian English literature. I am grateful to Atlantic Publishers and Distributors (P) Ltd, for the keen interest they have taken, and the co-operation they have extended to me in publishing this book.

Neeru Tandon

Contents

1

A Short History of Indian English Novel

It is a matter of common knowledge that the term 'Indo-Anglian Literature' was first used in a book published in Calcutta in 1883; with this title. The term became popular and confirmed when Dr. K.R. Srinivasa Iyenger published his books with the term in mind and V.K. Gokak published the *Golden Treasury of Indo-Anglian Poetry*.

Indian English fiction grew out of Indian soil through translation from literature into provincial languages, though the influence of foreign classics cannot all the same be denied. In the earlier days, the vernacular fiction writers like Tagore and Bankim Chandra Chatterjee often translated their own works from the regional language (Bengali) into English. These translated novels later inspired the writers to write short stories and novels originally in English. Indian English fiction is a major part of overall Indian literature as it is based on Indian themes, problems, mainly social and economic and Indian culture. This is proved by two Indian female Booker Prize winners; Arundhati Roy (*The God of Small Things*—depicts the life in Kerala) and Kiran Desai (*Inheritance of Loss*—depicts the life in the hills of Kanchenjunga).

The stage for novel writing or longer fiction was set by sketches, memoirs and short fiction. It is important to know those who tried the best to set the background for Indian English fiction. Dean Mohamed (1795-1851) has lately been discovered to have the greatest claims to have been the first

Indian writer in English with his travelogue laying claim to be the first published Indian English text. But usually the credit for this has been given to Cavelly Venkata Boriah (1776-1803) whose *Account of the Jains*, written in 1803, was published in 1809. But the first Indian prose writer of note in English is Raja Rammohan Roy (1772-1833). M.K. Naik regards his essay "A Defense of Hindu Theism" (1817) as the "first original publication of significance in Indian English Literature".[1]

If Raja Rammohan Roy is well-known as a social reformer for his essays as well as his belief in and advocacy of English as a tool to eradicate the ills of Hindu society. There were some other prose writers in the middle and later years of the 19th century too. Some of the writers like Krishna Mohan Banerji (1813-85) and Ram Gopal Ghose (1815-68) were early beneficiaries of English education. Both were students of Henry Derozio, the famous poet. Ram Gopal Ghose was also known as an orator. Expectedly many of the pieces are about social reform and more than a few are journalistic pieces or treatises. As in the case of other Indian languages, it was the establishment of journals and magazines and newspapers that contributed to the development of Indian English prose.

In western India, one of the major essayists was Behramji Malabari (1853-1912). Malabari was also a poet but here we are interested in his role as one of the pioneers of Indian journalism. Malabari wrote periodical essays in the style of Addison and Steele. His essays were collected in two volumes, *Gujarat and Gujaratis* (1882), and *The Indian Eye on English Life* (1895). His style and humour make him an essayist of a high calibre. He too was a social reformer with a steady eye. Nagesh Vishwanath Pai (1860-1920) was Malabari's contemporary and equal in prose writing. *His Stray Sketches from Chakmakpore* (1894) is a collection of character sketches drawn from different strata of society. According to Ramamurti, Chakmakpore is the forerunner of Narayan's Malgudi.

"A Journal of 48 Hours of the Year 1945" by Kailash Chunder Dutt was published in *The Calcutta Literary Gazette*

(6th June 1835). This is the tale of an unsuccessful revolt against the British. This piece of literary fantasy once again underlines how Indian English literature (think also of Henry Derozio's poetry) was nationalistic in nature from the very beginning. Or to put it differently, Indian English literature felt the need to distance itself from any sense of complicity in British rule. Writing in English perforce, meant critiquing the English as well as the local Indian reality.

Shoshee Chunder Dutt (1825-86) was a Justice of Peace (JP) and a Rai Bahadur. His short novel, "The Republic of Orissa: Annals from the Pages of the Twentieth Century", was published in the *Saturday Evening Hurkaru* on 25th May, 1845. The action in this takes place in the second decade of the twentieth century. The British are defeated and a republic is established in Orissa. Once again English is used against the English.

As a matter of fact, the famous Bengali novelist, Bankim Chandra (1838-94), wrote his first novel in English. This was *Rajmohan's Wife*, which was serialised as "Wife" in the Calcutta Weekly, *The Indian Field*, in 1864. This was published in book form only in the 1930s, and republished in 1990s. Bankim was much influenced by the English novelists that he had read, Sir Walter Scott and Charles Dickens in particular. *Rajmohan's Wife*, like his Bengali novels, deals with social issues of the day. In a sense, the main agenda of the Indian English novel was set in this first attempt itself. *Rajmohan's Wife* is about the effects of a bad marriage on the woman. The sufferings of a middle class housewife, Matangini at the hands of her husband, Rajmohan, in rural East Bengal forms the subject of the novel. This was the time of social reforms and it shouldn't surprise us that the first Indian English novel isn't a historical romance as has been suggested sometimes but a social novel. Bankim may not have written another novel in English but his Bengali novels were to influence the course of novels in India.

The second Indian English novel of note is also by a Bengali. Lal Behari Dey published *Govinda Samanta, or the History of a Bengal Raiyut* in 1874. The novel is set in

Burdwan district in mid-nineteenth century. The author's intention in his own prefatory words is to furnish "a plain and unvarnished tale of a plain peasant living in the plain country of Bengal." This novel is a family saga, which relates the life and times of Govinda Samanta, from his birth till death. We see the trials and vicissitudes of his extended family. The novel is said to have won a prize offered in 1871 for the best novel in Bengali or English illustrating the "Social and Domestic Life of the Rural Population and Working Classes of Bengal." What it therefore achieves and introduces into the Indian English novel is a high level of realism.

Lal Behari Dey was aware of the challenges of portraying Indian reality in the English language. How would you have Bengali peasants speak in English? Day, like R.K. Narayan later, makes his peasants speak in 'good' English. He realizes that his characters speak 'better' English than English peasants but as he says if he had made them speak in some kind of rural English dialect, "I should have turned them into English and not Bengali peasants." He writes elsewhere of cultural differences and like all Indian English writers deliberately cross pollinates the English language with Indián cultural markers. The challenge of the medium was best articulated more than sixty years later by Raja Rao in his famous "foreword" to *Kanthapura*.

Most of the writers named so far are from eastern India. This is after all a short introduction and can name only a few selected writers. But even so, the early writers in English all came from areas which had the greatest British influence, namely the Bengal region, the western coast, and the south.

Toru Dutt (1856-77) is better known as a poet. But she may very well be considered as the first woman novelist in Indian English, and perhaps the first Indian novelist in French. Her unfinished English novel, *Bianca or The Young Spanish Maiden*, was published in Calcutta in 1878. This is a romantic love story set in England. Malashri Lai believes that Toru Dutt couldn't finish this novel because it was autobiographical and "mirrored the turbulence in her young life" and that she was critiquing people close to her in it. Critics have felt it a great pity that the novel is incomplete, as K.S. Ramamurti puts it, if the novel had been completed, "it would have given us not only the first good Indian novel in English but a beautiful model for the Indian writers of English fiction, if not in terms of content, at least in terms of a natural graceful style." Because her setting is English and even the Spanish characters are settled in England, Toru Dutt did not face the usual challenges of the Indian English writer. Thus, she could exhibit her felicity in the language, which makes for good reading, as Ramamurti points out.

Mention must be made here of another woman writer, Krupabai Satthianandhan (1862-94). She was one of the earliest women medical students but unfortunately her health did not permit her to complete her education. She lived with her husband in Ooty and later Madras (now Chennai). She wrote for the *South Indian Observer* and the *National Indian Journal*. What she is known for, are her two novels. Both were published in the Journal of Madras Christian College. They were published in book form after her death. Both *Kamala: A Story of Hindu Life* (1894), and *Saguna: A Story of Native Christian Life* (1895) are autobiographical in nature. *Saguna* is about her earlier years and depicts the transformation of a Hindu Brahmin family into a Christian household. *Saguna* is set in present-day Maharashtra and Gujarat where Krupabai grew up. *Kamala* was written after the loss of her child and is about her sorrows and conflicts. Both these novels have been reprinted recently.

The impact of colonialism can be seen not only in the use of a new language to write in but also in concerns of the writers—from reform and defense of Hinduism and/or a new construction of India, to the depiction and sometimes celebration of conversion to Christianity. This is even more apparent in the genre of poetry.

While on the subject of women novelists, we must not ignore Shevantibai Nikambe, social reformer and educationist, who wrote *Ratnabai: A Sketch of a Bombay High Caste Hindu Wife* (1895). This short novel holds forth the ideal of a companionate marriage. A young married girl, whose husband is away in England, is sent to school against all opposition by her father. She suffers much at the hands of her in-laws but when her husband returns he finds a wife he can converse with and it ends happily. This was part of the larger discourse of reform and the treatment of women in Hindu society.

Other women writers who normally find mention in the history of Indian English fiction are Rajalakshmi Debi whose novel in verse form, *The Hindoo Wife or The Enchanted Fruit*, was published in 1876, and Cornelia Sorabji, a distinguished lawyer, who published three collections of short stories in the first decade of the twentieth century. These much admired collections, are *Love and Life Behind the Purdah* (1901), *Sun Babies* (1904), and *Between the Twilights* (1908). While Sorabji never wrote a novel, Rabindranath Tagore's sister Swarnakumari Ghosal (1855-1932) wrote three—*The Fatal Garland* (1910), *An Indian Love Story* (1910), and *An Unfinished Song* (1913). The first is a historical romance while the last is novel of sensibility that shows the influence of novelists like George Eliot.

To turn to male novelists of late-nineteenth and early-twentieth century, we find that many wrote historical romances. But, Shoshee Chunder Dutt, wrote *Shunkur: A Tale of Indian Mutiny* (1857), and *The Young Zamindar* (1883), both of which depict the greatness of the cultural heritage of the country and aim at raising the consciousness of the readers to fight for political freedom. H. Dutt wrote adventure fiction and is known for two novels—*Bijay Chand: An Indian Tale* (1888) and *Lieut. Suresh Biswas: His Life and Adventures* (1900). Some of the historical romances written around that time are—Chakravarti Khetrapal's *Sarala and Hingana* (1895), and T. Ramakrishna Pillai's *Padmini: An Indian Romance* (1903), and *The Dive for Death*: *An Indian Romance* (1911), S.M. Mitra's *Hindupore: A Peep Behind the Indian Unrest—An Anglo-Indian Romance* (1909), and Balkrishna's *The Love of Kusuma*: *An Eastern Love Story* (1910).

While Romesh Chunder Dutt translated his own Bengali novels into English—*The Lake of Palms: A Story of Indian Domestic Life* (1902), and *The Slave Girl of Agra: An Indian*

Historical Romance (1909)—one a novel of social reform and widow remarriage and the other a historical romance as promised in the title, Sarath Kumar Ghosh wrote a fantasy, *1001 Indian Nights: The Trials of Narayan Lai* (1906), and *The Prince of Destiny: The New Krishna* (1909). Ghosh's second novel is perhaps one of the earliest to explore the East-West encounter, a popular theme in the Indian English novel.

Two novelists from the early years of the twentieth century deserve mention here. They are Rajam Iyer and A. Madhaviah. Both writers from Madras were pioneers of the Tamil novel and published their first novels in Tamil in 1896. *True Greatness of Vasudeva Sastri*, which appeared as a serial in 1896-98, was published posthumously in book form in 1925. This religious novel about a vedantin is seen as a forerunner of novels by Raja Rao.

A Madhaviah wrote quite a few novels in English—*Satyananda* (1909), *Thillai Govindan* (1916)—which were published earlier, in 1908, under a different title (*A Posthumous Autobiography* edited by Pamba), *Clarinda* (1915), *Nanda, the Pariah who Overcame Caste* (1923), and *Lt. Panju—A Modern Indian* (1924). *Thillai Govindan* is about a contemporary Tamil Brahmin youth and the impact of western education on his life. It ends with his rediscovery of faith in Hinduism, Clarinda is a historical romance about a woman who was converted to Christianity in Tanjore. It is believed that she built the first church in that part of the country. According to Ramamurti, the church still stands in Palamcottah and is known as Gloriana Church. The novel traces the growth and development of a Maratha Brahmin girl from innocence and naivete to heroism. According to Ramamurti, one of the major achievements of Madhaviah is the language spoken by his characters. His Indian characters and his English characters speak very differently from each other even while he manages to make them speak in colloquial English. Ramamurti also feels that Madhaviah's humour is similar to that of R.K. Narayan's. He manages to portray the middle class India of his times with wonderful felicity and ease.

When the Gandhian whirlwind (phrase coined by Naik) struck India, many things changed including the novel. What we are talking about is the intensification of the sense of nationalism and the attempts to use all means to construct the idea of a modern India. Once again we begin with a novelist who was also a poet. This is K.S. Venkataramani (1891-1951). He has two novels—*Murugan, the Tiller* (1927), and *Kandan, the Patriot: A Novel of New India in the Making* (1932). *Murugan* contrasts the life of two friends, Kedari and Ramu, the former a materialist and the latter a Gandhian. A Gandhian colony is established at the end of the novel and the two friends settle down there. *Kandan* is set during the period of the Civil Disobedience Movement. Kandan, an ICS officer who has been educated in England, resigns from government service and joins the freedom movement only to be killed at the end.

The problem with Venkataramani's novels is that their narrative style leaves a lot to be desired. Venkataramani doesn't seem to have been impressed by any contemporary narrative model. This is true of his contemporary A.S.P. Ayyar as well. Ayyar, an ICS officer, was a dramatist as well. He couldn't write novels about contemporary politics because of his official position. So like nineteenth century poets, he resorts to Indian history to construct his idea of India. His novels are *Baladitya* (1930), and *Three Men of Destiny* (1939). He split the latter novel into two parts and published them separately as *The Legions Thunder Past* (1947), and *Chanakya and Chandragupta* (1951). *Baladitya* is set in the 5th century and is about the defeat of invading foreigners, in this case the Huns. *Three Men of Destiny* is about the aftermath of Alexander's invasion of India. The three men are Alexander, Chandragupta Maurya, and Chanakya.

Another novelist we should name before we talk of the trinity is K. Nagarajan. His *Athavar House* (1937) is a family saga that depicts a Maharashtrian Vaishnava Brahmin family settled in the south. It portrays a joint family, and explores the impact of modernity and Gandhism on the family. Nagarajan has another novel set in the thirties, but this, *Chronicle of Kedaram*, came out much later, in 1961.

The trinity of Mulk Raj Anand, R.K. Narayan, and Raja Rao began writing in the 1930s. Narayan's *Waiting for the Mahatma* (1955), or *Vendor of Sweets* (1967), treat Mahatma Gandhi and the impact of Gandhism quite differently. All three writers began writing during the freedom struggle soon after the Civil Disobedience Movement of early 1930s. The issues they tackled were all relevant issues of the time, issues that had to be depicted and debated in the quest to construct an ideal nation. Mulk Raj Anand's *Untouchable* (1935) and Rao's *Kanthapura* (1938) immediately tells the issues of caste and 'the upliftment of the downtrodden'. Modernity and religion, the role of religions, the effects of colonialism, the question of gender roles—mainly the place of women in society, the situation of the village and the peasantry, all find place in the Indian English novel as influenced by the trinity. Not that these issues had not entered the novel earlier but that these novelists had a great impact, which can be felt even today.

Mulk Raj Anand (1905-2004) was a prolific writer. He went to England in 1924 to do research in philosophy and came back as a committed socialist. He even took part in the Spanish Civil War. His other interest other than fiction has been art criticism. He is the founder editor of the art magazine, *Marg*. His first literary efforts were to chronicle the lives of the under-privileged. If *Untouchable* is about a sweeper Bakha, *Coolie* (1936) and *Two Leaves and a Bud* (1937) are about labourers. If *Coolie* depicts the lives of displaced labourers who are exploited by all kinds of economic forces including colonialism, *Two Leaves and a Bud* exposes the conditions of plantation life in British India. If in the first the protagonist comes down from the hills, in the second the protagonist is lured from Punjab to Assam. The trilogy—*The Village* (1939), *Across the Black Waters* (1941), and *The Sword and the Sickle* (1942)—on the Punjabi peasant followed next. The trilogy follows the life of Lal Singh who rebels against his village mores. He fights in the First World War in Flanders, is taken prisoner by the Germans, becomes a communist and ends up in prison again in India. In his last novel before Indian Independence, Mulk Raj Anand depicts one day in the life of a coppersmith. *The Big Heart* (1945) debates the virtue of the machine and modernity.

Anand is quite passionate about his causes. He displays what Naik calls "ruthless realism" (Naik, p. 160). He goes boldly where very few if any have gone before, inventing an English that has the flavour of Punjab. This is one of the major achievements of the trinity who each in his own way manages to write an English that is constructed by and constructs the geographical and social space depicted by their novels.

R.K. Narayan (b. 1906) is a very different writer from Anand. Narayan is one of the few Indian English writers of the earlier generation, or even any generation, who has been a full time writer. Thanks to television adaptations of his stories, his fictional town, Malgudi, is known to more than the readers of Indian English fiction. All his works have Malgudi as their setting, and he polishes and carves this one inch of ivory to perfection. His is the middle class world of the small town—modernity has impinged on this society but not whole sale westernisation. In his novels written before Independence, Narayan develops and fixes the ingredients of his recipe for his successful Section. "Swami and Friend" is a delightful tale about the escapedes of a schoolboy. *The Bachelor of Arts* (1937) is about the goings on in the life of a bachelor, Chandran, who rebelling against the idea of an arranged marriage even becomes a *sanyasi* for some time. He, of course, returns to a traditional arranged marriage. *The Dark Room* (1938) is Narayan's attempt at something different—a story about the suffering and abortive rebellion of a housewife. Narayan never attempted such serious fiction again though *The English Teacher* (1946), which was written after the tragic death of his wife, is a poignant novel about loss and reconciliation. This novel explores the world of the supernatural, again a subject that Narayan does not deal with seriously ever again. This was his last novel before Independence.

Raja Rao (b. 1908) who completes the trinity is as different from the other two as possible. *Kanthapura* is the only novel written by Raja Rao before Independence and this too shows a writer contemplating and depicting the changes that were taking place in the making of the modern nation. The "foreword" to *Kanthapura* is one of the most important documents in Indian English literature. It is here that an Indian English writer sets out as fully as Rao does the agenda for Indian English writers, their intents and the challenges they have to face. The problematic as he puts it is "to convey in a language not one's own but the spirit that is one's own". "So while the language is foreign, the experience is local. But the language isn't completely outside our ambit", he says. He identifies that English has the same position of power as Sanskrit or Persian had in their days. And the Indian English writer chooses to write in the language of power and the powerful. But, cautions Rao, this does not mean that the Indian English writer wants to be appropriated, he doesn't want to write like the English. The colonial encounter has changed all, and the Indian English writer has to use the space in between the coloniser's language and culture and the local traditional lives and experiences in order to create what the English writer cannot, and create what is made possible only because the writing is in English. Thus, the Indian English writer is duty bound to create and use Englishes that makes it impossible for the monolingual English reader to appropriate his/her experience with any degree of ease. "Don't write like the English, and don't write what can be easily written in the Indian language of your region." This is the agenda that Raja Rao sets forth.

One of the most interesting novels of this era is *Twilight in Delhi* (1940) by Ahmed Ali. Ahmed Ali portrays middle class Muslim life in early twentieth century Delhi, and attempts to capture the decay of a culture. Ahmed Ali became a Pakistani citizen after Partition, but this novel remains a landmark in Indian English fiction. Iqbalunnisa Hussain's *Purdah and Polygamy: Life in an Indian Muslim Household* (1944) delivers what it promises—an intimate picture of a way of life. Another novelist who deserves mention is K.A. Abbas who wrote many popular film scripts for Raj Kapoor, the noted Hindi film maker. His novel *Tomorrow is Ours: A Novel of the India of*

Today (1943), tries to construct an India with a role to play in world affairs. There are a number of other novelists who wrote novels on the freedom struggle and its impact.

The Trinity

The trinity have continued their long and distinguished career after Independence but there have also been a number of other major novelists during the period we are looking at.

Mulk Raj Anand returned to India for good in 1945 and didn't write for some time because of a nervous breakdown. *Seven Summers* (1951), his next book, was understandably a fictional recreation of his childhood, and was meant to be the first of a series of autobiographical novels with Krishan Chander as protagonist. After *Private Life of an Indian Prince* (1953), a novel about a milieu with which he did not have much familiarity, Anand returned to familiar territory with *The Old Woman and the Cow* (1960). *The Old Woman and the Cow* is about peasant life and the pressures on people that drives them to inhumanity in order to survive. The protagonist is Gauri, the 'cow' of the title, who is deserted by her husband and sold off by her grandmother who has to choose between her cow and Gauri. Gauri grows from a cow to a tigress.

Anand's next novel was *The Road* (1963) which travels the same territory as *Untouchable*. *The Death of Hero* (1964), which Anand reissued in the 1990s, is about Kashmir. His next two novels were part of his autobiographical series. *Morning Face* (1970), which won the Sahitya Akademi Award, and *Confessions of a Lover* (1976) follow the career of Krishan Chander through his schooldays, adolescence, college and an unsuccessful love affair, till he leaves for England.

R.K. Narayan achieved greater fame and fortune after Independence. He started off with *Mr. Sampath* (1949), a novel about the world of films, and then wrote *The Financial Expert* (1952), *Waiting for the Mahatma* (1955), *The Guide* (1958), *The Man-Eater of Malgudi* (1962), *The Vendor of Sweets* (1967), *The Painter of Signs* (1976), *A Tiger for Malgudi* (1983), and *The Talkative Man* (1986), *The World of Nagaraj* (1990), and *The Grandmother's Tale* (1993). Critics feel that Narayan was at the height of his powers from *The Financial Expert* till *The Vendor of Sweets*. Narayan is a delightful comic writer who studies middle class small town South Indian mores. *The Guide*, which won the Sahitya Akademi Award, is perhaps his most famous book and did very well in a movie version that R.K. Narayan himself did not feel too happy about.

Raja Rao has written more than he has been able to publish and his second book *Serpent and the Rope* (1960), which won him his Sahitya Akademi Award, showed him in very different light from *Kanthapura*. This novel, autobiographical in tone, is about the travels of a young man abroad and his life and loves till he understands that he needs to search for the true Guru for an understanding of life. This philosophical novel, in which, as Naik puts it, "the philosophy is not in the story—the philosophy is the story", signals the arrival of the philosopher novelist. Rao's *The Cat and Shakespeare* (1965) is a metaphysical comedy. Rao tries a different kind of novel in *Comrade Kirilov* (1976) where he looks at the life of an Indian intellectual, Padmanabha Iyer (the Kirilov of the title), in the 1930s and 40s in England. His recent work is the voluminous *The Chessmaster and His Moves* (1988). His attempt overall is to espouse an Indian philosophical point of view in the novel. Indian literature in English has journeyed a long way to achieve its present glory and grandeur. Today it is assimilated in the rubric of postcolonial literature. At present it is enriched by a sizeable number of women writers, read and acclaimed all over the world. The works of novelists like Anita Desai offer penetrative insight into the complex issues of life. Among these women writers Anita Desai has earned a separate space for her particular attention towards psychological insight and existential concerns. Her sensitive portrayal and understanding of intrinsic human nature makes her writings conspicuous and captivating. But there are many more before her.

Other Novelists

A major novelist who began writing in 1947 is Bhabani Bhattacharya (1906-88). Another social realist, he has said that every novel should have a social purpose. His first novel, *So Many Hungers* (1947), is set during the years of the Bengal famine. It depicts the various kinds of exploitations that took place during that period, from that of the colonial power to that of the local traders. *Music for Mohini* (1952) is an attempt to wed the city and the village, through the marriage of a city bred girl who has to then move to a village. In *He Who Rides a Tiger* (1952), Bhattacharya has Kalo, a blacksmith who is jailed for stealing a bunch of bananas, takes revenge on society by becoming a godman. *A Goddess Named Gold* is an allegory where a magic talisman raises false expectations. His next novel, *Shadow from Ladakh* (1966), which won him the Sahitya Akademi Award, is set against the background of the 1962 war with China. In this Gandhism is pitted against modern technology. *A Dream in Hawaii* (1978) is Bhattacharya's attempt to explore the East-West encounter. Bhattacharya has had a successful career with his novels being translated into many languages.

Another novelist from Bengal who was quite popular during that period was Sudhindranath Ghose (1899-1965). His tetralogy—*And Gazelles Leaping* (1949), *Cradle of the Clouds* (1951), *The Vermilion Boat* (1953), and *The Flame of the Forest* (1955)—follows the life of a nameless narrator-protagonist through about twenty years of his life. The central theme is the growth of the narrator's mind. This is a wonderful attempt in terms of narrative experimentation, written more like a magic realist tale (in other words, a traditional Indian story) than a western novel.

If Bhattacharya believes in the novel with a social purpose, the novelist who believes in complete entertainment is Manohar Malgonkar (b. 1913). Among his novels, *Distant Drum* (1960), his first novel, and *Bandicoot Run* (1982) are based in an army setting, a setting with which Malgonkar, as a retired army officer, is familiar. The latter novel is a spy thriller of a high order. He had written another competent espionage novel earlier, *Spy in Amber* (1971). *Combat of Shadows* (1962) is another attempt at writing a fast moving tale of passion and murder. *The Princes* (1963) is a picture of the times when the princely states merged with India and is considered a critical success because Malgonkar seems more interested in the issues than in just telling a fast tale. His novel on the Partition, *A Bend in the Ganges* (1964), is again a readable novel written on a large scale. *The Devil's Wind* (1972) is an attempt to portray the Revolt of 1857. In *Cactus Country* (1992), Malgonkar sees the 1971 war from the point of view of a Pakistani officer. Malgonkar is an exciting writer who deserves to be better known and deserves to be always in print. Among other novelists of this period are Khushwant Singh (b. 1918), Kamala Markandaya (b. 1924), Nayantara Sahgal (b. 1927), and Arun Joshi (1939-93). These are all novelists with a substantial amount of works. But perhaps this is the time to pause and look at certain novels which have had a great impact in Indian English fiction.

One such novel is G.V. Desani's *All About H. Hattler* (1948). This is a book that displays great comic virtuosity and anticipates many a post-modernist novel in form and style. It is not easy to summarise this novel which has to be read to be admired for all that it attempts and attempts successfully. Desani manages to use the language with great flexibility and it is a pity that neither he nor any of his contemporaries could pull it off again, or even tried to do so.

Another novel is Attia Hosain's *Sunlight on a Broken Column* (1961), which is an account of life in pre-Partition Lucknow. It is a classic of its kind, looking at the impact on the Muslim aristocracy of the winds of change brought about by the freedom struggle as well as notions of modernity.

Khushwant Singh's *Train to Pakistan* (1956), which has been made into a feature film recently, is his first and most famous novel. It is the story of the impact of Partition on a village in the western border and describes how the peaceful life of two communities is divided asunder. It is a wonderfully paced novel that also tells a love story as it delineates a society. In *I Shall Not Hear the Nightingale* (1959) Khushwant Singh's portrays a Sikh family and all that it goes through the freedom movement and the 1940s. Singh also has an enormously popular late novel, *Delhi*, to his credit.

Kamala Markandaya has a number of novels to her credit. As a diasporic writer her major concerns seem to be the East-West encounter and the different roles of women. Foreign characters people her fictional Indian world, which in any case shows the effect of processes of modernisation and urbanisation. *Nectar in a Sieve* (1954) is her first novel and critics have often wondered where in India such a village as depicted in the novel could be. Some of her other novels are: *Some Inner Fury* (1955), *Silence of Desire* (1960), *Possession* (1963), *A Handful of Rice* (1966), *The Coffer Dams* (1969), *The Nowhere Man* (1972), and *Two Virgins* (1973). Markandaya's output is substantial and her novels are eminently readable. Her last novel *Bombay Tiger* (2008) published posthumously by her daughter Kim Oliver is a great success.

Nayantara Sahgal, who belongs to the Nehru family, is the only political novelist in Indian English fiction. Her construction of the political space also includes the struggle for identity of the post-Independence Indian woman. *A Time to be Happy* (1958) is her first novel and it immediately announces the arrival of a fresh new voice. It deals with the last phase of the freedom struggle and the newly independent India. In *Maya*, it has the first of Sahgal's trapped-in-bad-marriage women. *This Time of Morning* (1968), and *Storm in Chandigarh* (1969) depict situations in Independent India and contain portraits of recognisable political figures. Both portray strains within marriage and the polity. *The Day in Shadow* (1971) is again about a marital breakdown as much as it is about political goings on, and *A Situation in New Delhi* (1977) deals with India after Nehru's death. Her finest and most ambitious novel so far has been *Rich Like Us* (1985). This novel deals with the entirety of the history of modern India culminating in the Emergency declared by Indira Gandhi. The novel tries to trace the almost inevitability of the journey from Mahatma Gandhi to Indira Gandhi. It is an extremely complex novel which cannot be summarised in this space. Her *Plans for Departure* came out in 1986.

Arun Joshi's *Strange Case of Billy Biswas* (1971) is a wonderful introduction to the world of post-Independence Indian English fiction. This is an extremely well paced book and tells the story of an Indian who returns from the west and where his search for identity takes him in the new nation. He ends up leading a tribe in so-called 'primitive' India and is shot dead by a policeman ironically during an effort to secure him by his well-wishers even his first book, *The Foreigner* (1968), was about a similar theme, of alienation. Joshi's heroes search for meaning in life, for an identity beyond the given. This holds true for two of his other novels, *The Apprentice* (1974), in which the life of an idealistic youth is delineated, and *The Last Labyrint* (1981), which won him the Sahitya Akdemi Award. But Joshi's *The City and the River* (1990) is a political allegory that shows the cyclical nature of human greed and deceit. Joshi is another of the novelists who deserve to be read by future generations.

Anita Desai (b. 1937) is a novelist whose career began in 1963 and is still going strong. To a large extent Desai's focus is on the inner world of her main characters, usually women. From Maya in *Cry, the Peacock* (1963) to Uma in *Fasting, Feasting* (1999), her main characters are essentially lonely and struggling with the forces of existence. Suffice to say that among women writers, Desai largely shifted the theme from the outer world to the inner space.

Rama Mehta in *Inside the Haveli* (1977), another winner of the Sahitya Akademi Award, portrays the married life of an urban educated woman who is forced into Purdah in a Rajput household. Very well written, the novel surprises the readers in advocating compromise with this way of life and presents a different picture of a woman fighting for her identity.

Rushdie and After

1980 is a watershed year in Indian English fiction. The preceding decade had seen the effervescence of Indian English poetry and a sense of ennui had actually descended on the novel. But the publication of *Midnight's Children* by Salman Rushdie (b. 1947) changed all that. This novel led to increased interest and market for Indian English writing and coupled with a governmental decision about import of books into India, and the entry of Penguin, led to a boom in publication of Indian English books. The novel articulates the viewpoint of a migrant who looks at all constructions of nation as fiction. If till *Midnight's Children* we have had Indian English novelists attempting to delineate continuities and define nationness, if they have tried to show life in Independent India so as to work towards redefinitions of good citizenship and governance, *Midnight Children (MC)* brings in the notion of the flawed imagination of nation, of the impossibility of a modern India. As an iconic text of postcolonial literature, *MC* (and Rushdie) celebrates the hybridity of the migrant and argues against alternate Indian visions of purity or continuity or possibility of cultural oneness. This fiction as true history has influenced many subsequent novels. His use of joyfully pollinated English language has had an equally great impact.

Among the host of novelists and novels that have come to the forefront after 1980, I must look briefly at the career of Amitav Ghosh (b. 1956). Beginning with *The Circle of Reason* (1986), and *The Shadow Lines* (1988), where he shows the constructed and thus shadowy nature of boundaries between states, this immensely talented writer has dissolved the boundaries between fiction and anthropological and historical research. *In an Antique Land* (1993) and *The Glass Palace* (2000) are examples of such uncategorisable writings. In between he wrote a science fiction mystery thriller, *The Calcutta Chromosome* (1996). He has also been an influential essayist writing on subjects as varied as the nuclear bomb and the jungles of Burma.

A writer who has been writing throughout this period and whose reputation has grown quietly is Shashi Deshpande. In her explorations of the lives of middle class women, Deshpande shows a different facet of society. Among her major novels are *The Dark Holds No Terrors* (1980) and *That Long Silence* (1988). Others are Upamanyu Chatterji (whose *English-August* explores the empty life of the upper-middle class Indian youth), Vikram Seth (whose *Golden Gate* is wonderful example of poetic skills used for narration and whose *A Suitable Boy* is a sprawling social realist book of the India of the fifties), Allen Sealy (whose *Trotter Nama* heralded the arrival of a great Anglo-Indian novelist, and who has followed it up with the critically acclaimed *Everest Hotel*) and Githa Hariharan (whose award winning debut novel *The Thousand Faces of Night* established her as a careful craftsperson, a reputation she has safeguarded through her other works). There are many other novelists—for example, the Booker Prize winner Arundhati Roy (*God of Small Things*), Mukul Kesavan (*Looking Through Glass*), Manju Kapoor (*Difficult Daughters*), Kiran Desai (*Inheritance of Loss*) and Aravind Adiga (*The White Tiger*). There are again a number of diasporic writers including Bharati Mukherjee (*Wife*) and Rohinton Mistry. The journey still continues and surely a long way to go.

NOTE

1. M.K. Naik, *A History of Indian English Literature,* New Delhi: Sahitya Academi, 1982, p. 14.

2

Anita Desai: Biographical Details

Anita Desai is indisputably one of the most powerful contemporary Indian novelists in English. She was born Anita Mazumdar in Mussoorie, a hill station near Dehradun in northern India to a Bengali father and a German mother on June 24, 1937. She grew up surrounded by Western literature and music. Her father D.N. Mazumdar was a Bengali businessman and her mother (Antionette) Toni Nime was of German origin. She began to write in English at the age of seven and published her first story at the age of nine. She made her own illustrations for them, securing them onto covers to move them appear as books. She says, "My family became aware of it when they became the hapless recipients of the little books I wrote, illustrated, stitched and bound into birthday gifts and resigned themselves to my future by calling me 'the writer in the Family'. I saw no alternative but to fill the role given to me."[1] Indeed, she continued her higher education in literature too, in Miranda House College at the University of Delhi where she went on to win the Pershad Memorial Prize for English. She received her BA in English Literature in 1957. She worked for one year after her graduation at Max Mueller Bhawan in Calcutta. The following year, she got married to Ashvin Desai, a businessman. The couple have four children—Rahul, Tani, Arjun, and the youngest, Kiran, who is the current toast of literary circles the world over, with her Booker win for *The Inheritance of Loss* and her first novel *Hullabaloo in the Guava Orchard*.

Anita Desai has two sisters and a brother. She spoke German as a child. She says in an interview with Jasbir Jain in 1979, "My parents spoke German with each other so probably it was my first language, I should think, as a child."[2] She was determined to be a writer, and it was prose, mainly fiction. Her stories appeared as favourite pieces in the children magazine and when she was in college she used to occasionally contribute short stories to the magazine. Desai herself describes her upbringing as "the greatest gift I could have been given as a writer!" She has lived in Calcutta, Chandigarh, Delhi and Pune and this accounts for the fact that all her novels are set in one or the other of these cities. She is, as Tilottama Tharoor puts it, immensely familiar with the contemporary Indian milieu, from which she derives the background and characters for her novels.

However, most of Desai's growing up years were spent in the city of Delhi, another pervasive presence in many of her tales. Her first acquaintance with English came about here, when she went to school (Queen Mary's School for Girls), and as the language in which she first learnt to read and write, it became, in essence, her literary language. When asked why she always chose to write in English, she says that since the first thing she saw written, and the first thing she ever read, was in English, it had seemed to her young mind, the language of books. Through her writing she wanted to belong to this world of books. Starting to write as early as at the age of seven, Anita Desai was the acknowledged 'writer' within the family.

Desai's mother, Toni Nime, had been from Berlin while her Bengali father, D.N. Mazumdar was originally from Dhaka. Apart from providing the young Desai a curious cultural milieu to grow up in, its other bequest, ancestral inheritances of displacements, may also be read between the lines of silences in her novels. Although her childhood home was a very 'Indian' set-up, her mother having accultured herself a lot, there were a lot of outside influences too. For instance, a lot more Western music was played in their home as compared to the average

Indian household! Years later, Desai was to describe her German mother as one who carried "a European core in her which protested against certain Indian tilings, which always maintained its independence and its separateness."[3] Perhaps it was this influence that provided, to the young writer's mind, the first unconscious impulse to portray and explore, notions of foreignness and 'separateness', and most of all, to grapple with certain ideas of solitude throughout her literary career. Delving deep into character and situation, working around the interior landscapes of people, whether Indian or foreign, she fashioned out of the dynamics of 'separateness', a metaphor for certain aspects of the human condition.

She admits "she prefers novels to short stories because the form of the novel gives her a good deal of thought and time (to) get round (the subject), see it from different angle and aspects. Whereas a short story demands something quite different. You have the whole of it quite clear in your mind and you just put it down at one throw."[4] As a novelist Desai made her debut in 1963 with *Cry, The Peacock*. She started writing short stories regularly before her marriage.

This novel was published in Britain by Peter Owen, a publisher specializing in literature of the British Commonwealth and continental Europe. She never tried to first get her work published in India because there was a belief that no publisher would be interested in fiction by an Indian writer and it was first in England that her work became noticed. U.S. readers were slower to discover her. This may be because of England's natural interest in India and the U.S.'s law of comprehension regarding the foreignness of her subject.

Desai writes in English only. This, she has repeatedly said, was a natural and unconscious choice for her: "I can state definitely that I did not choose English in a deliberate and conscious act and I'd say perhaps it was the language that chose me and I started writing stories in English at the age of seven and have been doing so for thirty years now without stopping to think why."[5]

She is considered the writer who introduced the psychological novel in the tradition of Virginia Woolf to India.

Included in this, is her pioneer status of writing of feminist issues. While many people today would not classify her work as feminist as in this post-feminist era the definition of a feminist is more wide. She said, "The feminist movement in India is very new and a younger generation of readers in India needs to be rather impatient of my books and to think of them as marks about completely helpless women, hopeless women. They find it somewhat unreal that the women don't fight back, but they don't seem to realize how very new this movement is."[6] Thus, she says, her writing is realistic: "Women think I am doing a disservice to the feminist movement by writing about women who have no control over their lives. But I was trying, as every writer tries to do, even in fiction, to get at the truth, write the truth. It would have been really fanciful if I had made Bim and Tara modern-day feminists."[7]

Desai considers *Clear Light of Day,* her most autobiographical novel, because she was writing about her neighbourhood in Delhi, although the characters are not based on her brother and sisters. What she was exploring in this novel, she has said, was the importance of childhood and memories as the source of a life. She wanted to start the book at the end and move backwards, into the characters' childhood and further, into the childhood of their parents, etc., but in the end when she had gone as far back as their infancy, the book just ground to a halt; it lost its momentum. She had a sense of disappointment about the book as her intention had been different. The character of Raja is identified with her in the sense that he is immersed in all different types of literature and culture, and is so concerned with protecting the multicultural heritage of India. Her worries about the Muslim neighbour family is not just about them particularly, but rather worry about the loss of all that the Muslim culture and literature contributes to India.

Anita Desai is a guide star for many bright young writers. Starting right at home she influenced her own daughter, Kiran Desai whose novel *Hullabaloo in the Guava Orchard* was a celebrated debut in 1997, and her second novel, *Inheritance of*

Loss became a classic as it received the famous Booker Prize. Kiran dedicated this novel to her mother 'Anita Desai'.

Kiran Desai was born in India in 1971, and educated in India, England and the United States. She is currently a student in Columbia University's Creative writing course. She went to high school in Massachusetts and then undergraduate in Vermont at Bennington and then to a writing program called Hollins, in Virginia. Anita Desai influenced her. Kiran Desai says in an interview, "All my life I've grown up hearing her talk about writing and literature and books. It was wonderful to have her (Anita Desai) around when I was writing this book, to talk to her through this whole process. She was wonderful through the whole thing. It's a big risk to take, spending years of your life doing something that you're not sure how it's going to turn out, and she was very good through that whole time, not providing critical support as much as emotional support. A very motherly role, really."[8]

Anita Desai grew up during World War II and could see the anxiety her German mother was experiencing about the situation and her family in Germany. After the War when she realized that the Germany she had known was devastated, her mother never returned there, nor had any desire to return. Anita Desai herself did not visit until she was an adult. Desai herself describes her upbringing as the greatest gift she could have been given as a writer.

Desai likes to lead a quiet life. Her colleagues who knew her in the 1950, describe her as intense and solitary. Even her choice of books reveals this tendency. She likes to read books which explore human nature. Her favourite authors are Chekhov, Henry James, Lawrence and Dostoevsky.

Truly speaking not much is known about her personal life and views on literature. She is hesitant talking about her personal life and biases. In her opinion, the creative art is a secret one. As sufficient material is not available we can just frame a picture of Anita Desai as a writer on the basis of various literary sources and her writings. Most of Professor Desai's novels are set in India and completely immersed in Indian life. According to Professor Alan Lightman, head of

WHS, her novels are distinguished by her focus on the inner lite of her characters and her concern with people previously marginalized in Indian fiction, primarily women, children and the elderly.

Professor Desai won the Winifred Holtby Prize of the Royal Society of Literature for the novel; *Fire on the Mountain* (1978) and the Guardian Award for Children's Literature for *Village by the Sea* (1984). She also received the Padma Sri Award from the Government of India and the Taraknath Das Award for promotion of Indo-US relations. She is a fellow of the Royal Society of Literature of London and was recently elected a fellow of the American Academy of Arts and Letters. She also won the Sahitya Academy Award and National Academy of Letters Award. Her three novels *Clear Light of Day, In Custody* and *Fasting Feasting* have been nominated for the Booker Prize. What is important is that her writing has not prevented her from looking after her family and her four children. She says, "I write for three and a half hours in the morning while the children are away at school. Once they are back my entire time is taken with them."[9] Thus, maintaining a proper balance between home and literary career. She has presented an ideal image of modern 'New Woman'. She is a member of the Advisory Board for English of the National Academy of Letters in Delhi and fellow of the Royal Society of Literature in London, The American Academy of Arts and Letters, Girton College, Cambridge and Clare Hall, Cambridge. Her major works are as follows:

Cry, The Peacock (*CTP*)—Peter Owen, 1963

Voices in the City (*VITC*)—Peter Owen, 1965

Where Shall We Go This Summer? (*WSWGTS*)—Vikas Publication, 1975

Fire on the Mountain (*FOTM*)—Heinemann, 1977

Games at Twilight and Other Stories (*GATAOS*)—Heinemann, 1978

The Peacock Garden (*TPG*)—Heinemann, 1979

Clear Light of Day (*CLOD*)—Heinemann, 1980

The Village by the Sea (*TVBTS*)—Heinemann, 1982

In Custody (*IC*)—Heinemann, 1984

Baumgartner's Bombay (*BB*)—Heinemann, 1987

Journey to Ithaca (*JTI*)—Heinemann, 1995

Fasting Feasting (*FF*)—Chalto and Windus, 1999

Diamond Dust and Other Stories (*DDAOS*)—Chalto and Windus, 2000

The Zigzag Way (TZW)—Chalto and Windus, 2004

Hill of Silver, Hill of Lead (*HOSHOL*)—Chalto and Windus, 2005

For Children:

The Peacock Garden—Bombay: Indian Book House, 1974

Cat on a Houseboat—Bombay: Orient Longman, 1976

Circus Cat, Alley Cat—Throught, 1957

How Gentle is the Mist—The Illustrated Weekly of India, 1958

Grand Mother—Miscellary, Calcutta; Writers Workshop, 1960

An Examination—Miscellary, 1960

To Seal a Picture—Miscellary, 1960

Guest House—Quest, 1961

Mr. Bose's Private Bliss—Envory, 1959

Private Tuition by Mr. Bose—Indian Litrerature, 1970

Descent from the Rooftop—The Illustrated Weekly of India, 1970

Surface Textures—Femine, 1974

The Accompanist—Quest, 1975

She has been awarded the Neil Gunn International Fellowship for 1944. Her novels have drawn worldwide attention and she stands in the forefront in the world of fiction, in the company of Iris Murdock, Doris Lessing, Margaret Atwood and Flora Nwapa.

The reader's first impression of reading Anita Desai is one of brave originality and uniqueness. Her novels are certainly reflective of social realities from a psychological perspective. She closely examines the emotional world of womankind. In dealing with the interior landscape and the psychic odyssey of her characters, Desai has extended and enlarged the thematic horizon of the Indian English novels. Dealing with the thoughts, emotions and sensations at various levels of consciousness, Anita Desai found the technique used by D.H. Lawrence, Virginia Woolf and Henry James, i.e. stream of consciousness technique and flashbacks in her novels.

According to Desai most marriages prove to be unions of incompatibility. Her women long for love and communion of the spirit which they perceive as the panacea of the ills of the world. In her novels one comes across a symbolic link between different images, which form an interface, a common bond. Imagery is primarily used to capture and crystallize a wide range of experiences. It lends clarity and vividness to the situation she describes, events she documents and characters she delineates. Most of the images used by Desai in her novels are so sharply condensed and chiselled that they resemble a piece of painting. She is a symbolist as well as an imagist. Her wide canvass, her experiences in various countries and places also contribute to it. Undoubtedly, she is a much travelled person.

Before coming to MIT, where she is professor at present, she was Purington Professor of English at Mount Holyoke College and divided her time between the United States, India and England. Philip S. Knoury, Dean of the School of Humanities and Social Science (MIT) said:

> Anita Desai is a tremendous addition to the humanities and to creative writing at MIT. She is a novelist of international distinction who brings a wonderfully bicultural approach to her fiction and teaching.[10]

No doubt, she is one of the world's best known authors, and a writer who has influenced generations of writers.

While Desai has taught for year at Mount Holyoke and MIT, and spends most of the years outside India. She does not consider herself part of the Indian diaspora. Although she does not fit in the Indian box anymore as she said, she considers herself lucky for having not left India until late in her life, because she feels that she has been drifting away from it ever since: "I can't really write of it with the same intensity and familiarity that I once had.[11] Yet she cannot feel at home any other place or society. Speaking about her initial years in India (she left India at 45), Desai confirms that her whole life was about family and neighbours. It was very difficult for a woman to experience anything else. She received 'Sahitya Academi Fellowhip' in Delhi in the year 2007, for her outstanding contribution in the field of Indian writing in English. My impressions and experiences about her are contained in this book in the form of questions and answers between us.

Anita Desai has attained an immense popularity as a novelist. Probably no other woman writer in the Indian English fiction has been admired by such different tastes and intellects, by whole classes of readers unlike each other. Anita Desai is solely conscious of her role as a woman writer and has tried her best to maintain the tradition for other women writers. As a person she has a belief and concern more with thought, emotion and sensation than with action and achievement.

NOTES

1. Anita Desai, *Commonwealth of Letters*, Vol. 2. No. 1, June 1990, p. 4.
2. web.net.edu/newsoffice/1993/novelist-0929-html
3. Shyam A. Asuani, *Critical Responses to Indian Fiction*. Delhi: M: Ital, 1985, p. 155.
4. *Ibid.*
5. *Ibid.*
6. *Ibid.*
7. www.nxiinternet.com
8. www.writers.com
9. web.nit.edu/newsoffice/1993/novelist-0929-html
10. www.nriinternet.com
11. www.writers.com

3

Anita Desai: A Novelist with a Difference

Anita Desai is one of the few distinguished Indian writers in English of international repute, whose works have been greatly admired both at home and abroad. Her contribution to fiction writing has been quite commendable and substantial. She comes face to face with the intangible realities of life, the innermost depths of the human psyche and the chaotic underworld of human mind through her novels. Her distinctive stature as novelist derives primarily from the fact that she has made extensive use of the stream of consciousness technique in her novels. Her achievement lies in the fact that she employs a relatively new technique in her fiction with a remarkable consummate skill. The fiction of Anita Desai has become self-analytical and introspective and the individual's quest for a personal meaning in life has become a theme of unavoidable interest for her. Her primary emphasis is thus on sights and sounds, on movements and patterns both physical and mental as they impinge on the consciousness of her protagonists.

Desai has got a distinguished place as her works are different from those of other Indian women writers, Kamala Markandaya, Ruth Prawer Jhabvala, Nayantara Sahgal, Shashi Deshpande, Shobhaa De and Kamla Das. Markandaya stresses more on the rural background. In Jhabvala's fiction the social background is more important than the characters who execute the various roles. Sahgal emphasizes on political and social awareness and Kamala Das moves between the man-woman relationship. Shobhaa De is more for physical desires and social framework while Shashi Deshpande follows Desai to a certain extent only. But in Desai's novels it is the exploration of sensibility, the inner working of mind that assumes the most important place and is unparalled. She unravels beautifully the mystery of the inner life of her characters. As a novelist she seems to be highly dissatisfied with most contemporary novelists' way of writing a novel. She voices her feelings in an article on 'women writers' with all the richness of material at hand. She made it clear that she would not be satisfied merely with uncritical prosaic documentation of social reality. Her real concern is nothing less than exploration of human psyche.

As a novelist, Desai excels in writing psychological novels. She would however call them surely subjective. Her writings reveal inner realities. She confides, "That my temperament and circumstances have combined to give me the shelter, privacy and solitude required for the writing of such novels thereby avoiding problems, a more objective writer has to deal with since he/she depends on observation rather than a private vision."[1] Desai's central pre-occupation as a novelist is with the existentialist-outlook on human life. Her characters are distinguished by the qualities of introspection, introversion and a refusal to surrender their individual selves. Deeply infected by the existential problems of modern industrial age, Anita Desai has created unique characters that are largely eccentric and abnormal in their mental make up and hence totally unable to conform. Rao has commented thus:

> Mrs. Desai brings something new to Indo-Anglian novel, instead of portraying character in terms of the environment of defining an individual in terms of his social or caste functions. Mrs. Desai creates character and the environment is important only in so far as it enables the reader to understand the character. Moreover the true artist that she is, Mrs. Desai presents each individual as an unsolved mystery.[2]

As a novelist Desai is unique as she has deviated from the path of realism and taken to the path of subtle psycho-analysis probing deeply into the inner working of a man's mind. She believes in the process of discovering the truth. She wrote:

> Writing is my way of plunging to the depths and exploring this underlying truth. All my writing is an effort to discover to underline and convey the true significance of things.[3]

Anita Desai has evoked mixed response from her readers. Critics have acclaimed her as a great artist, whose "writings reveal inner realities and psychic reverberations of her characters."[4] Her prose has won praise even from westerners. Desai is not interested so much in registering surface realities as in the probings of inner truths lying under the surface level. The single most distinction of the novelist is in suggesting (in quite a few of her novels), at times overtly, at times covertly, the small but significant change wrought in the perceptions of the other characters in the wake of the strivings of the central characters. Anita Desai's novels have excited both lay readers and critics alike. The central concerns in both the cases have not been very much dissimilar: alienation, the 'inscape' of a guest for the elusive self, existentialist yearnings in claustrophobic environs, the interaction between the old and the new, the dilemma of choosing between the instinct to conform and the urge to rebel. In her novels, there is no plot in the conventional sense of the term as she is never interested in telling a story, hence there is little plot and development of events in her novels. In the interview with Atma Ram she has herself made it clear, "I prefer the word pattern to plot as it sounds more natural...while plot sounds arbitrary, heavy handed and artificial all that I wish to avoid. One should have a pattern and then fit the characters, the setting and the scene into it—each piece in keeping with the others and so forming a balanced whole."[5]

It is really difficult to tell a tale without a well-structured plot for any writer. But Anita Desai does it and succeeds in it. Her forte as a novelist becomes, in the words of K.R.S. Iyengar, "The exploration of sensibility, the particular kind of Indian sensibility that is ill at ease among barbarous and the philistines, the anarchists and the moralists."[6]

Anita Desai is solely conscious of her role as a woman writer and has tried her best to maintain the tradition for other women writers. Her novels are documented with Indian settings, Indian culture and Indian background. Her younger character often try to imitate the Western culture but do not succeed in their lives. The elder generation in all respects are Indians and they adhere to Indian culture. It is unimaginable to think of Anita Desai without the portrayal of inner psyche of her characters. In her novels the inner workings, the inner sensibilities are more compelling than the outer weather or the visible action. Her strong point is an exploration of sensibilities. Desai's interest in the consciousness of the woman in her novels enables us to see the Indian woman adequately from the inside. She is occupied with interiorizing the consciousness of the woman and the economics of life do not bother her except when they are noticed as adding to the monotonous aspect of existence. In Desai's fictional world, living happily ever after in the old-fashioned sense, is the very fate her heroines struggle to escape. In fact Desai has fashioned a new concept of feminist fiction. The woman in her literary world is on a ceaseless quest, for a more meaningful life not only for herself but for humanity in general. Anita Desai has dealt with several types of severe psychological and social pressures. She has visualized society from the viewpoint of solitary individuals who look upon themselves as permanently uprooted beings. She has effectively used recurring images and symbols.

Anita Desai has found the artistic potential of the solitariness of the individual in an increasingly complex society. Desai's art as a novelist is praiseworthy because she is a meticulous artist. Most of her novels are about human relationships although it is rather their absence that is at the heart of the thematic impulse of her stories. Her characters, no matter to what age group they belong to seem to use one of Heideggar's phrases 'on the fringe of being' and then are debarred from evolving (to recall Kierkegaard) a purely aesthetic person. In fact in her novels she has dwelt upon the existentialist issues of the absurdity of human existence and the individuals trapped by circumstances. The great achievement of Desai rests on her beautifully recording the emotional turmoil, chaos and agonies of her oppressed protagonists. Another quality to note in her fiction is that there is not only a rejection of the passive acceptance of the traditional female role but also the deeply felt and suffered rebellion against the entire system of social relationship.

Anita Desai is a novelist of urban milieu. An uncrowned queen of the inner emotional world, she is endowed with soundless imaginative resourcefulness and creative vitality. She writes remarkably well about only those aspects of life that she has minutely observed and deeply experienced. Therefore, her fictional world full of imperfection and unfulfillment, hankering and helplessness, agony and anger, struggle and surrender is no doubt limited but within this limited world she reveals amazing variety and profundity.

Desai occupies an unassailable place in the galaxy of Indian English women novelists. She is one of the strongest voices of women writing in India today. Desai possesses sure and unerring satiric instincts. The several illuminating flashes of satire that break upon the narrative surface of her novels are evidence of her satiric mode. But satire with Anita Desai is only incidental. Her sense of irony embraces the whole emotional range of her characters. Unlike the satirists who distance themselves from their creatures and describe them from outside only, Desai probes into the inner psyche, inner recesses of her characters. That is why her whole style is ironical. Her delicate irony is the very essence of her style. Irony of style has been created by Desai deliberately.

It is not only in the use of subject matter, characterization and in presenting the atmosphere of minds but also in the use of narrative technique, symbols, images, flashback, the method of objective correlative and stream of consciousness, etc. that Anita Desai has achieved high recognition. In regard to the use of the stream of consciousness and interior monologue in her novels, she does it with a view to capturing the prismatic quality of life in her fiction. Every novel of Desai is unique in itself. In *Cry, The Peacock* the emotional disparity between

Maya and her husband Gautama is the basic cause of her sufferings. The lack of marital harmony in their lives leads to the contingent situation of Maya's life. Arjun's conflict with his father's bourgeois values of life creates a crisis of situation for him. In *Voices in the City* Nirode suspects his mother of adultery and his cherished image of his mother is shattered. Monisha experiences a sense or imprisonment in her in-law's house. This fact coupled with a lack of love and lack of natural trust in her marital life puts her in a predicament. Sarah, in *Bye, Bye Blackbird,* finds herself in a quandary as a result of her marriage with Adit, an Indian immigrant in London. His hope of going to India remains unfulfilled as Adit stays in England till he himself grows aware of his counterfeit life in England. The cause of Sita's predicament in *Where Shall We Go This Summer?* is rooted in her illusion about the magic personality of her deceased father and in the lack of love and communication in her marital and domestic life. Nanda Kaul in *Fire on the Mountain* also suffers as a result of the lack of love in her life because her husband neglects her in pursuit of his love affair with Miss David. In the state of despair and loneliness, she grows aware of the absurdity of human relationships. Raka, though a child, is also aware of the hostile forces of the world because she has often seen her father maltreating her mother. In *Clear Light of Day,* the parents spend their time playing cards at the club or at home and do not think of the emotional needs of their growing up children, Bim, Tara and Raja. This emotional starvation gives these children an awareness of the meaninglessness of their existence. Devan Sharma, the protagonist of Anita Desai's latest novel *In Custody* suffers as a result of inconsistency between activity and success. His unsuccessful interview of the great Urdu poet, Nur puts him in a quandary. Ithaca is presented in the novel *Journey to Ithaca. Fasting Feasting* tells the story of Arun, Anuna and Uma in a very interesting way. *Zigzag Way* is set in Mexico.

The comparative achievement of Anita Desai becomes clear when we notice that her fellow women writers like Kamala Markandaya, Ruth P. Jhabvala, Nayantara Sahgal,

Shashi Deshpande, seldom try to portray the psychic elements involved in their themes on outwardly level. Most of these writers have either overlooked the psychological reality or haven't gone so deep. Anita Desai thus clearly stands ahead the group in as much as she introduces a shift of focus from the outer in the inner part of human existence. She insists on analyzing her characters and the story is important only in so far as it reflects the obsessions of her characters. Each work of her is a haunting exploration of the psychic self.

Another quality of her fiction is her characters who are generally neurotic females, highly sensitive and alienated from their surroundings. Coming to her themes, Anita Desai seems to be quietly sliding in her scenes settings and characters without much of an advance preparation. In fact main cause of popularity is that in her fiction, life is depicted as it really is. In her world action is subordinated to psychology. In this respect the novelist shows close affinity with Virginia Woolf who also entered the consciousness of the characters. These qualities of her contribute a lot to understand how she has attained remarkable success as a novelist.

NOTES

1. Anita Desai, "Replies to the Questionnaire", *Kakatiya Journal in English Studies,* Vol. 3, No. 1, 1978.
2. B. Ramachandra Rao, *The Novels of Anita Desai: A Study*, New Delhi: Kalyani Publishers, 1972, p. 87.
3. Anita Desai, *Comments in Contemporary Novelists,* Ed. James Vinson, New York: St. Martin's Press, 1972, p. 348.
4. Usha Bande, *The Novels of Anita Desai,* New Delhi: Prestige Books, 1988, p. 7.
5. Anita Desai, in an interview with Atma Ram, *WLWE,* Vol. 30, No. 1, Spring 1990.
6. K.R.S. Iyengar, *Indian Writing in English,* New Delhi: Sterling Publishers Pvt. Ltd., 1985, p. 464.

4

Major Novels of Anita Desai

Anita Desai is one of the few distinguished Indian writers in English, whose works have been greatly admired both at home and abroad. The reader's first impression of reading Anita Desai is, therefore, one of brave originality and uniqueness. Her novels are certainly reflective of social realities from a psychological perspective. She closely examines the emotional world of womankind. She constantly highlights their individual traits, peculiar and tender instincts as crushed by the dehumanization of society. In dealing with the interior landscape and the psychic odyssey of the characters, Desai has extended and enlarged the thematic horizon of the Indo-Anglian novels. Dealing with the thoughts, emotions and sensations at various levels of consciousness, Anita Desai found the technique used by D.H. Lawrence, Virginia Woolf and Henry James. That's why she has used stream-of consciousness technique and flashback in her novels. Professor K.R. Srinivasa Iyengar rightly observes: "Since her preoccupation is with the inner world of sensibility rather than the outer world of action, she has tried to forge a style supple and suggestive enough to convey the fever and fretfulness of the stream-of-consciousness of her principal characters."[1]

Anita Desai portrays women as not totally cut off from families and societies but women who remain within these orbits and protest against monotony, injustice and humiliation. Woman in her novel is not a mere goddess or a robot but a self-actualising and self-realising individual. Unlike the other Indian novelists in English, Anita Desai's predominant concern is not with society or social forces but with the individual psyche and its interaction with social values. She creates an opulent gallery of characters, though dominated by the female. Prof. Jasbir Jain rightly points out.

> The world of Anita Desai's novels is an ambivalent one; it is a world where the central harmony is aspired to but not arrived at, and the desire to love and live clashes—at times violently—with the desire to withdraw and achieve harmony.[2]

Anita Desai took the literary world by a storm with the publication of her first novel, *Cry The Peacock* in 1963. The title of this novel refers to the exciting dance of the peacock at the approach of the rain bearing clouds. Maya, the heroine, is a neurotic young woman whose sanity is fast disintegrating under the pressures of marital discord and of certain vague but frightening childhood memories. Maya is a spoiled and pampered daughter of wealthy Brahman and is married to Gautama. He is insensitive, pragmatic and rational advocate who fails to understand her sensitive nature. She suffers from father-obsession and looks for the typical father image in her husband. In her childhood an albino astrologer had predicted that four years after her marriage one of them would die and the prediction makes her obsessed by the fear of death. As an after thought, she realizes that one of the two could be Gautama as well and she kills him by pushing him off the parapet and then commits suicide.

In *Voices in the City* (1965) Anita Desai presents a set of young educated people—Nirode Ray and his sisters Monisha and Amla. As signified by the title, the city which is here Calcutta with its dark pandemonium assumes the role of living spirit. It is the city of Death. It turns to the tragedy of man in a society where both art and life are devoid of love. Nirode is a rootless nihilist who meets failure after failure. And he refuses to make even the most necessary compromises that life demanded. He is alienated even from his mother. His elder sister. Monisha, finds him reduced to shrunken waste thing. Married against her will to a blind moralist she finds her life a virtual imprisonment and develops an incurable claustrophobia. The other members of the family are not very favourably placed either. The mother's plight is quite disturbing. The elder son, Arun, has married a clean, efficient, blue-eyed nurse never to return home. The younger daughter, Amla is like her brother and sister, an incurable extrovert. She decides to lead a contended life with the painter Dharma, but in vain. Thus they all are the product of the same social ethos and are subjected to the same kind of pressures.

Monisha's death has given Nirode a glimpse of the secret of life and death. But his ecstasy and relief soon vanish during the hours between Monisha's cremation and the arrival of his mother. Then he identifies his mother with Goddess Kali, who is the cause of both the existence and dissolution of this world.

The third novel *Bye-Bye Blackbird* (1971) deals with the immigrants' problem. The tri-section plan of the novel 'Arrival', 'Discovery and Recognition' and 'Departure'. It tells the tale of two Bengali youths—Dev and Adit's English wife Sarah. Dev, a new immigrant, comes to London to stay with the Sens in their claphan house. The absurdities of Dev's existence in England and its drab superficialities have been recorded by the novelist with accuracy and detachment in a poetic and humorous language. Dev is unhappy with the treatment accorded to immigrants in England. In his uncertainty, he develops a schizophrenic attitude to England. He changes place with Adit whom he called *spineless imperialist lover*. Later on, Adit longs to go back to India and Dev decides to stay on in England. The novel traces particularly Dev's responses to London and various phases through which Dev finally comes to accept his new home. In the final pages Anita Desai describes her female protagonist Sarah who has no choice and so she surrenders to the decision of her husband. The blackbird in the novel thus stands both for the temptation and the gloom that this temptation creates for the ex-colonial. The novel therefore, rightly bids the blackbird a 'bye-bye'.

Where Shall We Go This Summer deals with the boredom and loneliness experienced by married women, when they feel ignored and unwanted. Sita, the protagonist, living in her Bombay flat feels bored as the members of her family follow their own way of life. Minaka, her daughter, wants to be a scientist, her sons are often quarrelling among themselves and her husband Raman, factory owner, is a matter of fact person. He fails to understand his wife. Sita had lived with some satisfaction with her father at Manori with the determination not to give birth to her fifth baby. At last Raman visits her and they return to Bombay to face realities of the mundane existence.

Fire on the Mountain portrays three main female characters—the aged Nanda Kaul, Raka and Ila Das. Nanda Kaul lives in Summer Vila in the foothills of the Himalayas, after the death of her husband, a University Vice-Chancellor. Now she has withdrawn herself totally from the world and now wants to remain alone and nothing else. Both Nanda and her great grand daughter Raka try to live together avoiding each other, but the total seclusion of Raka brings a sort of self-realization and metamorphosis in Nanda's attitude and she begins to woo Raka with long stories—about her imaginary childhood. Raka is too wary to be caught.

Ila Das is Nanda's childhood friend, a ludicrous spinster. Her life represents another aspect of movement. Her barren unfulfilled life is contrasted with that of Nanda Kaul. There is an irony in her tragic death. We are trapped in a situation where there is no escape. The grim reality of Ila Das's rape and murder completely shatters the unreality of Nanda Kaul's projected reverie. The fire lit to the mountain stands for the funeral pyre that ultimately consumes and annihilates everything.

Clear Light of Day is about the growth of four children in an apparently absurd and grey world of New Delhi family. Two young girls, Bim and Tara have to cope up with a diabetic mother, a father and a mentally retarded brother. They are also burdened with the responsibility of tending to a young tubercular brother and an alcoholic old aunt. Tins domestic drama of absurdity takes place against the background of partition of the country, suggesting another pattern of violence, bloodshed and absurdity. The death of the parents leaves the children as emotional destitute; Tara gets married and goes abroad. Raja the elder brother gets married to the daughter of their Muslim neighbour Hyder Ali. He leaves Delhi and settles in Hyderabad. So that finally it is Bim who is left to look after the house and the mentally retarded Baba.

Deven, the protagonist of *In Custody* (1984) presents the stage next to Bim's in psychic balance and wholeness. He is a temporary lecturer in Hindi in a private college in Mirpore a suburb in Delhi. Deven is very-much interested in Urdu literature. As the novel opens, we see his friend Murad, now editor of an Urdu Magazine, requesting Deven to interview Nur Shahjehanabadi. The rest of the narrative shifts between Deven's success and failure, his enthusiasm and hesitancy and the final disaster he lands into. And finally he stands at a cross-road, not knowing where to turn to. In the end he finds strength in his inner self and restores to face life as it comes to him. All through the novel socio-economic factor colour his personality and mould his psyche.

In *Baumgartner's Bombay*, we see the loneliness and destitution of Hugo. Desai stresses Hugo's homelessness through the image of cats. The locale of the novel is Germany and India. The first chapter of the novel uses flashback technique from the present to past. His childhood is recalled through many German songs and poems which are scattered throughout the novel. Anita Desai has done justice to portray the mind of Baumgartner, his confusion, his maladjustment both in his own country and his adopted country.

Recently Anita Desai has produced two novels *Journey to Ithaca* and *Fasting Feasting*. These two novels she had written after she moved to New York, first novel is about Egyptian culture. It is a positive story and it is called superior religious and spiritual novel to the novels of Raja Roy. It is called a miracle work by the critics.

Journey to Ithaca exposes the theme of Indian spirituality. The novel begins with Cavafy's poem 'Ithaca' translated by Rac Dolven. In the novel India, more specifically spiritual India appears as a kind of Ithaca. Paranjape maintains that "Desai no doubt, intended India to be a type of Ithaca" (409). The main characters are Matteo and Sophie, a European couple who came to India together to share an adventure as hippies in the early 1970's. The story begins with Matteo lying sick in a hospital in India. Sophie who had deserted him, fed up with his foolish craving after Gurus, hurries to him to fetch him back home to live with her and her two children Giacomo and Istabel. Sophie is at the centre of the narrative. The novel documents the journey of two characters Matteo and Laila searching for enlightenment. The novel also portrays the pathetic conditions of Indian artists who have been selling Indian spirituality abroad. To a secular rational reader *Journey to Ithaca* remains a significant work.

Fasting Feasting believes in the dictum of *Bhagwad Gita* as the theme is no pleasure from pleasure and no pain from pain. In it essence of equality harmony and cheerfulness is everywhere to be found, "Balance of Mind" is the central theme. First half describes Arun, Sister Aruna and Uma who is mentally retarded. Marriage proposals are not coming, so later on she got married with a man who was father of four children. Uma leads a burdened life. Desai shows the psyche that divorced daughter is a very great burden more than even the unmarried daughter. Aruna got married to a very handsome, brilliant person. Trivial quality of joy in the Aruna's life is shown. She is equally unhappy. Feasting by Aruna never gives a good taste and fasting by Uma cannot give her satisfaction. Another character Melony, daughter of American family suffers from psychosis.[5] She eats too much and vomits. She is carried to psychotic centre and then cured over there.

The Zigzag Way—Desai has shifted to foreign land as to find the background of her latest novel *The Zigzag Way*. Desai again centres her attention on a male character Eric whose Psyche is displayed. Unlike *Fasting Feasting* where major characters were women like Uma, Aruna, Anamika or Melony; this novel presents Em, the girlfriend of Eric as a support to run the narrative. It reminds of Desai's novel *In Custody* where Deven's psyche is probed and his wife Sarla merely stands as a minor character. After describing the locale of Mirpore in *In Custody* Desai narrates Mexico, its culture, vision, practices in detail in her latest novel. *The Zigzag Way* (2004). It is a magical novel of elegiac beauty, which presents Mexico and in this Mexican landscape 'a young American Shimbles upon an unlikely path to self-discovery'.

Eric a New England born student in history at Harvard is a newly minted historian just out of graduate school, unsure of his past choices and future options. With no clear direction, he follows his lover, Em, when she travels to the Yucatan for her scientific research. But, unfortunately once she sets of with her colleagues to conduct fixed operations, Eric ends up alone and overwhelmed in this foreign place. Then he pursues his own private quest, tracing his family's history to a Mexican ghost town, where, a hundred years earlier, young Cornish Miners toiled to the death. With vivid sympathy, Desai conjures the struggles of Eric's grandparents and their community. The stories of Eric, his grandparents and Dona Vera—are interwoven into a short contemplative narrative. Eric is a passive narrator clambering his way through the beautiful but beguiling scenery, which is described in florid, dense prose. The novel's title comes from the zigzag way mines take on their way up out of mine shafts to prevent exhaustion. This is the first novel where the locale is not India but a foreign land Mexico which for long had fascinated the novelist and she wished to write about it. *The New York Times* notes that *The Zigzag Way* is not just a condensed course in 20th century Mexican history but a meditation on the futility of our efforts to outrun the past.

In addition to her widely celebrated novels, Anita Desai has authored two volumes of short stories—*Games at Twilight and Other Stories* (1979) and *Diamond Dust and Other Stories* (2000), alongwith some beautifully imaginative books for children. In 1983 she was awarded the Guardian Prize for children's fiction for *The Village by the Sea,* an adventurous fairy tale about a young boy living in a small fishing village in India. It was filmed as a six part serial by the BBC in 1992, and has been translated widely, including into Japanese, Russian and French. She has also written *The Peacock Garden* and *Cat on a Houseboat* for children, although she confesses that writing for young readers is possibly the most difficult literary feat of all, since one has to be conscious of one's readers continuously.

Anita Desai, fellow of the prestigious Royal Society of Literature, England and honorary member of the American Academy of Arts and Letters, and one of the most distinctive voices in the Indian literary scene has been the recipient of many awards. Apart from these already mentioned she has won the Neil Gunn Prize for International Literature, awarded by the Scottish Arts Council, in 1994, the 1999 Alberto Moravia Prize for Literature (Italy), the Grinzane-Cavour Prize, Italy, 2005, the Tomasi di Lampdusa Prize, Italy, 2006 and the CBE awarded by the British Government in 2006.

Over the years, Desai has occupied various prestigious academic positions across the world. She has been the Helen Cam Visiting Fellow at Girton College, Cambridge (1986-87), the Elizabeth Drew Visiting Professor at Smith College, U.S.A. (1987-88), the Purington Professor of English, Mount Holyoke College, U.S.A., 1988-93, the Gildersleeves Professor at Barnard College, New York, ('89), the Ashby Fellow at Clare Hall, Cambridge ('89), a visiting scholar at the Rockefeller Foundation, Bellagio, Italy in 1992 and a visiting professor at the American University of Cairo, 1992. She is also the John E. Burchard Professor of Humanities, Emeritus, at the Massachusetts Institute of Technology where she often guides aspiring writers in the creative writing program, an experience that she says has been both very challenging and enriching for her.

As an Indian fiction writer in English who has received wide acclaim from all over the world, Anita Desai occupies a unique place among the celebrated writers of this country. She is perhaps one of the few great writers of our times, who seems to be free from the restrictions of a particular region or locale in her work, and has acquired the kind of versatility that comes to writers who deal with both the interior world of characters and the exterior world of their actions and their settings, with such perfection and finesse. The whole of humanity is embraced by her all-pervasive vision. No wonder, then, that she has now been selected to adorn a most exalted position, that of a Fellow of Sahitya Akademi.

NOTES

1. K.R. Srinivasa Iyengar, *Indian Writing in English*, New Delhi, 1983, p. 464.
2. Jasbir Jain, The Use of Fantasy in the novels of Anita Desai (ed.) R.K. Dhawan, *Exploration in Modern Indo-English Fiction*. New Delhi, Bahari Publishers, 1982.

5

Anita Desai: A Psychological Novelist

Anita Desai's higher education has given her a deep insight into the human psyche and a clear critical perspective to re-examine tradition. She has shed her inhibitions in a marvelous fashion in order to show surprising frankness, boldness and honesty in the fictional treatment of the workings of the human psyche. Her novels throw light on inner climate, the climate of sensibility. Her primary intention as a novelist is to depict the psyche and emotional states of her protagonists. Anita Desai has a great significance to achieve and handle the nuances of human inner psyche beautifully. In her novels we do not find political and philosophical or social idea of characters but only characters with their observations, motivations, their consciences and their tensions.

Desai is blessed with good observations, sensitiveness and penetrating analysis of the characters, the qualities necessary for a psychological novelist. It becomes natural for her to make each work of hers a haunting discovery of the inner-self. As it is incumbent for an author who wants to point out the psychological aspects of characters to employ a certain design by which the interior working of the protagonist's mind is unfolded gradually with the progress of the narration, therefore Desai's endeavour is to discover the significance of reality by plunging below the surface and plumbing the depths, illuminating those depths till they become a more lucid, brilliant and explicable reflection of the apparent world.

Anita Desai is primarily a novelist of moods, of persistent states of mind or psyche. She is interested in the psychic life of her characters and her novels reveal that her real concern is with the exploration of human psyche. Her contribution to fiction writing has been quite commendable and substantial. She comes face to face with intangible realities of life, the innermost depths of the human psyche and the chaotic underworld of human mind through her novels. Her distinctive stature as a novelist derives primarily from the fact that she has made extensive use of the stream-of-consciousness technique in her novels. Her achievement lies in the fact that she employs a relatively new technique in Indian English fiction with a remarkable consummate skill. The fiction of Anita Desai has become self-analytical and introspective and the individual's quest for a personal meaning in life has become a theme of unavoidable interest for her. Her primary emphasis is thus on sights and sounds, on movements and patterns both physical and mental as they impinge on the consciousness of her protagonist. Her protagonists have usually sensitive sense of doom and withdraw into a sequestered world of their own.

Anita Desai has presented in her novels the predicament of sensitive women characters, who find it very difficult to adjust in the present mechanical and urbanised set-up. She sincerely broods over the fate and future of modern woman. She has explored different aspects of feminine psyche like man-woman dichotomy, their very personal relations, presentation of neurotic characters, etc. In fact, most of her novels are a study of feminine psyche, which comprises women of all ages. Images and symbols are employed freely to reveal the inner psyche of the characters and illuminated their obsession changing and contrasting moods, and psychic deviation besides emphasizing the obscure and weird atmosphere of her tale.

Desai portrays her female characters on the verge of psychological breakdown with a view to capture the prismatic quality of life in her fiction. She uses the stream of consciousness technique, flashbacks and interior monologues. Her female characters are educated, well to do and hypersensitive ladies burdened by chaotic milieu. Desai reflects the inner struggle of such characters, their desire to break the shackles and come out of their shells and assert themselves as human beings. Desai can be considered as the innovator of psychological study of alienated women in India. She deals with the problems of meaninglessness in life and lack of communication not from the philosophical or sociological but entirely from psychological point of view.

As a psychological novelist she tries to delve deep into the emotional built-up and crevices of her characters. She employs very beautifully all techniques of psychological novel like zigsaw puzzle, diary entries, self-analysis along with stream of consciousness and flashback.

She makes each work of hers an accelerating exploration of the psychic self. The psychological turmoil creates psychic imbalances, which in turn, handicap them in establishing harmonious and gratifying inter-personal relationships. There is a complete compatibility between her theme and technique. With the help of colour and symbols she reveals the hypersensitive nature of her heroines. Her language has three major characteristics—love of words, sensuous richness and sensitivity, which suit her expression of personal vision. She is much interested in life with its hopes, frustrations, negations, rejections and chaotic flow of events as she is concerned with the art of giving shape, purpose and wholeness to life.

The novelist's language and theme also reveal the meaningful correlations between the psychic conditions of the characters. Her deft handling of language, imagery and syntax in order to convey an acquainted expression of the interior psyche of her characters is superb and unique. She presents with a keen view that how moral values of women are conveniently altered to suit the demands of men who treat them as their objects of possession to be ruled and controlled by psychological insecurity nurtured in them through myths, customs and social discourse.

Desai's use of various linguistic devices in order to present the submerged psychic truth is unique in itself. Clusters of images, symbols, myths, fresh collocations, parallelisms, alliteration, consonance, rhyme, different levels of semantic interpretation are some of the devices used by her.

From the very beginning, her first novel *Cry, The Peacock* shows her interest in the psychology of her characters. Maya's psychic disintegration is presented and to do this Desai moulds images in such a way that the objects get increasingly blurred and confused. In the beginning only the edges of the images are mixed, e.g. the tail of the rat gets merged with father and father's voice becomes the voice of the peacock, yet they are recognizable. Later they all get mixed up leading to an imagistic disorder which sets forth effectively the chaos of Maya's psyche. Desai uses the stream of consciousness technique to explain the causes and growth of her despair. The second section of the novel reveals the gradual stages by which Maya moves from sanity to insanity. The final section which acts as the epilogue provides a powerful picture of the effect of the calamity on the important characters. Maya's heart craves for love and understanding, solace and support from her husband. Gautama is a normal gentleman interested in his profession of an advocate, perhaps too practical and materialistic to allot time for expressing his love. Maya does not tell him about the albino's prophecy for fear of hurting him. At the same time she is unable to bear the oppressive burden of the secret.

Because of Gautama's age and cold attitude to sex, Maya remains a much disappointed woman. The image of fighting and mating peacocks, apart from being the central motif of the novel, underlines Maya's sexual frustration too. Psychologists suggest that a healthy emotional and sexual life would have given Maya a sense of security and stopped her psyche from decaying. Fraud attributes neurosis of women to sexual dissatisfaction resulting from the rigours of civilized sexual morality. Various incidents representing her longing for outdoor life in which she bears frustration mainly by Gautama also affect her psyche. The neurotic defence mechanisms such as sleep rituals, hallucinatory visions and nightmares, experience of split personality, adverse somatic symptoms and religious avoidance of violence woefully fail to blunt the edge of her unconscious wish. At most places she appears to reel under the pressure and break to pieces as a result of the struggle within. And it resulted in psychosis which progressively moves towards a psychotic solution to Maya's neurotic struggle.

Monisha in *Voices in the City* seeks loneliness and privacy in order to be her ownself. She is oppressed by a sense of claustrophobia and longs to be free. Even her most private self is not spared by the members of the joint family. Love has no place in her relationship with her husband, Jiban. What she means by love is only a condition of conscience. She feels desperate and finds her life a conundrum that she shall brood for ever with passion and pain, never to arrive at a solution. She desires to be complete and fulfilled. Confronted by unconducive atmosphere, she turns inward and realizes that alone she can feel better. The gulf between expectations and reality throttles Monisha with the result that her bruised self withdraws into her private world where darkness is the natural element. She feels like a caged bird. Meenakshi Mukherjee rightly observes, "Monisha's claustrophobia and exasperation culminate in suicide and appropriately enough the style and imagery in the pages from Monisha's diary come closest to the language of the heroine of *Cry, The Peacock,* another desperate woman".[1]

Sleep cannot comfort her. The loneliness and the rejection of the uncongenial external world are the characteristic features of Monisha's life. In a sudden frenzy to experience desire and to experience feeling, she rushes to her room with a tin of kerosene, pours it over herself and sets fire. It is true, "Monisha's suicide is as much the result of her morbid nature and emotional insufficiency as the result of her uncongenial surroundings".[2] Thus, through this novel Desai portrays the agony, a sensitive soul experiences, in its quest for meaning and fulfillment in a hostile world.

In *Where Shall We Go This Summer*? the problem of Sita is again more a psychological problem than being external, that resulted from unfulfilled wishes. The husband-wife relationship is dragged into difficulties as they are opposite to each other. Raman is an extrovert and Sita is an introvert personality. She hates Raman for being cold. Her reactions like she starts smoking, abusing her children for trifles and her becoming extremely angry when the servants talk in the kitchen shows her hypersensitivity. Desai views her as a psychologist. Sita suffers from nervous disorders, a void in her life, emptiness, even in her married life resulting in her loss of identity. Her alienation from her surroundings, from the world around her forces her to live in a dream like world of fantasy which is the outcome of a serious psychological confusion. At a deeper psychological level Sita's quest for her identity is an outcome of the husband-wife conflict. Raman's insensitive nature causes serious libidinous problems to the mental life of Sita.

"Desai achieves the cohesive design of content and form in her psychological novels and bridges a thought-provoking harmony over different streams of feelings and sensibility, found in different settings of human society. On many places, she delves deeper and deeper in the inner world of her characters and brings out many realistic truths of psychological interest. For Desai, the inner climate, the climate of sensibility that lovers or dears or rumbles like thunder on suddenly blages forth like lightning, is more compelling than the outer weather, the physical geography or the visible action.[3]

We find that the structural pattern of this novel *Where Shall We Go This Summer?* is strikingly similar to that of Virginia Woolf's *To the Lighthouse*. Similar to Woolf's novel, it has three parts. Part one 'Monsoon' 67; Part two 'Winter' 47; Part three 'Monsoon' 67. Each section of this novel is concerned with a particular season, time and space. The psychological cosmos of Sita's life moves around the island and her father's fantasy. In the core of her heart, she believes that the magic of the island will wipe out the evil spell and her unborn child will remain within her womb for ever. Sita appears a bit abnormal and introvert. She wants to escape from the brutal realities and harsh facts of human life. She also thinks that no one cares for her. She becomes defiant in her words and deeds in the fit of depression. Sita has travelled a long distance from Maya and Monisha though she is yet to achieve perfection. She identifies herself with the jelly fish stranded on the shore. She becomes aware of the need to be related in order to gain protection. Her escape to Manori island symbolizes her need to acquire a 'place' for her 'self' both in the real and metaphorical sense of the term in order to maintain her mental equilibrium. Her urgent desire to leave the 'madness' of domesticity and the degree of triviality the outside world attaches to it sums up the traditional concept of the place destined for married women. In this novel Anita Desai follows the track of Bronte sisters, who chose to study the heart and mind of women from women's point of view.

The next novel *Fire on the Mountain* explores the inner emotional world of Nanda Kaul and Raka. Desai draws a picture of the tragedy of Nanda leading a segregated life like a recluse in lonely hill hut. In *Clear Light of Day,* again heroine prefers to lead a solitary life in a decaying house. We find that Desai penetrates into the hidden depth of mind of her characters, who are obsessed by nostalgic reminiscences of their past life and events. In this way Desai heralded a new era of psychological exploration of inner mind in her novels. We find that most of Desâi's protagonists pass through a psychological crisis which damages their value system. Some of them are lost, whereas some get out of their alienation. The psychological turmoil creates psychic imbalances, which in turn, handicap them in establishing harmonious and gratifying inter-personal relationships.

But it is wrong to say that Desai deals only with the female psyche. Her successfully probing into the male psyche establishes her as a psychological novelist whose interest is in human psychology. In her novel *In Custody* the main focus is shifted towards the male psychology. The major protagonist, Deven is the representation of male psyche. Deven comes from a lower-middle class family and his consciousness is directed towards a wide world beyond himself and his family. At thirty-five Deven feels already having spent all the empty years waiting for a break, waiting to do something worthwhile, something great. Deven is presented as a romantic and an escapist, a weak person incapable of facing crisis. A chanced visit by Murad brings about a dramatic change into the monotonous and purposeless existence of Deven. Murad's offer to take an interview of Nur appears the very summon, Deven has been waiting all these years.

> Deven felt another warm, moist tide of jubilation rise and increase inside him at being recognized, named and invited into the presence of a man so clearly a threshold into the house.[4]

To be successful has always been an anxiety with Deven. Nur in this sense is Deven's alter ego. In this novel there is a different category of psyche in the sense that here Desai attempts to study the helpless nature of male protagonists due to poverty, helplessness and lack of initiative. The diverse trends that affect the contemporary middle class Indian are unified into the sensibility of the protagonist, Deven. He undergoes experiences of various shades and complexities and eventually emerges as a wise man with a more mature and complete knowledge of being in this world. During the period of undergoing shades of various experiences, he suffers from the problem of marital dissonance. He is also disappointed with the atmosphere of the institution, Deven's psyche is probed. He is aware of his personal incompetency to fulfill his wife's desires and dreams. He lives with a sense of defeat and failure. The sense of defeat and failure bring disappointment in the lives of Sarla and Deven but it had not brought them any closer. The motif of despair, failure and mediocrity that underlines the lives of each of these people is repeated in several situations in the novel in the kind of homes, D-II types, that Deven a low paid employee in the same grade live in the phenomenon of 'brain drain' and migration to more prosperous countries for lucrative jobs. The prime characteristics of Deven that attract our attention are his helplessness, humility, suffering and nobility. Socio-economic factors colour his personality and mould his psyche. Desai uses some colour, bird, and animal images, relating to the character's despair, death and suffering. Except in the end, when Deven feels his epiphany that instills in him a new courage and clarity of vision. The novel by and large offers only negative images of characters and situations.

As a psychological novelist Desai has symbolically used the town of Mirpore. It symbolizes the basic nature of the entire class of society, to which the hero Deven belongs. Deven regards Mirpore as a prison where he is sentenced forever to live a gloomy and empty life.

In Custody is important as a psychological novel as it is recreation of the problems and the agonies of the wounded self. It is primarily about the functioning of human psyche. It is different from other novels as here we find neither a sensitive and highly strong woman protagonist nor any violent neurotic woman. It explores the psyche of male character whose problems are social. Similar kind of portrayal we find in *Baumgartner's Bombay*. Anita Desai, an expert in delineating the lacerated psyche portrays the ontological insecurity, alienation and anguish of uprooted individuals, in this novel too. It narrates the story of Hugo from his affluent childhood days in Germany to the horror of his murder in India by another German. This series of calamities losing his home, business and finally his mother makes him mute and accepting. When his frantic attempts to get connected to his mother fails, he withdraws into his own world, disinterested in the way of the world, in his own physical appearance, in anything except the company of his feline friends. Peer group experience is essential for the proper growth of child psyche. His complete schooling denied Hugo this opportunity, cultural uprooting, geographical displacement and failure to connect, torment his psyche. Frustrated with the world, with himself, having no where to go, not getting recognition for his simplicity and honesty the 'pagal firanghi' is saved out of his unpleasant past and unknown future by the German youth who murders him. He lived in doubt and distractions in his quest for identity, but he died in faith. The novelist peeps deeper into Baumgartner's mind and brings the inner fibers out of it. To force a way into the inside of human psyche is indeed an arduous work, but it fits into the narrative skill of Anita Desai. Desai's inside revelation of the character invites a wonderful parallel with

George Eliot who also displays the inner threads of human psyche. Hugo's urge to escape into a world of dream and memory from his childhood becomes a source of pleasure for his tense nervous system, but his leaning upon past memories creates an urge in him to escape the dreadful reality of his social existence. Like the characters of Virginia Woolf, Hugo too sometimes in a fit of his fear psychosis shifts from his present to his childhood memories. The use of nostalgia regulates the protagonist's language which conveys his inner experience and the true meaning of life. This way the sequestered world of the earlier novels now gives way to the socio-psychic entrapment of the self.

Thus Desai's fiction is symbolic, sensitive and psychological. Her fictional word reflects her concerns with psyche of her characters. Brati Biswas says in *Perspectives on Anita Desai:*

> By writing novels and stories that are psychological and purely subjective, She (Anita Desai) was free to employ, simply the language of the interior. She further states even when two characters meet, they use this particular type of language—the language of their thoughts, of their interior selves—which has nothing to do with geography.[5]

Anita Desai prefers simple words to polysyllabic words. A discreet mixture of Saxon and Latin words give her English a native touch. While writing about human psyche she uses more concrete nouns than abstract. This is to eliminate the 'disjunction of self and world'. As a result of this, her writing gains in authenticity, since man's two halves, the subjective and the objective make a whole. For vividness and visibility she includes adjectives, referring to physical and psychological tracts. The narrative voice is mirrored in evaluative epithets. A large number of adverbs of time, place, direction and degree give her writing a palpable quality and the adverbs of manner throw light on the personalities and the psychology of the characters. A balanced use of transitive and intransitive verbs adds speed to the progression of images, which are created in order to dramatize an inner conflict and symbolize it objectively through a situation or object. A well-known feature of her style is her use of figures of speech, metaphors and similes, personification, pathetic fallacies, alliteration and assonance are very common, but the towering figure employed by Desai is that of irony. Desai, in the garb of beautiful words and phrases, has tried to probe deep into human psyche. Few Indian English novelists have surpassed Anita Desai in psychological delineation of protagonists.

A characteristic use of symbols and images also helps the novelist like Desai to reveal her protagonists' psyche. Every colour, sound, odour, emotion and every visual image has its correspondence in tracts of human self. Whether it is the cry of peacock, or the city of death—Calcutta, or the locale of Manori island or sleepy Mirpore, Desai has used them symbolically. Her novels also abound in recurrent motifs. Her use of colour symbols convey the awareness of a confusing duality of existence. The two dominant colours in *Cry, the Peacock* are black and white. Red is probably symbolic of Maya's craving for a colourful life. In *Voices in the City*, however, scenes and characters have been presented in terms of black or dark. Black has been accentuated occasionally with streaks of white. "Everything is dark", clamours Sita, in *Where Shall We Go This Summer?* She finds her Manori house 'pitch dark', with its 'crowded darkness inside'.

We come to the conclusion after a close survey of her novels, that her novels are psychological dramas, surfacing an inner conflict through aesthetic objectivity. She has adopted a controlled method of stream of consciousness. Internal narration, a point of view within a character's consciousness, manifesting character's feelings about and evaluations of the events and characters of the story. In the novels of her first twenty years of writing, Desai has used a uniform structural pattern with marked features of a modern psychological novel. Meena Belliappa rightly says, "What is new in Anita Desai is the effort to delineate a sensitivity to locale, as it operates within the consciousness of her characters.... The nature of the central character is crucial to a fictional technique which places the centre of the novel within a single consciousness. The perceiver whose thoughts and feelings constitute the story, is also the instrument for registering the values of the objective world."[6]

'Free Indirect Thought' and 'Narrative Report of Thought Acts', dominate the writings of Anita Desai. The psychological nature of her novels makes it a natural choice. From the Spatio temporal point of view, the novels of Anita Desai give the impression of slow motion pictures with sharpness and perspicacity. The movement is in full control by the recurring monologues and implicit dialogue very frequent in her novels. Desai's writing gains in depth and intensity mainly due to her psychological perspective. The various kinds of discourses at different levels is a result of the combination of internal and external perspectives. The technique of 'Free Indirect Discourse', which has been freely used in these novels is a distinctive feature of her psychological novels. Madhusudan Prasad gives voices to our feelings when he says:

> She has added to Indian English fiction an existentialist dimension, a lyrical splendour and a technical richness that were hitherto lacking.[7]

NOTES

1. Meenakshi Mukherjee, *The Twice Born Fiction,* New Delhi: Arnold Heinemann, 1974, p. 190.
2. Meena Bulliappa, *Anita Desai: A Study of Her Fiction,* Calcutta: Writers Workshop, 1971, p. 51.
3. K.R. Srinivasa Iyengar, *Indian Writing in English,* New Delhi: Sterling Publishers, 1994, p. 464.
4. Desai Anita, *In Custody,* London: Heinemann, 1984.
5. K. Srivastava, *Perspectives on Anita Desai,* Ghaziabad: Vimal Prakashan, 1984, p. 147.
6. Meena Bulliappa, *op. cit.*, p. 27.
7. Madhusudan Prasad, *Anita Desai the Novelist,* Allahabad: New Horizons, 1981, p. 144.

6

Enduring Popularity of Anita Desai as a Novelist

Only 75 people have had the honour of winning the India's highest literary award since its inception in 1968. Of these, only two—M.R. Anand and R.K. Narayan have their body of work in English, who became Sahitya Akademi fellows. Desai has been given this honour 44 years after she published her first book *Cry, The Peacock* (1963), and 29 years after, she won the Sahitya Akademi Award for *Fire on the Mountain* Anita Desai has attained an immense popularity as a novelist. Probably no other woman writer in the Indian-English fiction has been admired by such different tastes and intellects by whole classes of readers unlike each other. Anita Desai is solely conscious of her role as a woman writer and has tried her best to maintain the tradition for other women writers. She has a belief and concern more with thought, emotion and sensation than with action, experience and achievement. Moreover, Desai's novels are documented with Indian setting. Indian culture and Indian background. Her younger character often try to imitate the western culture but do not succeed in their lives. The elder generation in all respects Indians and adherent to Indian culture. It is unimaginable to think of Anita Desai without the portrayal of inner psyche of her characters. In her novels the inner workings, the inner sensibilities are more compelling than the outer weather or the visible action. Her strong point is an exploration of sensibilities. Desai's interest in the consciousness of the woman in her novel enables us to see the Indian woman adequately from the inside. She is occupied with interiorizing the consciousness of the woman and the economics of life do not bother her except when they are noticed as adding to the monotonous aspect of existence. In Desai's fictional world, living happily ever after in the old fashioned sense in the very fate, her heroines struggle to escape. She shows us how the women have repeatedly to repress their emotions their finer impulses. And it is not of their own making but due to a social code. In fact, Desai has fashioned a new concept of feminist fiction. The woman in her literary world is on a ceaseless quest, for a more meaningful life not only for her self but for humanity in general. What fascinates her far more than the glittering surface of social life is the inner dynamics of her characters? Her art is found closer to that of Virginia Woolf and Henry James (Stream of consciousness technique) rather than that of Pope or Swift. From her novel *Cry, The Peacock* to *Fasting Feasting.* Anita Desai has dealt with several type of severe psychological and social pressures. She has visualized society from the viewpoint of solitary individuals who look upon themselves as permanently uprooted beings. She has effectively used recurring images and symbols.

Anita Desai has found the artistic potential of the isolateness of the individual in an increasingly complex society. Desai's art as a novelist is praiseworthy. She is a meticulous artist. And that's why most of her women characters feel exposed and utterly isolated. Her protagonists exhibit a lack of unquestionable and self-validating certainties. She portrays human beings as brutally victimized and no doubt women appear even worse than men. Most of her novels are about human relationship although it is rather their absence that is at the heart of the thematic impulse of her stories. Her characters, no matter to what age group they belong to, seem to use one of Heideggar's phrases "On the fringe of being and then are debarred from evolving (to recall Kierkegaard) a purely aesthetical person in fact in her novels she has dwelt upon the existentialist issues of the absurdity of human existence and the individuals trapped by circumstances. The great achievement of

Mrs. Desai rests on her beautifully recording the emotional turmoil, chaos and agonies of her oppressed protagonists." Another quality to note in her fiction is that there is not only a rejection of the passive acceptance of the traditional female role but also the deeply felt and suffered rebellion against the entire system of social relationship.

Anita Desai is a novelist of urban milieu. An uncrowned queen of the inner emotional world, she dexterously transcribes the subconscious the phan-tasmagoria of her highly sensitive protagonist terribly bewildered by the burden of living helplessly in the contemporary society bristling with absurd realities. Endowed with soundless imaginative resourcefulness and creative vitality, she writes remarkably well about only those aspects of life she has minutely observed and deeply experienced. Therefore, her fictional world full of imperfection and unfulfillment thankering and helplessness, agony and anger struggle and surrender is no doubt limited but within this limited world she reveals amazing variety and profundity.

> Anita Desai thus tries to introduce a modern psychological view and projects a sensibility generally not encountered in other Indo-Anglian writers of fiction. As a novelist her distinguishing qualities are many, the chief among them being the subordination of the background to the characters and the deft handling the language, imagery and syntax in order to convey an intimate expression of the inner world of her characters.

Desai occupies an unassailable place in the galaxy of Indian-English women novelists. She is one of the strongest voices of women writing in India today. Desai possesses sure and unerring satiric instincts. The several illuminating flashes of satire that break upon the narrative surface of her novels are evidence of her satiric mode. But satire with Anita Desai is only incidental. Her sense of irony embraces the whole emotional range of her characters. Unlike the satirists who distance themselves from their creatures and describe them from outside only. Desai, probes into the inner psyche inner recesses of her characters. That's why her whole style is ironical. Her delicate irony is the very essence of her style. Irony of style has been created by Desai deliberately. As weir, Ann Lowry, has written.

> Anita Desai is the Vanguard of a new generation of Indian writers who are experimenting with themes of inner consciousness—she gives her leaders valuable insights into the feminine consciousness though her memorable protagonists.

It is not only in the use of subject matter, characterization and in presenting the atmosphere of minds but also in the use of narrative technique symbols images flashback, the method of objective correlative and stream of consciousness, etc. that Anita Desai has achieved high recognition. In regard to the use of the stream of consciousness technique, flashbacks and interior monologue in her novels, she does it with a view to capturing the prismatic quality of life in her fiction. Every novel of Mrs. Desai is unique in itself. In *Cry, The Peacock* the emotional disparity between Maya and her husband. Gautam, is the basic cause of her sufferings. The lack of marital harmony in their lives leads to the contingent situation of Maya's life. Arjun's conflict with his father's bourgeois values of life and it creates a crisis of situation for him. In *Voice in the City* Nirode suspects his mother of adultery, and his cherished image of his mother is shattered. Monisha experiences a sense of imprisonment in her in laws house. This fact coupled with a lack of love and lack of natural trust in her marital life puts her in a predicament. Sarah, in *Bye-Bye Blackbird,* finds herself in a quandary as a result of her marriage with Adit, an Indian immigrant in London. His hopes of going to India remains unfulfilled as Adit stays in England till he himself grows aware of his counterfeit life in England. The cause of Sita's predicament in *Where Shall We Go This Summer*? is rooted in her illusion about the magic personality of her deceased father and in the lack of love and communication in her marital and domestic life, Nanda Kaul in *Fire on the Mountain* also suffers as a result of the lack of love in her life because her husband neglects her in pursuit of his love affair with Miss David. In the state of despair and loneliness, she grows aware of the absurdity of human relationships. Raka, though a child, is also aware of the hostile forces of the world because she has after seen her father maltreat her mother in *Clear Light of Day* the parents spend their time playing cards at the club or at home and do not think of the emotional needs of their growing up children, Bim, Tara and Raja. This emotional starvation gives these children an awareness of the meaninglessness of their existence. Deven Sharma, the protagonist of Anita Desai's latest novel *In Custody* suffers as a result of inconsistency between activity and success. His unsuccessful interview of the great Urdu poet, Nur puts him in a quandary.

The comparative achievement of Anita Desai becomes clear when we notice that her fellow women writers like Kamla Markandaya, Ruth Jhabvala, Nayantara Sahgal, Shashi Deshpande, seldom try to portray the psychic elements involved in their themes on outwardly level. But most of these writers have overlooked the psychological reality. Anita Desai thus clearly stands ahead the group in as much as she introduces a shift of focus from the outer in the inner part of human existence. Her main concern is to depict the psychic stages of her protagonist at some crucial juncture of their lives. To sustain her effort she has forged a style supple and suggestive enough, to convey the fever and fretfulness, to record the currents in the stream of consciousness of her character. The interplay of thoughts, feelings and emotion of characters are reflected in language syntax and imagery. She insists on analyzing her characters and the story is important only in so far as it reflects the obsessions of her characters. Each work of his is a haunting exploration of the psychic self.

Another quality of her fiction is her characters who are generally neurotic females highly sensitive and alienated from their surroundings. Coming to her themes Anita Desai seems to have opted for portraying various themes at a time in her novels and in each individual novel these themes seem to be occurring again and again. Her themes are thus original and entirely different from those of Indo-Anglian novelists. Her plots too are not repetitive. Each book has an individual structural pattern of its own. As the story advances, she seems to be quietly sliding in her scenes settings and characters without much of an advance preparation. In fact, main cause of popularity is that in her novel life is depicted as it really is. This ample knowledge of life is obtained through direct observation and insight. Her forte as novelist becomes in the words of K.R.S. Iyengar: "The exploration of sensibility—the particular kind of Indian sensibility that is ill at ease among barbarous and the philistines, the anarchists and the amoralists." Her preoccupation with the psyche of men, women and children diverts her complete attention to the question of being and the business of nausea of existence. They are traditional in their way of living but modern in their outlook and capacity to retain their individuality. Desai's preoccupation with woman's inner world and her sensibility bring her close to the novelist advocating for a new morality. Thus, the central theme of her novels automatically becomes the existential predicament of her protagonist as an individual.

Anita Desai is primarily a novelist of moods, of persistent states of mind or psyche. She is interested in the psychic life of her characters and her novels reveal that her real concern is with the exploration of human psyche. Her contribution to fiction writing has been quite commendable and substantial. She comes face to face with the intangible realities of life, the innermost depths of the human psyche and the chaotic underworld of human mind through her novels. Her distinctive stature as novelist derives primarily from the fact that she has made extensive use of the *stream-of consciousness technique* in her novels. Her achievement lies in the fact that she employs a relatively new technique in Indian-English fiction with a remarkable consummate skill. The fiction of Anita Desai has become self-analytical and introspective and the individual's quest for a personal meaning in life has become a theme of unavoidable interest for her. Her primary emphasis is thus on sights and sounds, on movements and patterns both physical and mental as they impinge on the consciousness of her protagonists. Her protagonists are usually sensitive women who, haunted by a peculiar sense of doom, withdraw into a sequestered world of their own.

In Desai's fiction we cannot ignore the woman as a subject because women have a significant place in her novels. In the majority of her works we have women narrators. The story is narrated through the feminine consciousness. Desai has a particular interest in analyzing women characters and suggesting the unusual poignancy of their fate. She investigates the actual, social and emotional bonds that shackle women. Here the setting is the upper and lower middle class Indian family life. It is in this atmosphere that she unravels the unhappy situation of the Indian women. She depicts the strong reactions of quiet, sensitive and intelligent Indian women married mostly to complacent, insensitive, uncaring, though dutiful men. Their lives turn into a bog of dull and drab matrimonial relationship with mostly no emotion and love on the part of the husband. Anita Desai is thus primarily concerned with fate of the married woman in Indian society. The theme of marital discord and an unhappy marriage causing loneliness and alienation in women characters is invariably repeated in most of her novels. The cord of harmony is never struck between Maya and Gautama, Monisha and Jiban, Sita and Raman, Sarah and Adit, Deven and Sarla, etc. Mostly her women fight for their freedom and emancipation from the clutches of a male dominated society.

K.R. Srinivasa Iyengar included a critical analysis of Anita Desai's fiction in the second edition of Indian writing in English (1973, first publication in 1963) in which he stated that Anita Desai through her first two novels *Cry, The Peacock* (1963) and *Voices in the City* (1965) was considered to have added a new dimension to the achievement of the Indian women writers in India. Her elegant and lucid novels which vividly evoke the atmosphere, society and landscapes of India, include *Fire on the Mountain* (1977) *Clear Light of Day* (1980) *Baumgartner's Bombay* (1985) *In Custody*, *Journey to Ithaca*, and *Fasting Feasting*. *Games at Twilight* (1978) and *Diamond Dust* (2000) are collections of short stories and her works for children include *Village by the Sea* (1982). The shift from the collective to the personal from the communal to the individual was conceived as the "new dimension". Desai's preoccupation with the woman's inner world; her sensibility, sulking frustration and storm raging inside her mind bring her closer to the novelists advocating for new morality. In almost each of her novels one can feel the author's urge for a way of living which would respond to the innermost yearning of the Indian woman for self-emancipation and self-dignity.

Desai has got a distinguished place as her works are different from those of other Indian women writers. Kamala, Markandaya. Ruth Jhabvala and Nayantara Sahgal. Markandaya stresses more on the rural background, in Jhabvala's fiction the social background is more important than the characters who enact the various roles, Sahgal emphasizes on political and social awareness, but in Desai's novels it is the exploration of sensibility the inner working of the mind that assumes the most important place. She unravels beautifully the mystery of the inner life of her characters. As a novelist she seems to be highly dissatisfied with most contemporary novelist's way of writing a novel. She voices her feelings in an article on 'women writers' with all the richness of material at hand. In their last few years of articulacy, they have been content to record and document. Thus, Desai has made it clear that she would not be satisfied merely with uncritical prosaic documentation of social reality. Her real concern is nothing less than exploration of human psyche.

As a novelist Desai excels in psychological novels. She would however call them purely subjective. Her writings reveal inner realities. She confides that "my temperament and circumstance have combined to give me the shelter, privacy and solitude required for the writing of such novels thereby avoiding problems, a more objective writer has to deal with, since he depends on observation rather than a private vision."

Desai's central preoccupation as a novelist is with the existentialist outlook on human life. Her characters are distinguished by the qualities of introspection, introversion and a refusal to surrender their individual selves. Deeply infected by the existential problems of modern industrial age. Anita Desai has created unique characters that are largely eccentric and abnormal in their mental make-up and hence totally unable to conform. Rao has commented thus:

> Mrs. Desai brings something new to Indo-Anglian novel, instead of portraying character in terms of the environment of defining an individual in terms of his social or caste functions, Mrs. Desai creates character and the environment is important only in so far as it enables the reader to understand the character. Moreover, the true artist that she is, Mrs. Desai presents each individual as an unsolved mystery. As a novelist Mrs. Desai is unique as she has deviated from the path of realism and taken to the path of subtle psycho-analysis, probing deeply into the inner working of a man's mind. She believes in the process of discovering the truth. She has herself stated: "Writing is my way of plunging to the depths and exploring this underlying truth. All my writing is an effort to discover to underline and convey the true significance of things."

Anita Desai employs the stream of consciousness device to portray a particular kind of sensibility. In this matter she is also influenced by Eliot, James Joyce and Virginia Woolf. She is unique as she has tried to forge a style supple and suggestive enough to convey the fever and fretfulness of the stream of consciousness of her principal characters. She has purposely adopted this technique to reveal forcefully the emotional needs of her haunted characters.

In her novels, there is no plot in the conventional sense of the term as she is never interested in telling a story, hence there is little plot and development of events in her novels. In the interview with Atma Ram she has herself made it clear "I prefer the word pattern to plot as it sounds more natural.. while plot sounds arbitrary, heavy handed and artificial all that I wish to avoid. One should have a pattern and then fit the characters, the setting and the scene into each piece in keeping with the others and so forming a balanced whole." It is really difficult to tell a tale without a well-structured plot for any writer. But Anita Desai does it and succeeds in it. A novel like

Cry, The Peacock, or *Fire on the Mountain* has nothing to narrate as such.

The mature artistry which can harmoniously blend matter with manner, form with content, design with detail, structure with texture, is a rare thing which Anita Desai has achieved. The interaction between poetic texture and the narrative structure has raised the Indian fiction in English to a higher level of artistic success. Anita Desai's gifts as prose stylist are now acknowledged. What is perhaps overlooked in the process is the fact that most of her problems as a fiction writer begin with the insistence on too much style on too small a canvas. Her limited canvas forces her to *strategies* which are not always conducive towards highly convincing fiction. In the technique of powerful reversal, Desai has acquired a peculiar mastery, sometimes though the effect is quite contrary to the one intended. This often creates a disturbing tragic awareness in the readers and this is how Mrs. Desai achieves the true function of art to disturb and remind us of basic realities ignored by the society. In the three major novels written by her in the later period Anita Desai continued to seize upon the shapelessness and meaninglessness of life and impose a particular design on them. The author consciously engages in the exploration of the human striation which often tends to be existential rather than bound by heredity, society, religion, moral or cultural values of the character or the authoress, for example in *In Custody* Desai's trouble are exactly like this. In *Fire on the Mountain*, Nanda Kaul has the choice to receive her great grand daughter and the friend Ila Das, but she doesn't. This leads to unpredictable situations. There in the novel action words parallelism auditory, kinetic and visual images arrest the action as if it were in painting. The novel ends abruptly, but at the same time artistically arresting trapping its honour and strange beauty. The plot of *Clear Light of Day* is more complex. The novel looks almost plotless. In *In Custody* Desai's fondness for quotes from various writers serves a definite purpose.

Thus while writing psychological and purely subjective novel, Desai uses freely the language of the interior, i.e. neither

German nor Bengali but English. And the use and the free play of this language amply suit the temperament of Anita Desai. Whatever she writes is a matter of instinct and waiting. As a novelist she represents the welcome creative release of the feminine sensibility. As a mature novelist she is able to narrate the story, to portray the characters, to convey the mood, to evoke the atmosphere and to probe the inner psyche of her character. The only thing that troubles us is her use of German songs and poetry in some of her novels, without giving English paraphrase. Even then one thing is sure that she makes use of various fictional techniques with success and they are always in accordance with the demands of the novels.

Desai's tremendous contribution to Indian-English fiction was recently recognized by the Sahitya Akademi fellowhip conferred on her in New Delhi in the year 2007. Although she is the seventy-fifth Fellow in the entire history of the Sahitya Akademi, she is only the third Indian writer in English, after Mulk Raj Anand and R.K. Narayan to be so honoured.

In his introduction to the new Random House edition of Anita Desai's novel *Baumgartner's Bombay*, Suketu Mehta rightly sums up the great literary debt owed to her by his generation of writers. He said, "Anita Desai is *godmother* to the current generation of prodigal Indian writers in English. She began writing at a time when Indian writers did not get big advances, weren't reviewed regularly in all the big papers, didn't win Bookers or Pulitzers. Teaching at American universities to support herself and her four children, she wrote steadily, consistently, and without fanfare. She championed Salman Rushdie from the beginning. She taught us, among other things, how to use spoken Indian-English it lapsing into parody."

7

Anita Desai's Art of Plot Characterization and Prose Style

Anita Desai is well established and has been esteemed highly for her positive contribution to Indian fiction in English. Her art of characterization has received much praise. She is an artist of a high order, and her concern for human lot has imparted a special charm to her novels. Desai's characterization is a wonder-work of genius. She possesses exuberant energy of creating characters. Her world is the world of richness, variety and complexity unmatched in the Indian-English fiction. She has never created common characters, instead, she has written about individual men and women—the solitary beings. Her characters, independent, agonized, frustrated and some what domineering make us feel as though we have noticed them in our neighborhood—and herein lies the charm of Desai's art of characterization. B. Ram Chandra Rao has commented thus.

> Mrs. Desai brings something new to Indo-Anglian novel. Instead of portraying character in terms of the environment of defining an individual in terms of his social or caste functions, Mrs. Desai creates characters, and the environment is important only in so far as it enables the reader to understand the character. Moreover, the true artist that she is, Mrs. Desai presents each individual as an unsolved mystery.

Mrs. Desai shows a remarkable skill in her use of a highly suggestive imagery and in handling the stream-of-consciousness techniques, which are her main technical instruments for portraying the psychic world of her characters. All the important characters are well developed. In the process of delineating her characters, she reveals their awareness of the absurdity of life, their agony and despair, their sense of isolation, their search for identity and meaning in life, and their sense of responsibility which accompanies their independent decisions. The modern scientific and technological progress which has transformed the conventional set up of society has undermined the words and dignity of human life. By probing into the psyche of her characters. Anita Desai has presented a living picture of the dullness and meaninglessness of today's society. That shows how the characters become much more unique and individual. Maya, Sita, Monisha, Sarah, Nanda, Raka and Tara, Deven, Hugo—all of them are created as the embodiment of an unsolved mystery never following the currents, always fighting against their surroundings and people for the sake of their freedom.

We find a lot of influence of the Existentialist thinkers—Camus, Sartre, Jaspers, Heidegger, Kierkegaard, Marcel, etc. on Anita Desai. Her keen interests in creating unique and individual characters, who decide their own course of action freely fighting for their emancipation from social and economic bondage, place her characterization on a unique platform. The psychological depths of her characters can be probed only by the technique of stream-of-consciousness or only by the impressionistic method. About her character-portrayal Shyam M. Asnani remarks as under:

> Anita Desai does not portray characters in a traditional manner. The characters come alive in their dynamic process always growing and changing viable and imitable. They are portrayed as preoccupied with the present, look backward in time and visualize failure as well. They have been represented in retrospect and fall back upon memory or the uncontrolled flow of thought.

> With this use of pure memory and flux Anita Desai may be said to be depicting reality.

Indeed as a creative artist, her central preoccupation is with the exploration and evaluation of the subjective reality of human individual. Deven Sharma, the protagonist of *In Custody,* is frantically busy in pursuit of his ideal, but the fact is that he also stands in the moment and passes through the agonizing states of anxiety, dread and concern. His dread of being ruined gives him an insight into his authentic existence, and he gains the courage of his convictions. Deven is an interesting study in characterization for he manifests inherent contradictions. He has an innate poetic sensibility but turns out to be a 'boring teacher', because he has distanced himself from the profession he has accepted.

Anita Desai's emphasis on the study of the individual as an aggregate of psychic and emotional impulses leads her to write what might be called novels of character. Her protagonists are basically tragic characters. They fail to cope with their surroundings and are cut off from their families and society. They are psychologically disturbed, morbid, self absorbed and incoherent in their manner and expression. They do not have the determination and the steadiness of will to pursue a definite line of action. They are introvert people, temporarily fallen into a stale of abnormal passiveness to sensation, in which again the association of ideas is not directed and controlled by a sense for conduct. Desai justifies her selection of solitary and introspective characters in the following words. "Well. I think, solitary and introspective people are always very aware of living on the brink—but perhaps my introspective characters arc more aware than others are of what lies on the others side." Desai's characters are creatures of habit, stubborn and unyielding. Some of them are defeated but most of them succeed in saying no to society. These characters are inevitably confronted with an unfriendly and hostile reality. They feel emotionally estranged from the family and environment. They turn inward and speak to themselves in long soliloquies and monologues. Maya, Monisha, Tara, Bim, Nirode, Deven all recollect their past. The language of the interior serves her purpose best when she dramatizes the innermost feelings of a character in long soliloquy. She is interested "delving deeper and deeper into a character or scene rather than going round about it."

In Desai's novels characters are set in binary opposition in terms of values, attitudes, temperaments and outlook on life. The male characters are also contrasted with each other as between Deven and Murad, Nirode and Dharma etc. The characters are polarized in terms of social status, success and quality of life. Like men, the women characters are also polarized; as Amla and Monisha, Tara and Bim, and Nanda and Raka.

Another important quality of Anita Desai's narrative mode is that it frequently roars into poetic heights in turn with the intending of perception embodied in the novels. Her minute observation of reality is reflected in her rich prose style. For example in *In Custody* she has used her observation to depict the situation:

> Turning his mind decisively away from their dangerous shoals, he paced up and down in his bare feet, his pajamas and the vest full holes, scratching at mosquito bites, smoking an occasional cigarette, refusing to entertain poetry and thinking in strict prose that he must look like a caged animal in a zoo to any creature that might be looking down at earth from other planet. Not that was all he was—a trapped animal.

Use of Language—Desai makes use of native words to evoke Indian atmosphere. Desai uses many Indian words in the novels. As a translation of these words in English words like *Puja*, *gup-shup*, *Samadhi*, *halwa*, *rotis*, *Neem Tree*, *Deven-bhai*, *bazzar*, *Kebabs and pilao bibi-ji*, *paise*, etc. Desai is also carried away by onomatopoeic words like *thrum*, *thrum*, *drip*, *drip*, *Ahh*, *roti and Dal*.

Desai's skill in sentence construction seems to be breaking down in the later novels. Somewhere very long sentences are also used. She also makes use of her rhetorical skill at several occasions. She also makes use of poetry to convey the meaning more effectively. Desai is no doubt a great artist with astounding technical dexterity. There is a happy fusion of structure, texture, technique and language. In each of her novels there is no conventional plot, instead, there are certain episodes which while creating a desired pattern and rhythm, contribute harmoniously to the overall structure of the novel, rendering it conspicuously coherent.

The narrative mode of Anita Desai's fiction is controlled by the characters, who in their freedom to act and think, weave a pattern of existence and a form of meaning through the various strategies of triptyche structure, first person and third person narrative, fantasy and poetic intensity.

Her characters are distinguished by the qualities of introspection, introversion and a refusal to compromise and their inability to accept the perspective of the partners inevitably results in isolation and loneliness. As in the case of Deven Sharma, (*In Custody*) who, in spite of so many obstacles refuses to surrender, does his work dutifully, faces failure, even then in the end refuses to compromise. He feels isolated, lonely as he is unable to develop mental sharing and compatibility with his wife Sarla.

Thus we can see that Desai develops her characters through circumstances. In other words, her characters are not flat; they change and grow psychologically under the stream-of-consciousness. They do not remain the same from beginning to the end. They are the fantastic creations of her fertile imagination. They have great deal of vigour and vitality. That's why they are dearly loved by the readers. R.S. Pathak has rightly commented, "Few Indian novelists in English have surpassed Anita Desai in psychological delineation of the protagonists."

Thus as for characterization, this novel, *In Custody*, as also most of Desai's novels, is very successful. All the important characters are well developed. Even Mr. Trivedi, a minor character is characterized sufficiently well. Of all the characters Murad, one of the chief protagonists in the novel, is unforgettable. He is very interesting. In her novels Desai is adept in creating characters like Deven, a diffident and awkward temporary lecturer, highly existentialist. Always looming in the background, doing her household duties, always complaining Sarla remains a silent yet the retaining presence. As her desires and consciousness is never properly depicted in the novel. One, often having read the novel hurriedly, forms the impression that Desai has failed to characterize her adequately well. But this impression proves wrong, as one reads the novel carefully, specially the later chapters.

In Custody is, by and large, a flawless creation of Desai's craft singularized by a happy fusion of structure, content and language. It reveals the remarkable measure of Desai's success in having dealt with a theme and male character, hitherto unexplored in her fictive world. We cannot but admire its novelistic excellences which even the western critics have come to recognize and accept.

8

Female Characters of Anita Desai

Anita Desai has contributed a lot in making Indian-English fiction popular the world over by shifting the domain of her fiction from outer to inner reality. G. Rai has announced her as "a writer with an original voice"; likewise Ramesh K. Srivastava rightly says, "Anita Desai has emerged as a very serious, skilled and promising novelist in India today."

Anita Desai looks at the predicament of women and visualizes life for a woman as a series of obligations and commitments. In addition to existentialistic reality of life she evokes the sentiment and sensibility of women for their role and respect in society. She closely examines the emotional world of womankind. She sets herself to voice the mute miseries and helplessness of millions of married women tormented by existentialist problems and predicaments. She focuses on how her heroines, in the contemporary urban milieu, are bravely, struggling against or helplessly submitting to the relentless forces of absurd life. Desai has natural preference for writing about women characters. She has written by and large about women characters and no wonder if most of her novels move around women characters. Although she is pre-occupied with the theme of incompatible marital couples yet we come across different kinds of women characters in her novels. She has explored the psyche of both the childless women, as of Maya in *Cry, The Peacock* of Monisha in *Voices in the City* and also of women with children like Sita in *Where Shall We Go This Summer?* and Nanda Kaul in *Fire on the Mountain*. The interesting thing to note is that Anita Desai has also portrayed the psyche of women in when that they don't want children.

Thus mostly Anita Desai portrays women as not totally cut off from familial and social ties but women who remain within these orbits and protest against monotony, injustice and humiliation. Her heroines are not mere goddesses or robots but also they are self actualizing and self realizing individuals. Delineating in novel after novel the pitiable and awful plight of the alienated self, especially of heroines like Sarla facing single handed the torments of their indifferent and temperamentally callous husbands, Anita Desai has rendered a new dimension to Indian fiction in English.

In fact, he has presented two extremes. If at one extreme there are sensitive women characters, on the other extreme, we also find thick-skinned women with blunt sensibility. In her very first novel *Cry, The Peacock* we find examples of two extremes. The dance of the peacock acquires a sinister significance to the heroine of the novel. Maya, the heroine is a neurotic young woman whose sanity is fast, disintegrating under the pressure of marital discord and of certain vague but frightening childhood memories. Maya, a spoiled and pampered daughter of wealthy Brahman is married to Gautama, a rather insensitive advocate who fails to understand her sensitive nature. She suffers from father-obsession and looks for the typical father image in her husband. Here Anita Desai has dealt with a sterile woman, highly sensitive and emotional. She is the pampered child of a Rai Saheb, and is brought up in an atmosphere of luxury. Though Gautama loves her in his own way yet Maya is never satisfied and happy. She feels that Gautama never cares for her and does not have any feelings for her. Being childless she is much attached to the dog. She comes before us as a hypersensitive woman, an introvert. Maya on the one extreme is fragile, with deep cultural roots and refined sensibilities. On the other extreme is her friend Pom who absolutely does not bother and is a typical woman with love for clothes, jewellery, colour, and looks.

Another women character is Maya's friend, Leila, who has married a tubercular man. She is gloomy and ascetic wearing no jewellery. She is a contrast to Pom. *Voices in the City* articulates Monisha's plight and psychic life and intimately shows the women like female birds in the cases, Monisha dies screaming for life, for the first experience of real feeling of pain awakens in her a desire to live. She loves to see herself as an unfettered individual and not to become at any stage a complacent, tame wife who adjusts herself to a gilded cage. "She is too silent for the family and the world distrusts her silence. She wants to be herself and not to compromise."

Sarah in the *Bye-Bye Blackbird* is alienated from her parents. Anita Desai treats Sarah with the sensitivity of a woman, always aware of those forces that change her destiny as a female. The glimpses she gives us into Sarah's inner struggle or that of her parents are full of pathos and human sympathy. Even with all her acceptance Sarah remains an outsider in her own chosen world.

Sita in *Where Shall We Go This Summer?* shudders at the idea of giving birth to a fifth child. She withdraws into her psyche of childhood days on the magic island. She lives in the world of fantasy thinking that going to the island and thereby to the world of childhood she could prevent the biological process of delivery. It is a strong case of neuroticism, finally she consents to the sane advice of her husband and comes back to Bombay to deliver. She is irrational, childish and petulant.

Through the character of Sita and Maya, Desai has portrayed the feminine psyche of neurotic women. They might be called sub-normal if not abnormal. Anita Desai's psychological probing of the women is that she includes females of different age groups. It is not that she confines herself to the young or the middle aged. She has also explored the psyche of girl Raka in *Fire on the Mountain.*

In Custody marks a departure from her earlier novels in the sense that the protagonist in this novel is not a female but a male. Centre of attraction is Deven and not his wife Sarla. Deven is married to Sarla who is not his choice. Sarla's domestic life is not a very happy one. Sarla is too prosaic for her husband who is poet by heart. Sarla is also a victim like her husband. She tries to discharge her duties as a housewife but there is nothing attractive either about her body or her temperament. She is usual, ordinary, compromising and a lady of normal temperament. That's why she is not like Maya or Sita or Amla, the typical heroines of Anita Desai. Sarla is a typical Indian housewife, she belongs to lower income group as her husband Deven is a temporary lecturer in a local college of Mirpore, near New Delhi. Her husband is the main protagonist, main sufferer but she is not less a victim as she suffers mentally, physically, economically and psychologically as well. Her husband never tries to understand her. Her marital life is not at all happy. She has a little son Manu. Her responsibilities as a mother makes her frustrated as she has no money in her hands. Her predicament is the lot of every second Indian woman. Sarla may not be the heroine in the sense Desai has Maya, Monisha, Amla and others but as far as *In Custody* is concerned Sarla's alienation, boredom and loneliness makes her a typical Desai's character.

Thus we had seen that Desai closely examines the emotional world of her heroines. She constantly highlights their individual traits, peculiar and tender instincts as crushed by the dehumanization of the society. Her heroines feel exposed, vulnerable and utterly isolated. They strain and shake the bars of their cage which is their home. But they do not contemplate leaving the threshold of their cage-home even in their wildest, bitterest moods as they are family women. But no doubt Desai's heroines are masterpieces.

9

Narrative Technique of Anita Desai

Anita Desai has emerged as a very serious, skilled and promising novelist in India today. Of all the contemporary Indian English novelists, Anita Desai is undisputably the most powerful novelist. She really deserves, compels and invites plenty of critical attention. She seriously sets herself to voice the mute miseries and helplessness of millions of men and women tormented by existentialist problems. An uncrowned queen of the inner emotional world she dexterously transcribes the subconscious, the phantasmagoria of her highly sensitive protagonists. Endowed with boundless imaginative resource fulness and creative vitality she reveals amazing variety and profundity in her fictional world. She has given a new dimension to the Indian novel in English by turning from outer to inner reality. G. Rai, has called her "writer with an original voice. Desai is well known for her use of technique."

The world 'Technique' is derived from the Greek word 'technique' meaning 'an art'. The method adopted by a writer to present life in the process of living may be described as the narrative technique. Though the novel gets its main sustenance from the story it intends to tell, its success depends on how it is narrated. The quality of readability, the most important of all the desirable qualities of a novel, may be achieved when there is compatibility between the narration and the narrative technique. Technique is a matter of predominant concern for Anita Desai. She has not only brought innovative changes in it but also makes use of flashbacks and stream-of-consciousness technique. She expresses her views on the skill of writing in the following words.

> Writing has become such a deeply ingrained habit, it is like chain smoking, I chain-smoke with words, with books.

Desai employs "the language of the interior to delineate the inner tensions and crises in the lives of her characters." That's why her novels are called forte of poetic sensibility. Desai's exploration of sensibility and distinctive technique made her novels celebrities. Anita Desai uses the technique of contrast between various settings, situations, characters and even between different stages of the same characters. Her achievement consists in beautifully recording the emotional turbulence and chaos of her oppressed protagonists with a remarkable fidelity and seriousness. Her fiction is not at all transparent and predictable, unlike the fiction of R.K. Narayan and Kamla Markandaya. Nor does she use the traditional plot structure with linear movement in terms of exposition, conflict, and resolution. She does not philosophize or indulge in self-conscious story telling in the manner of Raja Rao or Salman Rushdie, she declares—

> All my writing is an effort to discover to underline and convey the true significance of things.

Desai in her later novels, including *In Custody,* continues to seize upon the shapelessness and meaninglessness of life and impose a design on characters. Here, the author consciously engages in the exploration of the human situation which often tends to be existential rather than bond by heredity, social environment, religious, moral or cultural values of the character or the author. There is no determinism in Desai's novels—she seems to agree with Jean-Paul Sartre that man (or woman) is condemned to be free. Her fiction is bound by existentialist framework both in theme and technique. She declares:

> My novels are no reflection of Indian society, politics or character. They are a part of my private effort to seize

> upon the raw material of life—its shapelessness, it meaninglessness.

Desai has got different techniques as her novels lack the traditional plot structure with predictable linear movement in terms of exposition, conflict and its resolution. She often uses simple plot elements to propel plot development and depends on what may be called deconstructive devices for creations of meaning and atmosphere in her novels. She uses quotes from other writers and juxtaposes contradictory experiences for the reader by using technique such as value reversal and surrealistic effects. Within the existential framework, she creates people with dreams and wills who in turn create the story, action and drama of the novels. Her characters come alive as they find situation where choices and commitment are involved despite the meaninglessness and shapelessness of the human condition. One critic has written about the use of fantasy in narrative technique of her novels:

> It develops the theme of adventure, the attraction of the unusual...fantasy lies here in the narrative technique which combines the realistic and the romantic modes. It is not character which is important but incident or situation.

Desai's experiments with non-traditional materials and technique give her a distinct position among the Indian English novelists. Her fondness for quotes from various writers serves a definite purpose. Deven quotes Nur's words:

> My blood no more than a reed pen cut by the swords tip,
> Useless and dry till dipped in the Ink of life's blood.

These lines sum up the life and poetry of Nur. Life, blood and poetry are intertwined.

> Many sins, and much suffering, such is the pattern,
> Fate has traced on my tablet, with blood....

Sometimes, the poems are recited by Nur himself but significantly Nur's own poetry is never quoted; rather it is Nur's favourite English poets who are quoted. And the quoted poets are the famous romantics like Byron, Shelley and Keats and the lines quoted are from Ode to the West wind. Ode to Nightingale and La Belle Dame Sans Merci. The poems quoted have some bearing upon Nur's character as inferred by Deven:

> The recitation was so long, so filled with finely timed pauses and gestures, that Deven had begun to wonder....

The plot of the novel *In Custody* is intricately connected with the characters of Deven and Nur. In the beginning, it is Deven through whose action the plot moves but as soon as Murad asks him to interview the poet; the actions are more controlled by the poet than by Deven or Murad. The central incident of novel is the interview and all other actions are either related to it or subordinate to it. It is true that the main doer is Deven but all his actions, his long efforts and several trips to Delhi to interview the poet are subject to the will of Nur. The action of the whole novel is a long series of episodes related to the interview. And at long last when the interview does take place it does not come out well.

The tone of the novel is ironical in the sense that in spite of the best efforts of Deven his circumstances go against him and everything leads him to further trouble. Mr. Jain sells him a second hand tape-recorder and the boy Chiku who operates it, does it at the wrong time and what is finally recorded is worthless talks of Nur about biryani, pigeon flight, tales of his vagabond days. Thus from the point of view of technique *In Custody* is not a very significant novel, if we compare it with her more later novels like *Bye-Bye Blackbird*, *Journey to Ithaca* etc. But still it very well portrays the mind of an anti-hero Deven who is different, unsure of him, never able to fight and always a victim of people and circumstances. In the present novel, Desai, at occasion, achieves a fine blending of satire, irony and humour. The novel also makes use of poetry but ironically none of the poems recited are by Nur.

Desai also makes use of certain Hindi words in her dialogues but their use is justified. Justification for using foreign words is that either the words are untranslatable or the words come spontaneously when the characters are emotionally charged.

Thus we had seen that relegation of action to a secondary place enables us to understand more preferably how and why of a situation. In this respect the writer shows a close affinity with Virginia Woolf that also entered the consciousness of the characters. G. Rai puts the matter definitively.

> She is almost alone among Indo-Anglian writers who have used stream-of-consciousness technique in her novels and short stories to explore the working of the Indian mind.

Desai's style or technique of delivering the thematic thrust is the vital agent. Language is the main element of her style. Desai's use of language and dialogues is one of the features of her artistically conceived novels. She has tried to present her themes organically with appropriate adjustment and adaptations in spheres of style and point of view. Mrs. Desai is no doubt a great artist with a remarkable and astounding technical efficacy. It is not in the use of subject matter, characterization, and in presenting the atmosphere of minds but also in the use of narrative technique, symbols, images, flashbacks, and the method of objective co-relation and stream-of-consciousness etc. that Anita Desai has achieved high recognition. In regard to the use of the stream-of-consciousness technique, and interior monologue in the novel, she does it with a view to capturing the prismatic quality of life in her fiction. Desai finds this a more interesting technique rather than covering a large area superficially. For her, it is depth which is interesting, delving deeper and deeper in a character, a situation or a scene, rather than going round about it.

The credit goes to her technique as it enriches the novel by lifting it above the mere narration of a story or depiction of a character and provides it the very life, blood and the soul. Her technique does not only suit the existentialist theme dwelt upon in the novel but also go a long way in her externalizing the inner turmoil of her protagonists. This technique is deftly used by Mrs. Desai in capturing authentically a psychological realism, 'an intensified impressionism' a multiplied consciousness. Through its use, she aims at crystallizing the various complexities of man-woman relationship and the varying states of human psyche.

Meenakshi Mukherjee taking a note of Desai's language and style relates the novelist's manner of narration to the elements of her protagonist's personality. She believes that "Desai's style shows a strong individuality. About her language she observes that it is marked by three characteristics; sensuous richness, a high strong sensitiveness and a love for the sounds of words." The result is her comparative superiority over other Indian women novelists writing in English.

10

Various Critical Comments on Author and on the Novel

(1) "Anita Desai's fiction attests the validity of the Heracleitian doctrine that all living is essentially flux, and what is generally called being is merely a change form one state of consciousness to another." —R.N. Sinha

(2) "Anita Desai represents perhaps the finest blend of Indian and European sensibilities. A vivid reflection of this unique blend finds spontaneous expression in her novels and short-stories." —R.S. Sharma

(3) "I have been writing, since the age of seven as instinctively as I breathe. It is a necessity to me. I find it is in the process of writing that I am able to think, to feel and to realize at the highest pitch." —Anita Desai

(4) "That women writers are likely to place their emphasis differently from men, that their sense of values is likely to differ and that they will deal with what may appear trivial to male readers because it appears to have less consequence than the usual male actions do, with what is less solid and tangible than the concerns of most men—that is less with action, experience and achievement and more with thought, emotion and sensation." —Anita Desai

(5) "The beauty of *In Custody* is that what seems to be a story of inevitable tragedies turns out to be a tale of triumph over these tragedies...Magnificent."

—Salman Rushdie in the *Observer*

(6) "Resonant and Realistic" (about *In Custody*) Peter Kemp in the *Sunday Time*.

(7) *In Custody* "A deft, sometimes savage comedy", *The New York Times Book Review*.

(8) "A memorable book the best that Anita Desai has written" Paul Bailey in the *Evening Standard* about *In Custody*.

(9) "In Anita Desai's novels, imagery lends a poetic, lyrical coloring to the problems of the estranged self and project reality through artistic parallels more powerful and eloquent than common collocation of words." —Prasad

(10) "Anita Desai explores the disturbed psyche of the modern Indian woman. Her women characters try to strike a balance between instinctual needs and intellectual aspirations." —Santha Krishnaswamy

(11) "Anita Desai's gifts as a prose stylist are now acknowledged. What is perhaps overlooked in the process is the face that most of her problems as a fiction writer begin with her insistence on too much style on too small a canvas."

—R.S. Sharma

11

In Custody: An Introduction

In Custody: Introduction and Summary

> The beauty of *In Custody* is that what seems to be a story of inevitable tragedies turns out to be a tale of triumph over these tragedies Magnificent.
>
> —Salman Rushdie in the *Observer*

In Custody is a novel about an unassertive lecturer of Hindi in a Mofussil Degree College in Mirpore near·Delhi. His name is Deven Sharma. He is an Urdu enthusiast and wants to interview an established ageing poet of Urdu, named Nur. The whole novel is about the interview which is beset with many obstacles and mishaps and when at long last it materializes, the tape recorder is not operated well and what is recorded is a string of nonsense utterance of a senile poet about biryani, pigeon flight, wrestling and memories of his young days. Since the interview is financed by a grant from the college the tape of the interview is to be deposited in the college. But the irony is that there is nothing worth depositing in the tape. Deven is in a dilemma and he seems to be in custody of the poet.

In Custody marks the continuation of some of Desai's earlier themes and narrative tendencies as for example, the quest for identity, the theme of self-alienation, the problem and plight of alienated individuals caught in the crisis of a changing society. *In Custody* marks also a departure in the sense as it is not concerned with the inner world of female protagonists.

Rather it has an ineffectual young man whose problems are not just personal and private but public and social. The novel deals with issues like poetry, language and man-woman relationship even monetary problems. There is also a shift in her style of writing while her earlier novels were characterized by prose of a typical quality; *In Custody* reveals the absence of passages of lyrical beauty in it. This is probably due to the fact that in this novel, emphasis has shifted from the internal to the external. The narrative is organized in such a way that the cultural past of India becomes part and parcel of the bubbling and throbbing consciousness of Deven. The social and the cultural significance of the novel consists in Deven's honest efforts to surmount these insurmountable obstacles. In fact, the events that precede the hopeless position in which Deven is trapped emerge from a cultural matrix and a social milieu over which Deven has no control.

Major and Minor Characters of the Novel

(1)	Deven	The disingenuous unassertive lecturer of Hindi in a Degree College in Mirpore near New Delhi. He is a diffident, awkward and credulous character.
(2)	Muard	Childhood friend of Deven now editor of an Urdu Magazine, *Awaaz*.
(3)	Nur Shahajehanabadi	The great Urdu poet, caught between his two wives, is a weak grasping old man.
(4)	Sarla	A religious Hindu lady, a typical Indian house wife Sarla is married to Deven.
(5)	Imtiaz Begum	Second wife of great poet Nur. She is called by Deven a "Powdered and painted creature in black and silver.
(6)	Safia Begum	She is the first wife of the great poet Nur Shahjehanabadi. She is illiterate but highly money minded.

(7)	Abid Siddiqui	He is the kind, sympathetic lecturer of Urdu in Deven's college.
(8)	Mr. Tripathi	He is the Head of the Hindi Department in the same degree college at Mirpore. At times he becomes cruel and misuses his authority.
(9)	Mr. V.K. Sahay	Mr. V.K. Sahay son of K.K. Sahay patron and mentor of Murad. He was an elderly, bewhiskered man.
(10)	Manu	Manu is the only son of Deven and Sarla. He is a school going little boy.
(11)	Ali	Servant of Nur and Imtiaz Begum.
(12)	Rai Sahib	Finance Manager in the Deven's college.
(13)	Jaydev	Another lecturer in the Dept. of Hindi, Lala Ram College, Mirpore. He dreams to go to America to get a job there as Hindi Teacher.
(14)	Mr. Jain	A shopkeeper, who sold second hand tape-recorder to Deven.
(15)	Chiku	Nephew of Mr. Jain. Technical assistant of Deven for recording Nur's interview. Chiku has completed a course in electronics at the Sethi School of Electronics Cannaught Place, New Delhi.
(16)	Pintu	Another nephew of Mr. Jain, the shop-owner. He accompanied Deven to Mirpore, to play the tape over there. But he proved more imbecile than Chiku.
(17)	Dhanu	A Student of Deven, who had a gift for mechanics. He studied radio technology by correspondence course.

(18)	Raj	An old school friend of Deven, whose house is in Delhi. He is a handicapped born with one leg shorter.
(19)	Raj's aunt	She is widow, deeply religious, hospitable and homely lady, living in Delhi all alone.
(20)	Tailor	He lives near the house of Raj in Delhi. Ladies tailor, by profession, he acts as a devotional singer and gives company to Raj's aunt.

12

Chapterwise Summary of the Novel and Critical Comments

Chapter I

The novel opens with the arrival of Murad, Deven's old classmate and friend at Mirpore. He is the editor of an Urdu magazine *Awaaz*. He inspires Deven to interview Nur, the great poet of Urdu literature at his house in old Delhi. In attempt to escape the bullying Murad, he rushes to the classroom. But he loses interest in teaching the students as he is failure as a teacher. Together the two friends go out for lunch in a bazaar restaurant. During lunch they discuss their financial problems. Deven complains for the payment of his poems and reviews in Murad's magazine. Murad informs him that his magazine is not a success; he is simply carrying on with it to keep alive the glorious tradition of Urdu poetry. Murad wanted to publish some new work so he wanted a full feature on Nur. He instructs Deven, "Then do as I say. Find him. Go to him and interview him Discuss the scene with him." This chapter introduces us to two main characters of the novel Deven and Murad. Murad here sets background of Deven's tragic story. We find Deven as a teacher who is not at all comfortable in the class room as he is not confident about his knowledge of the subject being taught by him. He lacks interest in the subject too as his love is Urdu literature. Murad appears before us as a selfish giant in the garb of a friend. He is pushing Deven into such a web that it becomes impossible for him to come out of it. Murad is authoritative and unscrupulous.

Chapter II

The township of Mirpore, with its dreary mode of existence also breeds in him a sense of boredom and isolation. Deven's journey from Mirpore to Delhi commences to attain job-security. The meanness of his physical existence is paralleled by the meanness of the surroundings that he sees on his way to Delhi. The wasteland outside correlatives with wasteland of his mind.

However he reaches Delhi and meets Murad, takes an introductory letter from him, so that he can hold a formal meeting with the Urdu poet, Nur Shahjehanabadi. He wonders whether it is proper on his part to approach the greatest poet of Urdu with a letter of introduction from so unworthy person like Murad. Finally, after many more hustles he decides to meet the poet hesitatingly, being escorted by a boy of Murad's office. Even though Deven shrinks at the idea of possibly being exploited by his sharp and selfish friend Murad, the dream of meeting Nur draws him on. Nur used to be the inspiration for Deven once. Having always loved Urdu poetry and missed the chance to be an Urdu language professor, he is excited to go to Delhi.

Chapter III

Deven faces Nur at his residence. He is shocked to find that the poet, whom he so greatly admired and adored as God, enjoyed the company of the louts of *lafangas* of the bazaar world, and his second wife, Imtiaz Begum earlier belonged to a brothel. Nur rebukes Deven first of all for disturbing him and for being a lecturer in Hindi, intending to interview an Urdu poet. According to Nur, Urdu died long ago in 1947 and only its ghost exists in India.

Deven finds the atmosphere at Nur's house quite suffocating and the nature of his wife cruel and vulgar. His wife scolds Nur for drinking too much and scolds even visitor for being selfish. Disappointed, leaving the poet in immense pain and agony, Deven seems afraid of exploring the world of poetry any more. He thinks that it is better to live in the real world rather than in an imaginary one. We see that when Deven visits Nur, he becomes totally disappointed seeing his lifestyle. He is old, surrounded by flattering crawlers, married to a younger calculating wife who wants to use his glory to win her self fame. Deven's thoughts were totally shattered. At the same time the false beliefs of the people who developed a highly romantic attitude towards poetry and language also stand exposed in the novel.

Chapter IV

After his first unsatisfactory and unsuccessful meeting with Nur, on his way back to Mirpore in the bus, Deven's mind oscillates between his aspiration for poetry and its illusory nature. He decides, henceforth he would avoid that mirage, that dream that so easily twisted into nightmare. He reaches Mirpore and on the bus stand as he sees the face of one of his students he recalls again the verse of Nur. During the journey the dog crushed by the bus signals an ill omen. The neighbour sitting beside him philosophically reveals that the death of the dog is a blessing of God to living animal because for them there is only misery and suffering in the world between birth and death.

Night ends dawn breaks and sorrow reappears
Addressing us in morning light with a cock's shrill crows.

Then, just to save himself from Sarla's stony face, and her 'open fury' he decides that it would be better to go straight to his college. Later when he reaches home he sees the picture of an abandoned wife. She receives Deven with a look as if he were a stranger, an interloper. Deven looks for a redeemer who should help him come out of his trap—an enclosure of mental torture. He can't expect this kind of help from his wife: another victim of disappointment and bitter existence. He looks forward to his little son 'Manu'. He talks to him, inquires about his studies, plays and goes for walk with him. Manu and Sarla feel surprised at this unexpected turn in Deven's behaviour. "He walked as if he were walking away from the debris of his Delhi trip, his visit to Nur, the failed interview—leaving it all behind."

When he returns, he receives a letter from Nur in which the poet has agreed to allow Deven to work as his secretary. Deven is taken aback by Nur's decision. Nur's ailing body symbolically represents the sickening state of Urdu. The psychological pain of Deven is alter-ego of Nur's physical pain. Deven is torn between the conflict of dreams and duty. Murad, editor of *Awaaz* is in some better position than Deven as he has not surrendered to Hindi. Sincerity of purpose, zest, hero-worship of Nur help Deven in no way to realize his dreams. The sordid reality of the world clashes with Deven's brittle world of dreams. The collision smashes his hopes. He is caught in the middle of linguistic-politics. His meetings with Nur made him clear the essential absurdity of life and Desai is existential interpretation of human predicament.

Chapter V

Deven refuses to go to Nur as his secretary. He explains that he can't give up his job of lecturership at Mirpore and all other facilities he is enjoying there. He cannot understand the intention of Nur. Murad again persuades him to go to Nur with some courage and interview him for the next issue of the journal, *Awaaz*. This time, again Murad deceives him as Deven is cheated at Nur's house where he finds the arrangements of a soiree being made to celebrate the birthday of his second-wife, Imtiaz Bibi. Deven, in the birthday party, finds no reason for Imtiaz-Begum's stagy recitation of melodramatic and third-rate verses when the great Urdu poet sits silently, ignored and unnoticed. Nur and Deven leave the programme halfway and secretly retire to a room, where the poet tells Deven how Imtiaz-Begum has cheated him of his belongings and all other things that he possessed, even his audience. But Deven is not interested in anything now except in the interview which is urgently required. Nur agrees to help him in whatever way it is possible, by replying to his questions or by reciting some of his old and even unpublished verses. Deven promises to write memoir, and article or even a full book on the life and verses of Nur Shahjehanabadi, if the poet can spare sometime for him.

In the meantime, the two wives enter the scene and quarrel most spiritedly and Deven has to flee away once again.

Murad intends to devote a whole number of his journal to Nur Sahib's work. He is already behind the schedule. Deven does not have much time or courage to interview Nur again at his house. Murad advises him to take the help of a tape-recorded in collecting the speeches and recitation of Nur and then take them to his house and edit them Murad allures Deven that he may write a book like *My Days with Nur Shahjehanabadi* or a biography on the Urdu poet.

Chapter VI

Deven's college has an Urdu Department which often looks deserted. Mr. Siddiqui, a lovable, kind and compassionate man, is the head of this department. Deven goes to him for help and he even solves the problem of getting a tape-recorder by arranging funds from the college. But as the sum, he has been sanctioned from college authorities, is very small; Murad takes him to the shop and persuades him to purchase a second-hand tape-recorder. Murad seems to have had some prior deal with Jain Sahib, the shop-owner, which he does not reveal to Deven. Deven can't interfere with the purchase since he knows nothing about electronics. A technician Chiku is also given to assist him in the work of recording. Siddiqui, the head of Urdu department is symbolic of past grandeur Muslims. He is not entrusted with the job of custodian of Nur's poetry because he himself is living on the fringe of the society. Siddiqui's home in a dilapidated Villa has an air of impeccable royalty and majesty. He is the silent spectator scrutinizing the shifting interests of the society. His ancestral home is his lucrative commodity which he plans to sell to some landlord. He is unmarried and spends lavishly on himself and his friends. He is patronizing and encourages his servant for his melodious voice.

Chapter VII

After arranging tape Deven visits Nur's house to settle the important thing 'date and time' for interview. When he reaches there he finds that Nur's second wife, Imtiaz Begum, suddenly falls ill since the night of her birthday celebrations. She has high temperature and diarrhea. The poet is not in a position to be taken aside and be interviewed systematically. After all, he is forbidden to recite any poetry in the house. Imtiaz Begum will rebuke him for this. Moreover, according to Imtiaz Begum, nobody will like to listen to his shaking and faltering voice. His audience will rather like to listen to the song of a young voice like Imtiaz Begum herself. Once again, he is dejected in his attempt to persuade the poet for a revealing interview. When Nur expresses his desire to send her to the hospital for proper treatment, Deven is overjoyed to think of the possibility of finding the poet alone and conducting the awaited interview. But hope of achievement is again thwarted by Nur's confession that he has already failed in this attempt to send Imtiaz Begum to the hospital. In his enthusiasm to prove that he will make the interview a comfortable event, both for Nur and himself, Deven informs poet of his plan of recording everything on the tape. Nur is annoyed at the idea of having his poems recorded because he considers the act below his dignity. At the same time when Ali informs that Imtiaz Begum has sent for them, Deven is frightened by awareness that Imtiaz Begum is keeping a close watch on his activities to thwart his purpose. She rejects the plan of Deven very cruelly to discuss any subject regarding Nur's poetry. Later on, he is invited by Safia Begum to her room. She agrees to smuggle out Nur through the back door of her room and send him for the interview to the appointed place in the vicinity of Nur's house. Deven agrees and tells her that he'll inform her of the date and time for the interview. Safia Begum makes it clear to him that he will have to pay her for this interview. This new demand of money shocks him and finds his newly aroused hope of success shattered. Unable to find some way to meet her demand, he thinks of giving up the project.

Chapter VIII

Deven's repeated failure in his enterprise leads him to a mood of frustration and despair. At this his wife Sarla's sarcasm regarding his visit to Delhi pinches him more. Deven again grows aware of his unfulfilled ambition when he receives another letter from Nur inviting him to copy down the poet's new cycle of thirty-six couplets. But he is also aware that he cannot interview him unless he pays money to Safia Begum without whose help he sees no way of realizing his ambition. Torn by his ambition and his lack of resources, he is filled with anguish and despair. In this state of mental agony he compares the situation with that of Nur and discovers to his horror that both are trapped alike in their different circumstance. It is again Abid Siddiqui, who again rescues Deven from his present financial crisis. Taking advantage of his good relations with the Registrar, Siddiqui gets the fund released from the college for payment to Nur. Nevertheless, impelled by his sense of responsibility towards Siddiqui and the college and also by his irresistible love for Nur's poetry, he decides to go to Delhi once again. Then Deven is badly scolded by the head of the Hindi Department Mr. Trevedi for taking leave for a week and running after Urdu poetry so much like a mad man. He threatens to get him transferred to Urdu Department if he does not mend himself. Sarla was another hurdle in the way of Deven. Deven suggests Sarla to take the boy and go for her parent's home a week earlier. Still he is in a dilemma that all these efforts would lead him to yet another pile of refuse or to the clear shining horizon at last.

Chapter IX

Deven goes to Delhi in the hope of beginning the interview afresh. Deven goes to Safia Begum and pays her the money demanded by her. She directs him to the place where she has already hired a room on rent for the purpose of conducting the proposed interview. Deven and Chiku wait for Nur to arrive. But Nur does not come alone. Deven is dismayed to find that "he has brought along the same rabble that surrounded him every night on the terrace". It adds to Deven's distress when Nur starts talking of food and dinner instead of either reciting his poetry or speaking on the subject of poetry. Deven is upset by these excessive demands of Nur. He rushes out of the room to make an appeal to Murad for seeking financial help. Murad provides him with the money to feed Nur and his companions but threatens him with the words that he will deduct these expenses from his remuneration for the interview. Deven feels satisfied when the long hours of feasting and drinking become interspersed with certain periods of silence during which Nur recites his verse to a rapt audience. But he is exasperated to discover the imbecile Chiku fumbling with the machine and not taking any of it down. Since Chiku does not know what part of Nur's speech is to be recorded, he tapes all the irrelevant talks and gossips in which the poet frequently indulges. Deven's work is made difficult also by the idlers who accompany Nur on all occasions.

In his passion for Nur's poetry, Deven loses the sense of time. He drags on these sessions of feasting and poetry to a span of more than three weeks. On the last day of these quizzical session. Nur bursts into "a verse that Deven had never heard before, that no one in the room had heard before, that entered into their midst like some visitor from another element, silencing them all with wonder."

Finding Deven copy down the poem, Nur takes the note book from him and writes it himself for him. Deven realises his emotional and artistic relationship with Nur in these moments of sudden awareness, and is filled with the glory of sense fulfilment. But at the same time the tired Nur realises that his writing days are over and says, "What I have waiting for me six feet of earth in the cemetery by the mosque". And "all one can resume, at my age, is the primordial sleep. I am going to curl upon my bed like a child in its mother's womb and I shall sleep, shall wait for sleep to come". And the interview, the meeting, the *mehfil* has come to an end.

Chapter X

A new spell of miseries begins for Deven when he listens to the recording done by Chiku. After some initial difficulty the tape begins to play producing incoherent talks. Deven grows aware of the failure of this project. However, he sees a ray of hope in Murad's suggestion that he should take the tapes with him to Mirpore and give the recording a shape by editing it. Mr. Jain offers him the help of another nephew, Pintu, who looks even more imbecilic than Chiku.

The abandoned look of the college reminds him about his long neglected and almost forgotten duties. He gets the unexpected help from Dhanu, one of his students, in editing the tapes. But even then it was not worthwhile to present the tape before the college authorities. He again seeks the help of Mr. Siddiqui to escape punishment but he also rebukes him for having wasted the college funds. Deven feels isolated and hunted down. In order to overcome his anguish and sense of isolation he keeps awake in the night and evaluates the answer-books of the students. Deven is again thrown off his balance when he receives yet another letter from Nur with a bill for five hundred rupees as room rent. Feeling nervous and helpless, Deven goes to Murad's office in the hope of making him pay this bill. But he blatantly refuses to extend any help to him. Murad's callousness and treachery in this hour of need intensify Deven's anguish and sense of isolation. Instead of going back to Mirpore, Deven keeps walking aimlessly and reaches a park in Delhi where looking at the dome and the eastern walls of the "great Friday mosque". Deven finds an answer to his question about the significance of poetic art in the image of the dome which he perceives against the background of the sky in contrast to the earth.

Chapter XI

Deven's awareness of the nature and significance of artistic creation makes him view his life in a different perspective. When he reaches home, he does not feel annoyed by his wife's graceless looks. Instead, he feels sympathy for her as he identifies his own suffering with her frustrations. Though Deven is conscious of his sincerity and devotion to unsuccessful enterprise, he is unaware of his responsibility for his involvement in it. He continues to suffer because he shifts the responsibility of his failure to Murad and Mr. Jain, Chiku, Nur and his wives. He is unable to sleep on the night before the meeting of the board of the college authorities. He takes a long walk outside which reveals his anguish and despair and symbolize his desire to escape the threat of his present predicament. In these moments, death seems to him the only possibility of escape from his suffering. He remembers the students who have threatened him that in case he did not fulfill their demand of first division marks, they would pay him out for his treachery.

Unexpectedly Deven recalls Nur and tries to evaluate his genius apart from his senile demands and the ignoble aspects of his life. This evolution of his genies revives his faith in Nur's poetry and he receives his intimate relationship with Nur and is filled with a sense of gratitude for his poetry. He also becomes conscious of the eternal nature of his relationship with Nur. He learns that even his death cannot end this relationship because of emotional and spiritual bond with Nur. The fact is that in the act of inheriting his poetry, Deven becomes the custodian of Nur's very soul and spirit. Towards the end of the novel the hour of daybreak symbolizes the dawn of existentialist awareness in Deven. He becomes conscious of the true nature of his predicament.

He resolves to preserve the legacy of Nur, and gains courage to fight against the calamities, coming to him.

The special quality of Desai's literary voice is its ability to weave together several strands of feeling into a complex, affecting symphony. As Rushdie observes in his introduction to *In Custody*, when you first encounter it the prose seems to whisper, to speak so softly as to risk going unheard, bus as you bend you ear to listen you hear many unexpected notes of wicked comedy, of sharp, even biting perceptions about her fellow men and women, and of a clear-sighted unsentimentality about human nature that is anything but frail. The voice takes hold of the reader, gently, irresistibly and its strength and clarity soon come to seem like small miracles.

Like many romantic and post-romantic works Desai's *In Custody* in part derives its structure from a series of climatic and anti-climatic perfect moments, instants of vision, and epiphanies, which provide solace and meaning for Deven's life.

13

Critical Appreciation of the Novel *In Custody*

> Art could be responded to, understood, absorbed, identified with, but mystery it would still remain.
>
> —Jasbir Jain

In Custody really marks a turning point in Desai's career as it shows a significant broadening of the horizon of her views and ideas. It is known for dealing with male consciousness, which has not yielded the tense psychological drama of vitality and vibrancy, one of the distinctive features of Desai's earlier novels. The novel takes up different issues like language, controversy, plight of vanishing urdu poetry, lecturer's life and above all male psychology. Earlier her male characters subserved her design of being mere anchors to the plumb-lines into the feminine.

The novel reveals the story of the unsuspecting and worldly Deven Sharma, who is moved by an idea of creating the work of his life, but is unluckily frustrated by his own helplessness. The strained relationship between Deven and his wife Sarla is suggestively presented. Apparently, Deven's protest against her disappointment seems to be the outcome of his hurt male ego. He is over-aggressive in his behaviour at home, though outside it he is seek and humble. Deven feels so deserted by his fate that he censures himself for his insufficiency to make any excellence in life.

To Deven Nur is a significant poet not because he makes things immediate but because he removes them to a position where they become bearable. "That was what Nur's verse did—placed frightening and enexplicable experiences live time and death at a point where they could be seen and studied, in safety" (p. 54).

Decades ago, when a fledgling Salman Rushdie was starting out as a writer, one of the hands that guided and encouraged him was of Anita Desai's. Now the superstar writer pays his debt to her in a "Foreword" to Anita Desai's novel *In Custody*:

> When I think of Anita Desai I see her most clearly as a figure standing, as an equal, beside Jane Austen, that other great Indian novelist, creator of brave, brilliant women trapped by conservative social mores into becoming mere husband hunters, women who would be very recognizable to denizens of, for example, the Delhi of clear Light of Day. And because while she is wholly Indian she is also half-European I think of her in the company of other insider—outsiders such as the white Caribbean novelist Jean Rhys, or the half-sikh, half-Hungarian Paniter Amrita Sher-Gil. Nor should Anita Desai be placed in exclusively female company. As *In Custody* makes plain, she has cared as much about, and been shaped as deeply by the great (male) Urdu poets as by any woman's poems.
>
> *In Custody* was, therefore, a novel of transformation for its author, a doubly remarkable piece of work, because in this magnificent book Desai chose to write not of solitude but of friendship, of the perils and responsibilities of joining oneself to others rather than holding oneself apart. And at the same time she wrote, for the first time, a very public fiction, shedding the reserve of the earlier books to take on such sensitive themes as the unease of minority communities in modern India, the new imperialism of the Hindi language and the decay that, now even more than when the book was written, was and is all too tragically evident throughout

> the fissuring body of Indian society. The courage of the novel is considerable, and so is its prescience. "The slow death of my mother tongue, Urdu, is much further advanced than it was twenty-three years ago and much that was beautiful in the culture of Old Delhi has shipped away for ever."
>
> —Salman Rushdie

Anita Desai is acquainted with the dilemma of the modern woman who has to continue to play the role of the propagator of the human race and house wife. What fascinates her far more than the glittering surface of social life is the inner dynamics of her characters lives and motives. She excels particularly in highlighting the miserable plight of highly sensitive and emotional women, tortured by a humiliating sense of neglect, of loneliness and of desperation. Central characters in her novels are generally neurotic females, highly sensitive and alienated from this surroundings as a consequence of their failure or unwillingness to adjust with the reality.

In Custody marks a departure in these respects. In the first instance, this is a male protagonist and a male-central narrative and point of view. And unlike the earlier novels *In Custody* has an ineffectual but well-meaning young man whose problems are not just personal and private but public and social. Here we find neither a sensitive and highly-strung woman protagonist nor any intense introspection bordering on neurosis. The main themes of the novel revolve around issues like poetry, language and even monetary problems. Consequently, there is a shift even in Desai's inner realms and rhythms of the feminine. There is also a shift in her style of writing; while her earlier novels were characterized by prose of a lyrical quality in *In Custody* there is absence of lyrical beauty. This maybe due to the shifting of the emphasis from the internal to the external.

Further the novels end in a positive note unlike most of earlier novels. The main protagonist is not a female but a male like Deven Sharma. But here comes a natural question.

In providing a male version through the story of Deven's entrapment Desai negates any feministic verdict based on the other female versions of entrapment that is likely put the blame on the male-centered society. Thus Anita Desai, often described as one of the finest writers of this country, has novel from her earlier typical way of sympathy with her female characters. Desai herself speaks out in recent interview that she has been deliberately shifting her focus from female character to male characters. She rather feels the needs to address and voice out themes which concern males too.

Epigraph—Prefixed to the Novel

The epigraph prefixed to the novel, taken from Wordsworth's "Rob Roy's Grave", suggests the in ironic perspective that controls the narrative. In Wordsworth's poem, the speaker feels that Scotch thief, who was brave and wise, entered society "an age too late:/ Or shall we say an age too soon?" 'For the obvious reason that his love of freedom, or liberty, has to encounter a society dominated by "rents and factors, rights of chance,/ Sheriff, and lairds and their domains." Rob Roy felt that books and statutes are the barriers that man himself placed against the self. Like Rob Roy, the free spirit of Deven longs for freshness and stimulation at the time when social civility has deteriorated into social incivility. It is not social incivility that wounds Deven, but his intrinsic compulsions. The compulsions emerge from his domestic and financial circumstances, which make it impossible for him to keep what he has achieved. The locale and the atmosphere which are fore-grounded in the text consist of a city with endless slums, hawkers, beggars, shopkeepers, and swindlers, all busy in their own way, transforming poetry into shocking and turbulent prose. Cold-shouldered by one of his colleagues when he approaches him for help, Deven feels:

> He could not see why anyone should help him. He no longer knew if he ought to be—or even if he wanted to be helped. Were these people really helping him to succeed in a unique and wonderful enterprise or simply locking him up more and more firmly in a barred trap? And was the trap set by Murad, by Siddiqui, or by Nur

> and his wives. All he knew was that he who had set out to hunt Nur down, was being hunted down himself, the prey.

If we gloss the passage in terms of the epigraph prefixed to the novel, it becomes ironical, in the sense that among Deven and his friends neither Rob Roy's neither primitive social dynamic nor that of the French revolutionists, who are alluded to in the poem, prevails. But what is significant and revealing is Deven's determined effort to keep what he has achieved and, in the process, heal the wounded self. While Wordsworth's Rob Roy thought of vindicating the self by visualizing a state of society much later described and advocated by Rousseau, Deven tries to salvage the self by patiently resisting the social and anti-social forces. In spite of the crisis he faces, "the thought of Nur's poetry being read, the sound of it softly murmuring in his ear." The ups and downs of human life, the upheavals in relationship are nicely crafted in this novel. *In Custody* a novel of shattered emotion and scattered dreams in custody reflects the intricacies of relationships.

Language Controversy

As a child, Desai used to speak German at home and Hindi, Bengali or Urdu outside, while learning English in school. For someone who could switch from any one of these to another in a jiffy, the knowledge of language was a natural, un-self-conscious one. It is only with her 1984 novel, *In Custody,* that the conscious discourse of languages began to appear through the narrative. Also shortlisted for the Booker, *In Custody* is woven around the life of Deven, a mild-mannered professor who seeks to interview Nur, the greatest living Urdu poet of the generation. It is a profound commentary on the many meanings and colours of language, as it unfolds through life and art. The old Nur seems to suggest the fall from glory of Urdu, the mellifluous language of great poets, and thus the history of a language emerges as the subtext of the novel. Desai's courageous attempt to render one language through another—in this case, Urdu through English—becomes a metaphor of inter-cultural translations. Indeed, in this novel as in others, she also tries to translate, from an Indian language into English, without falling into the dangerous trap of reducing serious characters into caricatures or stereotypes!

Novel into Film

Ismail Merchant made the film on this novel in 1993. When Anita Desai saw the opening scenes of this film, she was surprised "my first reaction was, but it is in colour and I had visualized the scenes in black and white." Desai co-wrote the screenplay of the film with Shahrukh Husain for Merchant Ivory Productions.

When Merchant first read Desai's novel, he was attracted to the book's focus on Urdu poetry and the atmosphere of a decaying culture. "I was drawn to the character of Nur (played in the film by Shashi Kapoor) the atmosphere of his family, especially his two wives and his disciples." Merchant said, "I felt strongly about the writing and could see the book in cinematic terms."

Desai said she never sees a book in terms of a film and so she described her experience of writing the screenplay of *In Custody* as an interesting experiment a challenge and a painful experience. At the end of the process of cutting and "cutting and hacking the book", Desai realized that the screenplay was no longer like her novel—just a mere skeletion. However she remained committed to the project, since she had faith in Merchant's ability to give a heart and soul to the screenplay. She remarked in an interview given to me on the eve of her Sahitya Akademi Fellowship programme in Sahitya Akademi, New Delhi (Nov. 2007) that after writing this screenplay she recognized that film was not her medium of expression. In her words, "Writing the screenplay was live obliterating the text rather than creating it."

"When you write for the screen, you have to learn to give up control; she said, admitting that she soon discovered that there are other creative forces—including the director, actor, music, cinematography that add colour to the script written in black and white."

In the film, Merchant used poems of Faiz Ahmed. Faiz, written way before the film was conceived. Faiz's work is used in everything from popular Hindi film songs and ads to classical ghazal and quawwalis. In an interview with Ameena Meer, Ismail Merchant said, "I always wanted to do a film about the Urdu language, which is disappearing. It is the most gracious and expressive language and the poetry is so sublime, the thoughts are so great, that it is impossible to supplant it. When I read Anita Desai's novel I thought that I would be able to say so much through the character of Nur, the dying Urdu poet, so I immediately bought the rights to it. It has taken six years since Anita wrote the first draft of the screenplay to get the film made. Some of it I ended up improvising like the character of the old woman, who sits there and curses and smokes a hookah." The film portrays Bhopal rather than Delhi.

Desai as a High Priest of Nature

The fiction of Anita Desai from *Cry, The Peacock* (1963) to her latest mind blowing novel *Journey to Ithaca* (2001) have natural environment in which she embroiders dreams of despair, defeats and illusions of individual characters. It is amazing that critics and scholars have overlooked this aspect of her fiction. In fact the nature and the natural environment are the material on which she weaves her tragic tales. Admitting the importance of nature in her fiction she says in an interview.

They (natural objects) are of primary importance to me. The visual images and sounds, smells and textures of the places I knew, are my material.

Nature is a familiar presence in Desai's novels. Natural landscape fuses with the character's inner milieu and provides a new dimension to her narrative. Her feminine sensibility imparts an edge and dimension to her view of nature. Her love for and obsession with nature is not superficial. It is deep-seated in her mental make-up and is part of a large vision which guides her novels. In the stark barren and lifeless lives of the protagonists Nature acts both as a metaphor of hope and life and as an ironical presence that sharpens the awareness of a grim existence in the hollow metropolis. Desai's perception of the city is deeply interfused with a subtle awareness of Nature in all its diversity—the flower and the grass, the seasons and the hills, the animals and the birds. While Desai's perception of Nature is in itself quite delightful. Nature also provides a symbolic dimension to the total meaning of her fiction and thus becomes a sharpening element of her form and style. In fact Nature in Anita Desai's novels appears basically in two forms (a) as timid and enclosed, perceived through the metaphor of the garden, (b) as open and benign, perceived through sight and sounds.

Nature in Anita Desai's fiction plays an important role in sharpening the spirit of the protagonists. Through its different moods and elements Nature casts a deep shadow over the spirits of the characters who are but helpless victims of a cruel, indifferent and malignant nature.

In the novel *In Custody* Nature is symbolized by the neem tree growing outside the wall of the courtyard of Deven's house. It does not provide any peaceful shade to Deven, but only obstructs the free flow of fresh air. Desai shows that even Nature is not able to help a person escape from this trap and get full freedom. Again, a cricket chirping incessantly stands for Deven's unconscious mind. It suggests that his unconscious self is greatly agitated under strong pressure from all sides. On his way to Delhi, Deven sees all around him nature without any sign of joy. Thus the novelist suggestively projects his impending disappointment through Nature imagery effectively and artistically. Bushes and grasses all appeared to have died, the land was shorn or shrouded.

The thrust of summer, the parched and barren atmosphere of summer correspond to the dry and parched existence of the protagonist Deven. When Deven returns to Delhi he stands near the doorway and sees the sparrows nesting in the skylight twitter and quarrel, scattering twigs as they rustle about their nests. The coming of the devastating summer announced by 'SURAHI' hawker outside is already a felt experience for Deven. But the summer with its dryness, its heat and thrust is not going to continue for ever. When the heat becomes unbearable for Deven, he hears thunders in the distance, perhaps, announcing that the monsoon is drawing closer. Deven thinks it has come because he cannot endure the heat.

Nature takes a different colour with the change of outlook of the main protagonist. Deven could never see any beauty or comfort even in the landscape. The sky is gradually filled with a grey light. It is no longer dark. The grey light slowly dissolves the 'dense blackness' of the night. Consequent upon the resolution of the protagonist's inner drama, nature is seen to cover itself with beauty and spelendour, The sunlight dissolving the darkness of the night before, is symbolic of the emergence of the new courageous 'self' of Deven dispersing his previous timid self. There is delightful fusion of colour, light and sound reflecting the regenerated spirit of Deven.

Thus we had seen that the human world always interacts with the world of nature in novels of Anita Desai. Nature in the novels acts both as a consoling agent and also as a disturbing presence. There is a constant interaction between the inner world of the protagonist and the outer world of nature and in the process of this interaction, an intense vision of the life is projected. In the novels of Anita Desai Nature thus appears as an ironic presence that pervades the life of the main characters of the novel.

Desai's Dealing with Minor Characters

Raj was the old-school friend of Deven. He is handicapped. "Born with one leg shorter than the other, he had been the least intimidating of his school-fellows." He wore orthopaedic boot and played the game of cricket with Raj and Murad. Sometimes they were found copying down each-other's home work. Deven had lost touch with Raj after he went to live in Mirpore. One day Deven received a postcard from Cairo. Through that he came to know that Raj was teaching in a school in Cairo. Desai says: "The exotic notion of his handicapped friend fetching up in Egypt had struck him speechless; he had not replied."

Raj's aunt still lived in Delhi, in the same house. She was a religious, pious and humble lady. She was widow, living alone in the house. The most notable thing about her is that she was very hospitable and generous. She had one helper with her who was a tailor. She gave him food and he acted as her protector and sang holy songs according to her directions Desai narrates.

"She wore not only widow's white clothes but also the chain of wooden beads and other such insignia of the initiated. It was with the gestures of a trained devotee that she bade him sit down and with a gratifying variety of foods. When he politely protested, the spectacled man who was shoveling in rice and pickles by the handfuls, told him, 'Eat, eat'. She enjoys when you eat, so he did." Desai has used the character of Raj's aunt to display the Indian women's religious bent of mind. She describes in detail even about this minor character. "The old lady's piety consisted not only in the feeding of whoever came to be fed—large numbers of Sadhus in white or saffron, carrying begging bowls came regularly for the purpose of helping her to fulfil her earthly duties and earn her merit in her next incarnation—but also in performing long and elaborate Pujas at dawn and dusk. Possibly at other hours as well but it was these occasion that Deven witnessed. She had one wall of the kitchen turned into a veritable temple, with tinted oleographs of saints, plaster images of her pet gods, incense holders, fresh garlands. Saucers of offerings and lamps ranged along the shelves and in the niches. While she sat, or stood, or bowed and tended this family of domesticated gods, the tailor played the role she had assigned him of a devotional singer."

The aunt after doing her Puja cooked meal for them. She had taken a great care of Deven during his short stay over there at her house. No doubt she is a minor character but Desai had made her memorable as she had done full justice with her character.

Desai's Use of Religion

In the novel *In Custody* Anita Desai narrates the narrative in and around the locale of Mirpore, a small town near Delhi. It is an area of mixed community. Comparative descriptions of mosques and temples in Mirpore and of Hindu-Muslim antagonism and riots and the resulting chaos give thematic depth to the novel and enhance lifelikeness. Religious sentiments are depicted in the mention of the early morning hymns sung by groups walking in towns to awaken the spiritually idle people in India. Vital religious feelings of human service and eternal prayers to God for redemption are delineated in the character of Rai's aunt, who stands for Hinduism; while mention of Siddiqui family and the way of the life at Nur's and the history of Mirpore enrich the Muslim background of the theme. The religious clash is somehow represented through the clash between languages Hindi and Urdu also. But no hard feelings against the public of other caste is shown vividly in the novel except a few utterances, like Nur says "Safe, simple Hindi language, safe comfortable ideas of cow-worship and caste and the romance of Krishna" (p. 55). Particularly some persons are deeply religious in the novel. On one hand there are Mrs. Bhalla, Raj's aunt, Sarla, tailor and of course Mr. Trevedi, the religious people practicing Hindu way of life, Nur and Mr. Siddiqui practicing the Muslim dharma, on the other. Mrs. Bhalla and party are trying to work for their religion by singing morning hymns during the processions. Raj's aunt is working to attain God through prayers and services to mankind. She fed large number of 'sadhus' in white or 'saffron' and prays with the tailor like this,

> I shall make my body into a clay lamp.
> My soul its wick and my blood oil.
> Ah, the light of this lamp would reveal
> The face of my Beloved to me.

Nur also believes in his Muslim religion. He has two wives as his religion permits for that. His belief in atonement of sins through suffering is essentially a religious idea. He also wants to go for 'Huz' and demands money from Deven for the same. Mr. Trevedi is a staunch believer in Hinduism. He calls Deven as 'Muslim toadies' and puts the charge that Deven will ruin the students with his Muslim ideas and Urdu language. He says 'I'll warn the R.S.S., you are a traitor'. Mr. Trevedi, being Brahmin and R.S.S. man, is anti-Muslim.

His violent reaction to Deven's request clarifies how language becomes a signifier of religious identity and national loyalty. This linguistic confrontation often leads to communal riots in India. The novel presents the Hindi/Urdu controversy that involves communal implications and does not allow the languages to become objective medium of communication.

Mrs. Desai has shown the part played by religion in the lives of various characters. She has shown Sarla as a religious Hindu lady. She explains "Sarla regularly performed Puja before a tinted oleograph of the goddess Lakshmi that hung in the corner by her dressing table, offering it flow incense and candles" (p. 143). This shows the religious practices of Hindus. Lakshmi Puja is symbolic also as it shows Sarla's bent of mind that she requires the materialistic wealth. In the same way Anita Desai describes details the religious practices of the old lady, living in Delhi. Desai's comment about Raj's aunt, "The old lady's piety consisted not only in the feeding whoever came to be fed-large numbers of sadhus in white or saffron, carry begging bowls came regularly for the purpose of helping her to fulfil earthly duties and earn her merit in her next incarnation, but also in performing long and elaborate pujas at dawn and dusk."

Ending of the Novel

Critics believe that *In Custody* ends with a positive note. Deven is able to perceive a ray of hope even in his boundless suffering and humiliation. Towards the end of the novel, he becomes convinced that perhaps when everyone "had cut him off and he was absolutely alone he would begin to find himself and his own strength." He realizes that life is different from geometry, in which every question had its answer and every problem its solution. In fact the novel has an open ending which suggests the eternal troubles in the life of an insignificant teacher.

Deven thinks that he had accepted the gifts of Nur's poetry and he was custodian of Nur's soul and spirit. He is not in the position to deny or abandon. Here Deven's strength to face the calamities that would begin with the day and he would run to meet them, makes the novel's ending melodramatic. Some critics openly say about the ending that had left Deven struggling with a world where evil dominates and the innocents suffer in poverty. But in fact only when Deven decides to accept and endure whatever disasters befall him, he reaches a kind of grateful inner strength. "Soon the sun would be up and blazing. The day would begin, with its calamities. They would flash out of the sky and cut him down like swords. He would run to meet them." (p. 296)

REFERENCE

Jain, Jasbir. "Anita Desai Indian English Novelists: Anthology of Critical Essays". Ed. Madhusudan Prasad. New Delhi: Sterling, 1982, p. 111.

14

Structure and Theme

> The thematic concern of *In Custody* is Deven's quest for scholarship to win bread of minimal comfort to his small family and permanency on his job, but instead he comforts himself with the stone of superior idealism of being the sole custodian of Nur's poetry and with spurious dignity springing from it.
>
> —F.A. Inamdar

The theme of the novel is probed through nature, the city, the house, the circus, and the comet and stars. In fact we can easily identify that Anita Desai has systematically fused three thematic threads in the novel, *In Custody;* craze for freedom, problem of love and marriage and imprisonment and death in life through various apparent objects. The novelist here tries to discover the true significance of things in life. Her search for meanings, value or truth will explain the wider concerns.

In reality, Desai here explores the psyche of male protagonist outside the circumscriptions of familial ties and obligations. She makes a departure from her earlier obsessive pre-occupation with the interior landscape of hypersensitive and neurotic women. Deven is endowed with different kind of sensibility. He is not an alienated self in the sense the female protagonists of Desai's earlier novels are. This novel focuses on a pathetic, trapped male character whose wife despises his inability to succeed financially. A terrified, insignificant person, Deven moves from mediocrity as a college lecturer to impending professional and financial ruin as he incurs increasing monetary debts, which he finally decides to endure rather than committing suicide. Later Desai makes clear that just as the male characters are trapped in a world that offers no possibility for success, the female characters have even more right to feel frustrated with a sexist society that reduces them to clinging to these men who cannot provide them with what they really need.

Anita Desai focuses her attention on the subjective reality of existence. The various experiences and the emotional sufferings of the protagonist, Deven Sharma, reveal the inconsistency between activity and success. The main theme of the novel *In Custody* revolves round Deven and focuses on his awareness of the meaninglessness of his existence, his yearning to discover meaning in the world of Urdu poetry. Deven Sharma, the protagonist of *In Custody* is frantically busy in pursuit of his ideal, but the fact is that he also stands in the moment and passes through the agonizing states of anxiety, dread and concern. His dread of being ruined gives him an insight into his authentic existence, and he gains the courage of his convictions. Emphasis on the unique and particular in human experience is an important feature of the existentialist writings. *In Custody* bears testimony to this fact. The centrality of self in Anita Desai is concentrated in terrifying isolation, finding it hard to reconcile with world around 'self'. Deven and Sarla therefore, are constantly confronted with the stupendous task of defining their relation to themselves and to their immediate human context. Acceptable behavioral pattern is alien to them. The root is not far to find. He craves for freedom. Deven by and large has strange childhood from which he develops a negative self-image and aversion. The immediate result is, his fragmented psyche to view world as a hostile place. For him the domestic life is not his world, rather it is a trap where his individuality is endangered and thus complete lack of interest and dissonance in his relationship bring solitary confinement and show his reluctance to face reality. He knows how he has been trapped and how he can begin to live afresh. He cries, he tries and he flies too but all in vain. There are many obstacles too. Soon he is caught by fantasy. The next thing is marital disharmony. It is one of the main issues dealt in the novel. Desai's existential crisis is conceptualized as a see-saw balance on a central fulcrum with women sitting on one end, men on the other. She refuses male as super power. Even Deven plays negative role in his relation with Sarla. They have an unhappy married life. Deven is married to Sarla but they are not able to get along happily as husband and wife. Both of them are frustrated in their own way, but they're unable to do anything for each-other. Deven feels as if he were in trap. Marriage, his family responsibilities and his job have placed him in a sort of cage and there was no way out of it. Desai's main concern is to depict the psychic and social status of Deven at this crucial juncture of his life. To do this more effectively Desai has forged a style supple and suggestive enough, to convey the fever and fretfulness of Deven and Sarla's life. All her efforts are visible through language syntax and imagery.

We already know that Anita Desai seems to have opted for portraying various themes at a time in the novel. These themes seem to be occurring again and again. Major characters in the novel resist the demand of society and turn out to be rebels. Not finding a proper channel of communication Deven becomes alienated and starts brooding on this life. All his wanderings and reflections finally bring him into new vistas of understanding that he had formerly ignored or rejected.

The novel is a burning epitome of life-history caught in the morass of mean and impoverished existence, yearning to redeem it. Deven is cheated and bullied with a project that ends in his disaster and ruin. The whole narrative oscillates between Deven's dreams and realities, his aspiration for poetry and its illusory nature and finally into ultimate disaster. Defeated aims, frustrated ends, and thwarted wishes full Deven's heart with gloomy darkness. The financial and social factors are mostly responsible for the drooping spirit of Deven. Self-pity resulting from his self-defeat weakens him further. Deven is further humiliated, cheated, bullied and thrown away. The idea of death occurs in his mind. In the process of visualizing Nur's death Deven becomes conscious of the eternal nature of his relationship with Nur. He learns that even his death cannot end this relationship. At the same time during his morning-walk beside canal, he wishes that it would have been good if his student were to emerge to stab him. There is an insistent longing for death as a possible exit out of this ordeal, but very soon this longing for death is sought by an all pervasive awareness and consciousness.

Like many romantics and post-romantic works, Desai's *In Custody* in part derives its structures from a series of climatic and anticlimactic perfect moments, instants of vision and epiphanies, which provide solace and meaning for Deven's life. Readers's problem involves deciding how to take these epiphanic moments since the context in which they appear or the events that quickly follow clearly invalidate these powerful experiences or at least limit their significance. Such moments in the novel include his entrance into Nur's house, Interview of Nur for which he had been waiting all these empty years (31) his encounter with the vomiting poet and his furious wife (59) and his rare play with his son Manu, during which Deven recalls and fantasizes his own fame (pp. 73-74). Desai carefully presents one of these apparently climatic epiphanies at the close of the tenth chapter when Deven walks through the heat after Murad has betrayed him yet once more by refusing to pay for the room in which Nur's interview took place. Walking past the Red Fort and other famous sight of Delhi, he enters a small park and sits on a bench.

The sun was behind it, a great brassy conflagration, dazzling his eyes, clearly. The white and black marble facing of the eastern doorway made a graceful caligraphic pattern. The enormous arched doorway soared upwards to the dome which rose like a vast bubble that the flat earth had sent out into the dusty yellow grey sky, a silent exhalation of stone. It was absolutely still, very serene. It was in fact the silent answer to his questioning. Since it was silent, he could not hear it, but he felt it impress its shape upon his eyelids, very gently, very lightly, like fingertips pressing them to sleep. Gradually, the sky disappeared, the sun and light and the glare, and the shape became clearer and sharper till it was all there was cool, high minded and remote (pp. 191-92).

Anita Desai's themes are thus original and entirely different from those of other contemporary Indian-English novelists. Her themes tend to wedge off the tracks of other novelists. Each aspect merges with the other and sometimes one finds a number of themes woven together. Using these themes as a foundation the writer is able to build up her characters into significant whole. The issue of alienation and isolation finally emerges out as integral part of the central theme of the novel. The special quality of Desai's literary voice is its ability to weave together several strands of feeling into a complex structure, affecting symphony. As Rushdie observes in his introduction to *In Custody*: "When you first encounter it the prose seems to whisper, to speak so softly as to risk going unheard, but as you bend your ear to listen you hear, many unexpected notes of wicked comedy, of sharp, even biting perceptions about her fellow men and women, and of a clear-sighted unsentimentality about human nature that is anything but frail. The voice takes hold of the reader, gently, irresistibly, and its strength and clarity soon come to seem like small miracles." (www.rediffmail.com). Mrs. Desai is no doubt a great artist with a remarkable and astounding technical efficacy.

15

Deven Sharma: An Unheroic Hero

In Custody is a novel about an unheroic, unimpressive and unassertive lecturer of Hindi. Meek and self-effacing, Deven is resigned to his life as a lecturer in an obscure college in the dusty, shapeless town of Mirpore. "He had little gift for speech, for conversation, so little practice in it, and know only how to stumble awkwardly to the point, gracelessly." That's why Deven is never successful in convincing others. Deven comes from a lower-middle class background. His father was a school teacher, a scholar and lover of Urdu poetry. Urdu was taught to Deven by his father. As a child he has observed closely the bitter asthamatic father for his failure in measuring up to his expectations. He is married to an insipid wife Sarla who is miles away from her husband's literary taste and intellectual pursuit. Deven is an Urdu enthusiast and great fan of the Urdu poetry and wants to interview an established ageing poet of 'Urdu' named Nur. According to Bipin B. Panigrahi and Viney Kirpal "Deven is portrayed as a marginal character, dangling on the periphery of action incapable of forcing his way to the centre of things." Deven's social role is that of a teacher but because of his poor personality he commands no respect from his students. While taking class, instead of looking at the students he would be looking outside the class towards an imaginary audience. No wonder he is an unsuccessful teacher, who could not command attention, let alone the regard of his unruly class (p. 13). Deven is quite opposite of the traditional image of Guru. Though his students are rowdy and take no interest in studies, yet in a way he is also responsible for his failure as a teacher. He had been for years practising the trick of focusing his eyes upon the door at the end of the room, the door that opened on the passage, freedom and release (1C, p. 12). His desire for freedom from mundane existence is also visible in the romantic notions he fosters about himself and his job of teaching. Such an assumption has imparted on him a sense of defeat which prevented him from total absorption in his ill-paid profession.

Deven's background is also responsible for his personality type developed in a different way. All through his childhood and youth he had known only one way to deal with life and, that was to lie low and remain invisible. That's why Deven is always unsure of himself and because of his simplicity and tactlessness bordering on being a simpleton he always lands in some odd situation. Deven is very timid as well. So timid that he can hardly make friends with any girl. He seeks to reach out into the wider world in the hope of self-fulfilment. He suffers from the problem of marital disonence.

Financially Deven is not well off. He lives in a colony DII/69, made for the lower income group and named after a leader of Harijans. He is not at all comfortable in his ill-matched marriage. Deven as a husband is also a failure. His martial life is boring and unpalatable. Deven had been more a poet than a professor when he married Sarla—he had only been taken on as a temporary lecturer and still had confidence in his verse—and for the wife of a poet she seemed too prosaic. Of course, she had not been his choice but that of his mother and aunts crafty and cautious women. She was the daughter of a friend of an aunt's, she lived in the same street as that family, they had observed her for years and found her suitable in every way, easy, plain, penny-pinching and congenitally pessimistic (1C, p. 67).

Deven comes from Delhi and settles down at Mirpore, a small town, along with his wife Sarla and son Manu and leads an unhappy domestic life. The place he lives looks like a trap or prison. Desai narrates:

> After he graduated and married and came Mirpore to teach, it became for him the impassable desert that lay between him and the capital with its lost treasures of friendships, entertainment, attractions and opportunities. It turned into that strip of no man's land that lies around a prison, threatening in its desolution. (1C, p. 24)

In fact, his consciousness is essentially directed towards a wider world beyond himself and his family. On the familial front, Deven finds himself as an angry self. The repressive atmosphere of a lower-middle class ethos offers him on suitable avenues for recognition. He is aware of his personal incompetency to fulfil his wife's desire and dreams on the material level. Like his father he feels apologetic because he cannot do better. He lives with a sense of defeat and failure. Overtly, his irritability with Sarla appears to be the outcome of his hurt male ego. Deep down, his rage is, in a way, an externalization of self-hate, born out of an unconscious self accusation. He finds nothing attractive either about Sarla, her body or her temperament. Deven's preoccupation with his literary pursuit and supercillions attitude towards his wife makes things even worse. His married life does not provide any welcome change. In the company of his wife Sarla, he feels as if he were a stranger, an interloper (p. 66). He is painted to notice the dereliction of his marriage. He has his little son 'Manu' who was very often querulous with hunger and sleeps by the time Deven comes back from work.

Deven is by nature an introvert when, unexpectedly, an old friend Murad invites him to go to Delhi to interview the greatest living Urdu poet, Deven sees a chance both to achieve fame and to fulfill his dreams. Deven's world is full of imperfection and unfulfilment, hankering and helplessness, agony and anger and struggle, is no doubt limited, but within this limited world of Deven, Anita Desai reveals amazing variety and profundity. He becomes nervous while taking to Murad. He feels embarrassed and cannot tolerate his students staring at him. The forces working in him side by side show his tendency to subordinate himself to the wishes of other. There is a conflict in him between his idealized self and actual self. In fact, he is an existentialist hero, he thinks that his life is empty and he is in a cage. Self-pity—resulting from his self-defeat weakens him further, "No one ever listens me, My hard work leads nowhere to nothing, Nothing" (p. 185).

Deven is an unheroic hero in the context of the novel. But he is the central character and it is mainly through Deven that the story has been narrated. "His idealized image of himself is that of an upright teacher in the college, a humble man in society outside and victimized self in his home, turning aggressive often" (*Usha Bande*, The novel of Anita Desai, p. 155). He is presented as the diffident and awkward temporary lecturer in a private college. He is a nondescript teacher of Hindi stricken with a rare devotion for Urdu poetry. He makes a confession before Murad, "I never said I was looking for a guru; I have given up thinking I can ever write poetry. I am only a poor lecturer, temporary, earning my living. I tell you I haven't time I can't serve Nur." Deven suffers from job-insecurity. His journey from Mirpore to Delhi commences to attain job security. His journey back to Mirpore is journey from ignorance of reality to its awareness. He intends to replace nightmare by reality, illusion by life. Ironically he is happy to free himself from it but does not know that he is landing himself into another labyrinth. He leads the life of a victim, a victim of the ordinary life. Whenever he sees Sarla, he is reminded of a victim figure. The real and free life has always been beyond Deven's reach. The lack of togetherness combined with his idea of being a victim alienates him both from his wife and his only child Manu.

Deven's character is an interesting study in characterization for his manifest inherent contradictions. He has an innate poetic sensibility but turns out to be a boring teacher because he has distanced himself from the profession he has accepted. Deven has himself been a timid creature and conscious of his inadequacies, but indulges in a vain enthusiasm for poetry. In taking on the task of a custodian, Deven must sideline his own creative output in favour of the living poetic legend. But in fulfilling his duty as a custodian he has to overcome many obstacles. In getting close to the poet Nur, he finds himself embroiled in the small, trifling details of Nur's domestic life, an involvement which ultimately goes out of his control.

Deven is self-minimizing and self-reducing, as he cannot make assertive or expansive moves. He even avoids triumph or success because it is presumptions. He places taboos on his thought and feelings, so acute and unconscious is his self minimizing attitude that he dubs himself a fool in his first interview with Nur. He is overpowered by doubts having a little confidence in his qualities.

Deven is a frustrated guy. His frustrations arise out of his inability to make a timely escape from complexities with which he would not have known how to contend. He admits to be totally inadequate, incompetent and unconfident (p. 114). He suffers from certain complexes also. He is 'he felt, a trapped animal' and there is no way out of the cage. When Siddiqui calls him a lucky chap he pounces upon him saying that "All his life he had never even glimpsed the beautiful face of the goddess of luck" (p. 142). Deven finds it difficult to sort out the problems of his life. His struggles are not different from those of a swimmer in unknown water (p. 191). He is effective and fruitless and his problem are not just personal and private but public and social.

Deven's great rootless, restless mobility, loneliness, and his paralyzing helplessness are objectified by the people with whom he comes in contact. His wife Sarla, his friends, Murad, his derelict poet, Nur, the businessman Mr. Jain, and his two nephews, his colleague Mr. Siddiqui, the head of his department Mr. Trevedi, and the two wives of the poet. He is simpleton by nature. He believes Murad's words, his childhood friend who comes from the metropolis of Delhi to meet him and ask him to take an interview of the great poet Nur. He never doubts his intentions though he was conscious of the deceptive ways of Murad who has always exploited him and has never paid for his book review and poems. His timidity and inefficacy go to such an extent that he cannot even buy the tape-recorder leave alone operating it. But quite late he realises a lack of sympathy in Murad whose friendship with him is nothing but customary, "nothing but long custom, and custom could be a well from which one never rose, a trap from which there was no release." (p. 175)

Actually Deven's main limitation is the lack of critical faculty. Living in Mirpore he has almost become a villager. He is even hesitant to enter the city or go towards Kashmiri Gate in search of Murad's office. Deven's trips to Delhi teach him a great deal both about art and human nature and take him outside his limited experience. Deven appears as an ineffectual but reasonable young man whose problems are not just personal and private but public and social as well. In fact the whole novel reveals individual human nature, the relationships between people and the relationship of the individual to society. For his failure many social factors are responsible, such as debts have piled up, students threaten to beat him up and the college authorities demand an explanation for misspent money. In fact even in his childhood and youth, social and familial factors were responsible for his drooping spirits. He remains invisible as he never gets recognition, neither by his family nor by the society. Under the circumstances his married life, too, does not provide any welcome change. His house represents his prison. In fact, his is the case of an alienated individuals caught in the crisis of changing society.

Deven's idealised self is of an upright teacher, a respected man in the society, a great lover and an eminent critic of Urdu poetry. But his actual self is completely different from this idealized image. He comes from a lower-middle class family and his consciousness is directed towards a wide world beyond himself and his family. Deven is the portrait of an ordinary average human being who had high aspirations to achieve some status in life. At thirty-five he feels already having spent all the empty years waiting for a break, waiting to do something worthwhile, something great. Actually Deven is a romantic and an escapist, a weak person incapable of facing the crisis. He loves Urdu and Urdu poetry but has to choose Hindi as a subject for teaching because of its value in the job market. He says, "I am only a teacher...must teach to support my family." In fact we find Deven torn between the conflict of dreams and duty.

His idealized self is of a respected husband and a loving and dutiful father. But actually we find him a contradiction to it. On the familial self Deven finds himself as an angry self. His job and family is oppressive enough for him as he believes that he is chained to me necessity of "earning a livelihood" in order to support his family. Such an assumption has imparted on to him a sense of defeat which prevents him from total absorption in his ill paid profession, where he is popularly known as a 'thrifty', domesticated and a two cigarette man.... To achieve his ideal image and to fulfill his dreams he readily castes off his role as a teacher, as a husband and a father and seeks to add a new dimension to his existence. The desire to achieve distinction and to transcend the barriers in his way of interviewing Nur, Deven does everything possible for a common man like him. Ultimately he realizes that reality is always quite depressing but the answer does not lie in escapist measurers. Deven reaches wholeness of life and achieves spontaneity when he marches away from a self-created trap to the joyous affirmations of life. And he accepts the human conditions as it is and reaches to an existential dimension of personality. Though he could not achieve the idealised image of himself, yet he is able to recognise his actual self. Towards the end of the novel he is a changed person altogether. As the novel ends with a positive note, Deven is able to perceive a ray of hope even in his boundless suffering and humiliation. He is convinced that "perhaps when everyone had cut him off and he was absolutely alone, he would begin to find himself and his own strength". (p. 181)

Deven's suffering gave him a philosophical outlook. In fact each new misfortune and calamity fill him with the iron for resistance. He undergoes experiences of various shades and complexities and eventually emerges as a wiser man with a more complete knowledge of being in this world.

Thus we see that Deven Sharma, the unheroic hero of this novel *In Custody* is cheated and bullied with a project that ends in his disaster and ruin. It explores an extraordinary and unique individual life that sets to attain Himalayan glory but finds relegated to a very meagre and factual position. But at the same time we have a lot of sympathy for this diffident, awkward, credulous and disingenuous character. His character is very important as the whole narrative oscillates between Deven's dreams and realities, his success and failure, his enthusiastic and vacillation and the ultimate disaster into which he lands.

The main tragic factor is that Deven does not possess confidence and courage to rise equal to the occasion. He thinks that it is some sort of madness which carries him to Delhi for a task which he is incapable of doing. He finds that he is neither qualified nor has experience for this challenging pursuit. All his suffering is caused by his friendship with Murad and Nur. That friendship still exists though in custody only. He had accepted the gift of Nur's poetry and that means that he is the custodian of Nur's very soul and spirit.

The great Indian-English poet Keki-N Daruwalla finds fault with the novel's ending regarding the character of Deven as the reader does not know what exactly happens to Deven at the close of the novels.

"And the ending, whether one takes it that Deven commits suicide or refrains from committing it frankly left me surprised and untouched" (Daruwalla, *loc. cit.*). Desai evokes the dominant attributes of contemporary Indian society through the character of Deven who acquires symbolic cannotations besides his role as the central figure.

The whole undertaking begins as an adventure but soon becomes crusade. Deven's attitude is one of diffidence; he has neither the sense of excitement which accompanies an adventure nor the sense of courage which is involved in crusade. Though he has devotion enough for both. N. Ramchandran Nair remarks, "*In Custody* is a poor exception. Deven's crisis in *In Custody* lacks in purpose and intensity. Neither his passion for the decadent Urdu poetry nor his concern for the ageing noble poet. Nur is sufficient to provoke such agony and ecstasy in Deven."

Ismail Merchant said, "He (Deven) is not a mechanically minded man.... His intentions are so pure that he's not going to give up his passion for poetry because he can't use a tape recorder and Nur realizes that Deven is the one who can be custodian of his work. He doesn't give it to his wives, he has found someone who feels passionately about it."

Thus to conclude we can say that Deven fails as an artist because he is alienated from life and its realities and he considers art to be separate from life. His growth into an artist through the encounters with the Urdu poet Nur, is characterized by the transformation of his earlier perception of the separateness of art, life and the artist into a wider vision of their inseparability and mutual compatibility. But towards the end of the novel when everyone deserts him, Deven suddenly finds his own inner strength and learns to accept his responsibilities with fortitude.

Deven—A Contrast to Murad

Deven is the hero of the novel *In Custody*. His father was a school teacher. Deven is portrayed as a marginal character that "dangles on the periphery of action". Murad is his childhood friend. He is a great manipulator, frequently violent and invariably unscrupulous character. In comparing Deven with Murad novelist presents a contrasting picture. "Murad had been the spoilt rich boy with money in his pocket for cinema shows and cigarettes and Deven the poor widow's son who could be bribed and bought to do anything for him, and although this had been the basis of their friendship, it had grown and altered and stood the test of time." Both of them know each other since their school time and their basis of friendship is not natural because they differ in nature and status. This difference of status in their friendship is of symbolic significance.

At one stage Murad and Deven appear to be two aspects of the same person. Deven is the deprived one, a widow's son, working in a mundane job, while Murad is the rich man's son and doing a job close to his heart. Murad provides the opportunity to Deven to interview Nur, the famous Urdu poet. As far as Deven is concerned, a miracle does come to pass and despite all his forebodings he finds himself pushed by some inner madness towards his goal which is set by Murad. We can see its glimpse in his encounter with Murad in the college.

While Murad is free and frank even in an alien atmosphere where he is only a casual visitor, Deven, who belongs to it, appears subdued and inferior to contrast. He becomes nervous while talking to Murad. And Murad is successful in gaining upper hand whenever he deals with Deven. That's why in his attempt to escape bullying Murad, he rushes to the classroom. But there also he proves once again a failure as a teacher. Sincerity of purpose, zest, hero-worhip of Nur, help Deven in no way to realize his dreams. Deven's failure is reminiscent of Desai's tragic vision. He is caught in the middle of linguistic-politics. The debunking to Urdu from mainstream is equally painful to him. But his Hindu religion stands in the way to his loyalty.

Murad, editor of *Awaaz*, is in same better position than Deven as he has not surrendered to Hindi. He wishes to crown Urdu its coveted crown.

Deven suffers from job insecurity while Murad is running his own business very cunningly. It is clear as Desai narrates "He is a great manipulator in the final examination. At school Murad had scored higher marks than Deven, although he had borrowed Deven's notes and often asked for Deven's help."

Through a series of coincidences, Deven is assumed by Murad to fulfill his task by immortalizing the verse of Nur in an audio recording. Initially, Deven dismisses this idea as he thinks that this gesture will belittle the great art of the great poet reducing his poetry to 'some song for the cinema, or radio' (p. 91).

However Murad criticizes his small-turn sensibility and sarcastically convinces him by saying, 'This is the age of electronics, haven't you heard? Or hasn't the news travelled to Mirpore yet? (p. 91). Murad continues to champion the forces of change and modernity in Deven's life and Deven, despite suspecting his sincerity, submits to his friend's oratory, only to reflect nearer the end of the novel, when things go wrong, whether their friendship too is another meaningless symbol of a lost custom. Despite his many journeys to Urdu's custodian Deven is unable to budge the metaphorical desert which separates the small regional turn of Mirpore and the national capital Delhi.

Thus Deven and Murad both are interesting characters. Deven, the hero is the major character, and the whole narrative revolves around him. But at the same time it is impossible to deny the importance of Murad's character as he is the one who has set the goal for Deven and it is very much because of him that Deven had suffered so much. He is the background against which Deven's personality appears in all different shades and colours.

REFERENCES

Nair, N. Ramchandran. *In Custody:* The Road Not Town: Indian Women Novelist, Set I, Vol. 4, Ed. R.K. Dhawan, New Delhi, Prestige Books, 1991.

Ismail Merchant in an interview with Ameena meer, April 1994 title. The star in India, B net.com

16

Characterization

Like Fernando's *Three Women,* Anita Desai's *In Custody* criticizes traditional society, but her novel focuses on two pathetic, trapped male characters whose wives despise their ability to come up to their expectations. A terrified, insignificant person, Deven moves from mediocrity as a college lecturer to impending professional and financial ruin as he incurs increasing monetary debts, which he finally decides to endure rather than committing suicide. His wife gives him little support—in fact, the women in the book seem rather nasty, especially the enraged young wife of Deven's hero, the poet Nur. As the story progresses, however, Desai makes clear that just as the male characters are trapped in a world that offers no possibility for success, the female characters have even more right to feel frustrated with a sexist society that reduces them to mere caricatures and provides no opportunity to prove their identity.

Desai's characters seem justified when they act out of self-preservation. But in fact, Desai does more than simply subvert a male society's attitude towards women, since she portrays a flawed Site-like image in her main male character Deven. Deven suffers bitterly throughout as he has too weak a character and personality to refuse the burdens others place upon him. He could never manage fiery rebellion. In contrast, he becomes noble at the end of the book by taking upon himself tremendous responsibilities. "He had accepted the gift of Nur's poetry and that meant he was custodian of Nur's very soul and spirit." Deven is a somewhat pitiful character—although one you desperately want to see succeed.

Other important characters to be known are Murad, Nur Sahajehanabadi, Abid Siddiqui, Mr. Trevedi, Sarla and Imtiaz Begum.

Murad

Murad is the central character of the novel *In Custody* next only to Deven, the hero of the novel. Murad is the childhood friend of Deven. They have studied together. Now at Delhi, Murad is a contrast to Deven. He is a great manipulator. The son of a wealthy Kashmiri carpet seller, Murad had been the rich spoilt boy with lots of money to spend on films and cigarettes. He projects that now he is not very rich as his father has disinherited him. He lives in Delhi with his mother. Murad regards his mother a saint. He says to Deven, "In the end even my sainted mother became suspicious and wanted to know why I needed so much money. She is willing to indulge me so far but no further."

Murad is a great manipulator. Deven and Murad know each other since their schooldays and basis of their friendship is not natural because they differ in nature and status:

> [....] Murad had been the spoilt rich boy with money in his pocket for cinema shows and cigarettes and Deven the poor widow's so who could be bribed and brought to do anything for him [....] (p. 11)
>
> [....] In the final examination at school, Murad had scored higher marks than Deven "although he had borrowed Deven's notes and often asked for Deven's help."

Murad is the editor of Urdu magazine *Awaaz*. He projects that he runs *Awaaz* to save the glorious traditions of Urdu from being extinguished by the Hindi Wallas. Murad's name means 'Heart's Desire' and he is concerned only to fulfil his heart's desires at any cost. Murad's face serves as a metaphor. He is facially disfigured by pockmarks; he epitomizes an Urdu speaker who is tainted by his contempt for Hindi. He is slippery, frequently violent and invariably unscrupulous and always complacently exclusive. Even the poet Nur says about Murad, "That jokar he should paint his face, wear false noose and perform in a traveling circus."

Murad frequently visits Deven's college and disturbs him for company. It is he who sets the goal for Deven. Murad is free and frank even in an alien atmosphere where he is only a casual visitor. Deven who belongs to it (college) appears subdued and inferior to contrast. Murad has always exploited Deven and has never paid for his book reviews and poems. Throughout the novel he catches weak aspects of Deven's personality and knows how to manipulate things to his own advantage. Murad overwhelms him by a show of false sympathy for the poorly paid intellectuals.

> It is too bad, how badly our lecturers are paid. How can the intellectuals of this country do any worthwhile work if no one shows them any respect or compensates them for all the sufferings.

Murad also takes advantage of this emotional state of Deven and strikes at his dormant love of Urdu poetry. He inspires Deven to go to Nur and interview him at his house in Old Delhi before he dies and vanishes, like a comet into the dark. He deceives Deven again and again. When Deven reaches Murad's office, Murad tortures him by his crafted behaviour and uncertain replies to his questions. He tells Deven that he does not know Nur's address. Deven grows nervous and feels shocked at the loss of his time and money only because of Murad. Truly speaking Murad enjoys torturing Deven. He has treated him in this manner since their boyhood. Seeing his dismay, Murad writes a letter of introduction to Nur and sends his office boy to help Deven find out the poet's house. At his second meeting with Nur, "Deven cried, stabbed to the heart by the thought that Murad had deceived him once again, had known something he had not divulged."

Unlike Deven, he is resourceful and aggressive. Even so there is something quite pitiable about his attempts to get things out of people and maintain an appearance of decent living. A.N. Dwevedi remarks, "Murad is a very cunning and crafty fellow". But perhaps Murad's way is the only way to get

Deven to do something. And Murad's bullying can thus be viewed as a strategy used by an adult of forcing child into growing up. Murad has to bully him and tell him, "Go back to your village, rot there with your buffaloes and your dung heaps. Go away, don't waste my time."

Murad has a self-congratulatory attitude toward Urdu. He considered himself a patron and well-wisher of Urdu language and feels great pride in saying that he is trying to keep alive the delicate language. He says, "Now I am planning special issue on Urdu poetry. Someone has to keep alive the glorious tradition of Urdu literature." But later on when he had to pay money he has number of complaints. He himself complains of the excessive bills from hotels and restaurants for drinks and other materials to the whole party. Murad wants now the sole right of the tape to sell it to HMV or Polyder so as to pay the bill and clear the debts.

We cannot easily forget the characters like Murad with his impish facetiousness somber profundity and verbal flippancy. He has been rightly compared by the critics with Shakespeare's *Iago*.

Nur Shahjehanabadi

Nur Shahjehanabadi is the renowned yet temperamental Urdu poet. He is the ideal of Deven, the main protagonist of the novel *In Custody*. Murad, the friend of Deven wants to publish his interview in the latest issue of his journal *Awaaz* as Deven says "But no special issue on Urdu poetry would be complete if it did not have some verse by Nur". But actually we find Nur being reduced to an old, whining figure. Murad and Deven have described him in different texture. While Deven is of the view that no special issue on Urdu poetry would be complete without Nur, Murad says in contrast "poor man, he is very old and ill—he has written nothing new. He is finished." But at the same time Murad informs Deven that he has sent the name of Nur to the Noble prize committee for its award for literature once again.

Nur has two wives. Safia Begum is the elder one, old and uneducated, while Imtiaz Begum is the younger one, a powdered and painted creature. Deven finds his house messy, disorganized, and shrouded in 'semi-darkness' and shadowy gloom. In fact 'Nur's house is *this home of ferocious felines*'. For the very first time when Deven enters and sees three things, a tap dripped, a broken bicycle and a cat slept. These images explore Nur's indisciplined life and Nur as a broken and useless man and his wives as ferocious as tigresses. His pigs like life, his unclean and greedy habit of mind are hinted at by his wife:

> "You have reduced him to that, making him eat and drink like some animal, like a pig." (pp. 59-60). His is compared with "fish-like skin and fish like spattering of the brown freckles of age". His imaginative urge to live beyond his means is hinted by calling him "a whale in a pail of water".

Nur changes Deven's recording sessions into mehfils which were attended by Nur's rowdy companions where lots of liquor, biryani and kebabs were consumed all at Deven's cost. Nur's talk is digressive even abusive during the recording sessions.

For Deven, Nur is nothing but the poet. Instead of finding the genius in his creations, Deven tries to seek him in the man. Nur's portrait, as a superhuman poet is similar to that of the freedom fighter farmer of *Where Shall We Go This Summer?* But Nur is not at all angelic. In the past, he was connected with nonentities and bad characters. His suffering from piles indicates his irregular eating habits. His excessive drinking and eating in such a garish company are all repulsive to Deven. Nur's family life is found to be equally disgusting. He, as a man, is full of surprises and contradictions—hurt and hurting in turn, pathetic, drunk and controlled by the women he lives with. Nur's love of pigeons ennobles him and connects him with ancient Muslim nobility. We see the pigeons hungry for Nur's flesh and blood with their gluttonous beaks "as if they would tear the flesh from his bones and devour it if he had nothing else to give them. Their greed was monstrous; they coated him with their gluttony."

In Chandni Chowk; in his own room on the terrace, he is the presiding deity of poetry. and all the chaotic audience are like obscure fairies of the literary sky. Many of the miniature poets recite their verses to Nur for his appreciation and guidance and Nur plays, comically, the role of the director of Urdù poets.

Nur appears as a true lover of his second wife Imtiaz Begum. Though she adores and sometimes she hates Nur but helpless Nur, knowing the fangs of her venomous malice, is yet, in love with her and cannot go against her will. He is very much concerned regarding the health of Imtiaz Begum. He goes and feeds her spoon by spoon. At this Deven's reaction is noteworthy. "Deven withdrew, frowning feeling more than a little impatient with the old man's weakness and gullibility."

Knowing all her feelings from her heart, Nur like a gentle conscience murmurs to himself patiently, "I would nurse her myself". It seems that such a feeling symbolizes his depth of love for his Begum later his heart breaks into emotional excitement. He tries to calm down the overflowing emotions of her heart and consoles her, "Dear heart, I will not, no I will not recite" Nur assured her coming closer to bed with his hands outstretched. "I am giving. No recitation" again. Deven understands him, his expectations, his desires and his way of exploiting others. In Desai's narration Nur holds the key to Urdu's revival. However, it is difficult to say whether Desai's guiding muse in this novels is Faiz since the Nur we meet—a poet at the end of his career is very reluctant to part with the old metaphors and lifestyle of an aristocratic lineage and seems to be untouched by a progressive outlook. He is obsessed with his pigeons, his body is saturated with an excess of rich foods and alcohol, he lives in a dusty faded house with his two wives. His poetic nurse sustains itself through the poetry of Byron and Shelley.

In fact, Nur the poet represents to Deven all that, he has idealized in himself. But Nur has uninhibitedly and unashamedly revealed his true life before Deven. That's why Deven says to Murad. "You think I'll give up a job...my salary to be that—that mad man's secretary to fill his inkpots, take down his curses and abuses? How could you tell him a thing, Murad, how?"

In the long confession which occurs on the day of the birthday celebrations, Nur tells Deven the whole story, of how Imtiaz Begum wanted the proper setting for herself and her fame, how she has raided his house, and stole away his audience and his friends.

Nur has a distinct attitude towards the language Hindi and Urdu and he gives absolutely no credit to academics for the well-being of the language. He is so disgusted with the universities that he calls them graveyards of the language. The occasion for his outburst is a gathering of young poets who are reciting their poems in Tarennum at Nur's house, "I tell you we must get over this rolling of Urdu verses into little sugar pills for babies to suck".

Before us there are two Nur, Nur the poet and Nur the senile, greedy, lustful man constantly making claims on Deven. Deven is attracted by one and repelled by the other.

Nur is not a man of his words. He never tries to keep his promises. He appears as a weak willed character, who is controlled by his senses. When Deven requests for the interview, which is urgently required, Nur agrees to help him in whatever way it is possible by replying his questions or by reciting some of his old and even unpublished verses. But later on it proves to be a fiasco as he tortures Deven in every possible way of quoting other English poets, by extracting money, by forcing him to arrange for his drink, food etc. It is Nur's person and poetry which have caused a thrust and stir in the life of Deven. Whenever there is shortage of drinks and other things, Nur's recitation of poetry stops. Nur mingles his own poetry with that of the great poets of the past. He quotes Byron and Shelley frequently. The best poem ever written by any poet recited by Nur reveals his awful loneliness and estranged existence which Deven has watched in his house.

O what can ail thee knight—at arms.
Alone and palely loitering?

Nur is so demanding and cruel to Deven that through his letter he declares that his death will occur shortly and requests Deven to arrange for some funds from the college for his family and children. It should be said to the credit of Desai that "she has created for the first time in Indian English fiction a figure like Nur, a poet born out of nervousness, impatience and regret." Finally we see Nur is not the ascetic, magical genius of Deven's imagining, but a weak grasping old man whose creative days are long since ever. Nur, who is an ideal for lovers of Urdu poetry and Nur whose mean mentality, greedy nature and behaviour, create repulsiveness in the onlookers is an interesting character to study.

Mr. Abid Siddiqui

Mr. Siddiqui is a lecturer in the college of Mirpore. He is an utterly lovable man. He is related with the family of Nawab of Mirpore with a crumbling palacial house. He is extravagant and wide-hearted like Nawabs. Siddiqui is a bachelor. He lives alone in his ancestral home, of which he is the sole guardian. Although to Deven he looks like an owner of big property, but in reality he represents a very lonely, meaningless and colourless life. He heads the withering Urdu Department. But he is resourceful and worldly wise and takes Deven out of his impasse. He often celebrates his Eden while presiding over a party of feasting, drinking and gambling. When Deven enters Siddiqui's house for the first time, he feels uncomfortable to see Siddiqui sitting in his house in an unexpected grandeur. Siddiqui is happy to see him, for he leads a very lonely life.

Mr. Siddiqui's house is at the other end of the bazaar. This symbolic house is symbolic of his imprisoned life. He wants to escape to Delhi. Therefore he asks Deven, "someone would do me the favour of seizing and destroying my property here so I would be free to make the return journey to Delhi". His inner discontent and alienated self is evoked through the house which is blackened and which has neither lights nor curtains to colour the gloom and the kitchen which is filthy. When Deven goes to his house he finds Siddiqui sitting out on the terrace in a cane chair. His attitude is of a grand landowner, Deven calls him a man of leisure and plenty. Though now things are quite different with Mr. Siddiqui as all his motor cars and carriages are old. Deven visits him and calls him "the recognizable yet unfamiliar figure of the little professor of Urdu seated on the terrace."

To Deven, Mr. Siddiqui is a very helpful, kind and compassionate person. Deven, whenever feels neglected and dejected, finds consolation in the warm welcome of Mr. Siddiqui. Siddiqui meets him with open arms and gives a cordial welcome with these words of appreciation "what an honor, what a pleasure, what an occasion, please come up come up". This sympathetic attitude and these consolatory words make Deven think about Siddiqui very firmly. Even in Delhi whenever in trouble he recalls, "Might Siddiqui, that sourceful little bird with the black bright eye come to aid once more".

Siddiqui is a wonderful host. Desai narrates, "Siddiqui's manner as a host was as impeccable as if all were still in order, still functioning in another, more opulent age." When Deven visits his house, he offers everything that he can, including Rum, Kebabs and pulao. Deven finds Siddiqui living 'very drearily domesticated and thrifty'. In fact Mr. Siddiqui is also not very well off. Cane chair in his house is tattered and broken. House is not painted for decades. Kitchen roof has fallen. There is no cooking at home. He explains "But my friend, who am I to spend my miserable earnings on except myself?"

Siddiqui has dual personality. While as a teacher in the college he is neat, trim and circumspect, at home he is transformed into a hedonist, a sybarite, a connoisseur of music and food and even a gambler. As Deven says, "he wondered how he had remained unacquainted so long with Siddiqui's talent for remaking fact into more acceptable, more attractive fiction. It had never displayed itself in college where he was only what he was, nothing else."

Siddiqui is very manipulative, calculative and clever, having various connections. He has power to convince others. He does it for Deven so many times. As Desai says, "Deven felt almost shattered by his agreeableness, by Siddiqui's cleverness, by the success of the whole mad venture in which he himself had scarcely dared to believe" (p. 105). At one point of time Siddiqui becomes more important than Deven himself for this project. As he insists that Deven must make his project a success because it is at his request that the funds have been made available to Deven and if Deven fails in his venture he will be considered responsible for Deven's deception and misuses of college-funds. With this change in situation, Deven grows aware of Siddiqui's importance in the enterprise and wonders at his exchange of role with Siddiqui. He feels that he has already lost his place of the central figure in this venture to Siddiqui. Because no one can deny that it is Siddiqui, through whose efforts, he could get the financial help. And without financial help it could not be possible for him to start and complete his project.

Siddiqui has a heart full of the milk of human kindness. He proves it in the case of Deven as well as in the Chotu's case. As Chotu helps him so he is there to think about Chotu's future. He has nobody else except Chotu in his family. He takes care of Chotu's present and also Chotu's future needs. He is also very much concerned about the present and future of Urdu. He realizes and says—"Yes. Urdu is becoming a rarity—it is only grown for export to Pakistan, or to the Gulf. Have you heard Faiz has gone to Beirut, to edit an Urdu magazine there?" (p. 97) Another example can be seen when Deven speaks to him about his project, Mr. Siddiqui appreciates his efforts to enrich and consolidates Urdu literature and poetry.

But Mr. Siddiqui has some negative aspects too. He is not a devout Muslim. As in the Quran it is prohibited to drink wine but Mr. Abid Siddiqui drinks, gambles and enjoys himself. He is never shown worshipping or doing any sort of religious activity. He has no sentimental attachment with his ancestral property. Siddiqui desires to go away from Mirpore to enjoy life elsewhere. He sometimes appears like Nur. Siddiqui also tries to buy the company of people by offering them good food, wine and money. At the same time because Deven could not fulfill his promises he becomes cruel with Deven. He talks very severely and cruelly. At times Deven finds some similarities between Nur and Siddiqui. He compares Nur's Mehfil with the sitting at Mr. Siddiqui's house. It was too like the Mehfil at Nur's house, "was the discreet and cautious Siddiqui not inviting disaster by allowing Chotu to turn from servant boy to singing star" (p. 138). This bachelor is in fact a hedonist and a romantic, who has the talent for remaking fact into more acceptable, more attractive victim.

In short Mr. Siddiqui is an interesting character, he gives vitality to the novel. He is somehow a realistic character. That's why he is in the list of Desai's loveable characters.

Mr. Trevedi

Mr. Trevedi is a minor character and appears for a very short time in the eighth chapter of the novel *In Custody*. He is the head of the Hindi Department in the Lala Ram College, Mirpore.

Mr. Trevedi is the major obstacle to be cleared for Deven before taking the interview of Nur Shahjehanabadi, a poet who is symbol of poetry, success and immortality for Deven. Mr. Trevedi has been teaching at the Mirpore College since long before Deven joined. Mr. Trevedi is also an ordinary teacher. There is nothing extraordinary in his career as lecturer, as Deven says. "He had long ago published a few short stories in a women's magazine now defunct and which no one remembered."

Mr. Trevedi is known as "a small vicious ferret of a man called Trevedi". He has not maintained very good and cordial relationship with anybody. Desai narrates, "When he looked at everyone with the same expression of manic hatred and as if he were calculating the right time to dart out and bite." Deven is also of the same view regarding the manner and behaviour of Mr. Trevedi. He has also faced the aggressive behaviour of Mr. Trevedi so often. Even when he makes the request for a week's leave to go to Delhi for the interview, he seems ready to bear the aggression of Mr. Trevedi. This is exactly what happened. He puts a number of questions in return. When Deven narrates the long incoherent explanation, Mr. Trevedi "pulled dreadful faces, like an actor practicing the rudra-rasa, the furious temper—opening his mouth, baring his teeth narrowing his eyes, cupping his ear with one hand and scowling."

It's not only Deven who holds such views about Mr. Trevedi, even his students have faced all these tantrums so many times and "found these a subject for hilarity but Deven's risibility had long ago been numbed and paralyzed".

Mr. Trevedi has a very bad opinion about the teachers and students of the college. According to him they are mad. He says. "Have you gone mad? All of you, I always thought a mad dog must have run through this college, biting staff and students alike-you are all mad." He even threatens Deven to demote him and to transfer him to Urdu department if he does not mend himself. He calls Deven as 'Muslim toadies' and puts the charge that Deven will ruin his students with his Muslims ideas and Urdu language. He says, "I'll complain to the principal. I'll warn the R.S.S., you are a traitor." Thus we had seen that Mr. Trevedi is representing those persons in the society who have no sympathetic outlook for others who are sufferers and who need help. Mr. Trevedi being Brahmin is anti-Muslim. He is not only against Muslims but also against their language Urdu. He is a staunch believer in R.S.S. and because of his unsympathetic and rash temperament is neither liked by his students nor by his colleagues. He is a very ordinary and common character that can be felt by anybody, anywhere.

Sarla

Sarla is the wife of the Deven, the hero of the novel *In Custody*. But Sarla is not the heroine, in the sense that she is not the central character of the novel *In Custody* unlike Maya, Amla, Monisha and other heroines of Anita Desai. Sarla appears not as an individual but just as the wife of Deven. She is the typical Hindu wife, simple, timid, obscure and domineered. As Deven's bride, she is his mother's and aunt's choice. Sarla's marital and material ambitions remain unfulfilled. For Deven, as a wife, she is unsympathetic, indignant, misunderstanding and sarcastic. Even though being the wife of a Hindi lecturer she has absolutely no interest in literature, or her husband's frequent visits to Delhi to interview the poet. Sarla is a religious Hindu lady. Desai explains, "Sarla regularly performed Puja before a tinted Oleograph of the goddess Lakshmi that hung in the corner by her dressing table, offering it flowers, incense and candles."

Just like any other common girl Sarla too had some dreams for her married life. She desires love, affection, comfort and understanding from her husband. Before marriage, she has wished for a life full of luxuries: the car, fridge, servants, etc. "The thwarting of her aspirations had cut two dark furrows from the corners of her nostril to the corners of her mouth, as deep and permanent as surgical scars. The drop of her thin, straight hair on either side of her head repeated these twin lines of disappointment."

Sarla a plain, penny-pinching and congenitally pessimistic woman presents the picture of an abandoned wife. Moreover she is anguished as she has no charm in her life except tedium and boredom. Her husband has failed to cater to her needs, be it physical, material or emotional. Her aspirations were thwarted and she, naturally felt embittered. For satisfaction, Deven takes recourse to poetry but she has nothing. Her area is limited. Her world revolves around her husband Deven, her son Manu and her house.

Sarla's marital life is unhappy. She cannot look beyond the four walls of her house. There is lack of communication and sense of belongingness between husband and wife. Her husband finds himself in her company as if he were a stranger, an interloper. Both are sore with each-other and their anger is reflected in Sarla's occasional silence and sullenness. Even at the end of the novel Deven admits that his wife's untidiness, her shabbiness and sullen expression were the results of his own misdoing.

Often Sarla feels embittered, as she feels everybody neglects her company. In fact, Sarla is a victim of circumstances. She has absolutely no idea about her husband's preoccupation and suspects that his frequent visits to Delhi are in order to meet his girl friend. Sarla as a wife knows nothing but to fret and sulk leading a dry existence always cross with her husband.

Sarla tries to discharge her duties as a housewife but she fails to attract Deven as he finds that there is nothing attractive about her. She is called an insipid wife who is miles away from her literary taste and intellectual pursuit. Sarla has a miserable, routine life, full of labour, "the shabbiness of her limp, worn clothes or her hunched twisted posture, her untidy hair or sullen expression" were integral parts of her humiliation. Sarla represents the destiny of most of the Desai's women characters.

She is an ordinary woman with ordinary looks and very ordinary thoughts. That's why she is unlike the other heroines of Desai. Sarla never lifted her voice in his (Deven's) presence—"countless generations of Hindu womanhood behind her stood in her way, preventing her from displaying open rebellion. Deven knows she would scream and abuse only when she was safely out of the way, preferably in the kitchen, her own domain."

Through Sarla, Anita Desai has revealed glimpses of the repressed condition of women in society. Sarla's method of defence in her house was to go into the bedroom and snivel. She will refuse to speak at all. She'll do this to incite their child to wail in sympathy. Deven notices and points out and that Sarla is not a good housewife. She never manages the house properly. As Deven feels when he comes home from Delhi in the absence of Sarla. Desai says, "Sarla had neglected to empty the dustbin in the kitchen before she left it. Contents had turned putrid, and stank." Moreover she never tries to update herself or do the things in a better way. The reason behind this may be her frustrations, and dissatisfaction from Deven.

Sarla is sarcastic in tone while talking to Deven. When she returns from her parent's house, she shows Deven the new clothes of Manu given by her parents and other things in such a sarcastic way that Deven feels hurt. Sarla never tries to understand and share or solve the problems of her husband. She blames him every time. Even she suspects that Deven's visits to Delhi are in order to meet some girl over there. This also shows her lack of faith in her husband and in her marital life.

Thus we see that though Desai has not presented Sarla as main character but she conveys through her an image of suffering wife, by adding sensitive nature to her and exploring her circumstances. She feels lonely and unhappy as she is traditional wife and mother. She is shown to suffer more because of the incompatibility between her individuality and awareness of herself and the traditional views of her husband. She suffers and feels more deeply the harsh sting of dislocation between aspirations and reality. The discrepancy between what she aspires or sets out to do in life and harsh reality confronting her, plunges her into abysmal anguish. She is a character, an exception in the world of Desai's women, who is drawn from the mainstream of life and as such is the representative of the common lot of women. Sarla, appears little on the surface of the narrative but she is there to reveal Deven as a frustrated man with familialties and to measure his sense of responsibility towards his son and life-partner. Sarla is a victim of her husband's weakness and helplessness. J.P. Tripathi feels that "Sarla is the typical Hindu wife, simple, timid, obscure, domineered, undemanding and co-operative, Sarla feels herself insecure and unattended. One night during summer all the three of them sleep in a room enduring suffocation. Sarla is not interested in shifting cots to the courtyard as she had a nightmare of robbers attacking them in sleep. In the eyes of Sarla, Deven is not paying due attention to them, with the result Sarla experiences terrible dissatisfaction in her married life as she wanted Deven to be the custodian of her family. We may conclude....richer texture" (pp. 1-138).

Imtiaz Begum

Imtiaz Begum is the second wife of famous Urdu poet, Nur. She is composed of two opposite elements, fascination and jealousy, for the poet. By her intellect, beauty, skill in singing and dancing, she has won the heart of Nur. For her, art is a means of earning money and livelihood unlike Deven and Nur to whom art means total selfless dedication. She appears accusing the poet of cowardice in her hoarse, exhausted voice. She taunted her husband, "A tortoise that sticks its head in the mud at the bottom of the pond." She shows her husband the money she has earned by singing lyrics. The husband-wife isolation is much obvious as she tries to stop the usual poetic session of Nur at the terrace, and plots against his publicity, interview and book-publication on him. She adores and hates Nur for his superior talent. She accuses Nur, "That is why you cannot abide my voice, cannot abide to hear me sing and so you insult me by getting up and leaving my performance. You insult me." It seems that the book does offer an alternative vision through the poetry of Nur's second wife, but this vision is rejected by Deven because he sees her as a snake, an impostor who has stolen her husband's verse. Again Imtiaz Begum's character is problematic because it wavers between the typecast intellectual poet, who is a chosen companion of the programme. Muslim poet as his second wife and the woman who sends her manuscript to Deven for critical perusal. But finally it seems that Urdu cannot sustain the modernty of a female narrative.

Foppery, pretensions and stratagems characterize her nature. To receive appreciation and assert her superiority over Nur, she celebrates her birthday and sings verse composed by her to Nur's admirers. She uses all dancers' tricks to win the audience with her relatives planted in it to praise her. Nur revolts against his wife's vain glory and retires, as he feels that his 'jewels' are taken away by her. Her driving away of Nur's secretary is another example of conspiratorial rivalry. Safia Begum's (Nur's first wife) accusation of Imtiaz makes it clear. "You have taken his name and his reputation and today even his admirers". For Deven she is a threatening presence with her evil interruptions; that's way Deven becomes so happy with the idea that Imtiaz Begum will go to Hospital leaving Nur and him alone. Only then they will be able to conduct the taped interview in peace. Deven experiences mixed feelings of relief and regret as he hurries out of the threatening presence of Imtiaz Begum. "He feels...regret at having left without making any arrangements...for the interview." "She has no control over her temper. She is frank, open and blunt to the extent that she grows hysteric with anger in the presence of Deven and calls him jackals from the so called universities that are really asylums for failures, trained to feed upon our carcasses." She even forbids Nur to recite his poems or meet his friends in future.

Imtiaz begum rages at her limitations and writes in her own defense, stands out as the most outrageous of these women. In fact, the radically redefines her experience by insisting on telling her story. Desai shocks us near the end of the novel when she presents Imtiaz Begum's point of view in a letter to Deven, in which she claims that Nur married her because of her 'gifts and abilities', not because of sexual entrapment as was guessed by all in the novel. She challenges him to read her enclosed Urdu poems:

> Let me see if you are strong enough to face them and admit to their merit. Or if they fill you with fear and insecurity because they threaten you with danger—danger that your superiority to women may become questionable.... Are you not guilty of assuming that because you are a male, you have a right to brains, talent, reputation, and achievement, while I, because I was born a female, am condemned to find what satisfaction I can in being maligned, mocked, ignored and neglected? Is it not you who has made me play the role of the loose woman in gaudy garments by refusing to take my work seriously and giving me just that much regard that you would extend to even a failure in the arts as long as the artist was male? (p. 196)

Her angry statements make the readers reevaluate what they previously had only seen through the eyes of a male perspective. Finally somewhere she gains respect as a character by arresting her rights and abilities.

We may conclude in the words of Malashri Lai. "Had Desai developed in Sarla, the conflict between traditional 'wifely' acceptances and her perceptive opposition to Deven's foolhardiness, the novel In Custody may have had a richer texture."

17

Existentialism in Anita Desai's Fiction

The key note of existentialism is that "existence precedes essence". It grapples with the problems of man who is uprooted; lonely, forlorn, dismayed, anguished, fighting against destiny just to prove his identity. It is normally applied to writing that emphasizes man's responsibility for forming his own nature and that stresses the prime importance of personal decision, personal freedom and personal goals. The instinct of revolt and rebellion is at the very core of existentialism. The uncertainty of 'to be or not to be' haunts the mind of the character. Anita Desai has used this technique very beautifully to express the inner-most thoughts and special characteristics of her major characters in her novels. Soren Kierkegaard stresses that uniting himself with God is necessary. *Gabriel Marcel* perceived that inhuman values had reduced man to a meaningless code of words. Karl Jaspers believes that morbid search for identity lies at the core of all philosophical thought while Heidegger's theory is that Man is thrown in a particular situation, not chosen by him, but *Sartre* believes in the supremacy of man's existence in a Godless world. Albert Camus emphasizes individual experiences.

Anita Desai is mainly influenced by Jasper, Camus, Heidegger and Kafka. Her major characters are tormented by their fears and phobias, as they feel circumscribed by the frightening conditions of their existence. Jaspers' existentialist concept of the border line situation figures prominently in the novels of Anita Desai. As in *Cry, The Peacock*. Maya's morbid and constant fear of death place her in a border line situation. Monisha in *Voice in the City,* unable to bear the absurdity of her existence, commits suicide.

Heidegger's concept of temporality manifests itself in Bim's character *Clear Light of Day*. Nirode's desire to move from failure to failure and Sita's endeavor to retain her unborn baby is unique in itself. Camus' concept of the absurdity of human existence and his concept of the problem of murder and suicide are evident in the shape of Maya's murder of Gautama, Monisha's suicide, and Murder and Rape of Ila Das, etc.

Anita Desai was influenced by one another important existentialist *Nietzsche*. He declared that 'God is dead for the modern man'. He had no trust in reason because it makes man a calculating coward and withdraws him from an active participation in life. Sartre also believes in the supremacy of man's existence, in a Godless world. He declared that 'man is alone in a Godless universe'. Anita Desai's novels are apt illustrations of these aspect of the existentialist view of life. In her novels, she has ably dwelt upon such existentialist themes as maladjustment, alienation, absurdity of human existence, quest for the ultimate meaning in life. Decision, detachment, isolation, and time as a fourth dimension focusing on how men and women in the contemporary urban milieu are bravely "struggling against or helplessly submitting to the relentless forces of absurd life. As for the themes in her novels, she has been deeply influenced by the existentialists. Desai's achievement consists in beautifully recording the emotional turbulence and chaos of her oppressed protagonist with a remarkable fidelity and seriousness. A fear of uncertainty hangs on the minds of her characters because they visualize some tragedy that threatens their existence. They encounter the harsh reality of existence single handedly. Deven Sharma, the protagonist of *In Custody* gets an insight into his authentic existence through his dread of being ruined and he finally gains the courage of his convictions.

Time, place and causation are the three basic factors governing all existence. In describing Deven's predicament in relation to time and place Anita Desai reveals the existential significances of the two basic factors Time and Place. She does not mention causation the third basic factor. Her emphasis on the external aspect of time and place clearly suggests that even the realization of existentialist awareness is possible within the limits of time and space only. Apart from the problem of choosing the appropriate time and place for the interview, Deven's diffidence is another obstacle that stands in the way of the fulfillment of his ambition. He goes to Nur's house at an hour of the day. When he expects to find the poet alone; but he is surprised to find a crowd of people in the courtyard of Nur's house. Later on while interviewing the poet in his passion for his poetry, Deven forgets the sense of time. He drags on these sessions of feasting and poetry to a span of more than three weeks, whereas he intended to complete this project in a week's time. Thus these basic feators mean a lot as far as the narrative of the novel is concerned.

Deven is frantically busy in pursuit of his ideal, but the fact is that he also stands in the moment and passes through the agonizing states of anxiety, dread and concern. In describing Deven's predicament in relation to time and place, Anita Desai reveals the existential significance of these two factors which govern all existence. Although she does not mention causation, the third basis factor governing existence, her emphasis on the eternal aspect of time and place clearly suggests that even the realization of existentialist awareness is possible within the limits of time and space only. Apart from the problem of choosing the appropriate time and place for the interview Deven's diffidence is another obstacle that stands in the way of the fulfillment of his ambition.

Deven's repeated failure in his enterprise leads him to mood of frustration and despair. As he reviews his past in contrast to his ambition and despair for success, he is distressed to discover that his life has been a series of failures. He feels defeated and grows listless. "Every effort he had made had ended in defeat: most of the poems he had written and sent to Murad had been rejected, his monograph never published, his wife and son eyed him with blatant disappointment, nor had he won the regard of his colleagues or students...it. He felt it inside him like an empty hole one he had been staring at all his years, intimidated by its blackness and blankness."

Torn by his ambition and his lack of resources, he is filled with anguish and despair. In this state of mental agony he compares his situation with that of Nur and discovers to his horror that both are trapped alike in their different circumstances. While depicting Deven's anguish and despair at his sense of circumscription, Anita Desai reveals the illusory aspect of freedom. Deven's anguish and despair in his present circumstances are genuinely existentialist, but he cherishes an illusion about his free will. He is yet unaware of the sense of moral responsibility that results from the strength of one's inner convictions, and in the absence of which use of free will leads only to illusion or absurdity.

"And that was all he was—a trapped animal. In his youth, he had the illusion of having free will, not knowing he was in a trap. Marriage, a family and a job had placed hurt in this cage, now there was no way out of it." The unexpected friendship with Nur had given him the illusion that the door of the trap had opened and he could escape after all into a wider world that lay outside but a closer familiarity with poet had shown him that what he thought of as the wider world was an illusion too—it was only another kind of zoo in which he could not hope to find freedom, he would only blunder into another cage inhabited by some other trapped animals. In such moments of unbearable anguish, death seems to him the only possibility of escape from his sufferings. Deven thinks that some; student leaping out of the bushes with a knife would be a simple solution, one to be hoped for by comparison.

Unexpectedly, Deven recalls Nur and tries to evaluate his genius apart from his senile demands. This evaluation of his genius revives his faith in his poetry. In this process Deven becomes conscious of the eternal nature of his relationship with Nur. He learns that even his death can not end this relationship.

Towards the end of the novel, the hour of daybreak symbolizes the dawn of existentialist awareness in Deven. He becomes conscious of the true nature of his predicament. The strength of his inner convictions gives him the courage and confidence to make his choice. He resolves to preserve the legacy of Nur and gains courage to fight against the calamities that may befall him with the beginning of the next day. As he rushes back to its home, he stops only to pull a branch of thorns from under his foot. It is through the symbol of thorns that Anita Desai crystallizes the change in Deven's attitude to the assault of existence.

> His present misfortune is no more than a prick of thorns to him and he has the courage of an existentialist to face it.
>
> —Anita Desai

Indeed, as a creative artist her central preoccupation is with the exploration and evaluation of the subjective reality of human individual. The novel *In Custody* like her many other novels bears the testimony to this fact. Her concern with human subjectivity naturally involves her interest in the existentialist predicament of modern man. Therefore, a study of her treatment of the existentialist problems of life is central to the correct understanding and appraisal of her writings. It is to the credit of Anita Desai that in concentrating on the inner being of human individual, she has given a new dimension to the Indian English novel.

18

Isolation and Alienation

Anita Desai holds a unique place among modern Indian English novelists. *In Custody* marks a departure as here for the first time Desai's preoccupation of writing about sensitive women 'in an insensitive world' takes a back seat and male characters occupy the centre stage. Her writings from *Cry, The Peacock* (1963) to *Clear Light of Day* (1980) expose inner realities and psychic echoes of her characters, as her forte is the quest of sensibility. She is interested in peculiar and eccentric characters rather than everyday, average ones. Obviously, all Desai's earlier novels are characterized by a quality of introversion, for she has been interested in capturing the atmosphere of the mind and she writes about the inner world of thoughts and emotions of her characters rather than their external world only.

In Custody presents before us a young man Deven, psychologically tense and yearning to indulge in some literary endeavous. The prime characteristics of Deven that attract our attention are his helplessness, humility, suffering and nobility. Here in the novel Desai had experimented with the theme of alienation with a new set of characters and situations. The theme of alienation is reinforced herein with great ingenuity and skill. It focuses our attention on the mental agonies and dilemmas of Deven, whose fanatic love of Urdu drives him into the clutches of his so-called friend Murad. Having only a poor helpless mother, Deven naturally grows into a week, uncertain person. He is not satiable with his life and just because of it he becomes a victim of unhappiness and inferiority complex. As a child, he had watched closely the bitter disappointment of his mother, and the apologetic smile of his father for his failure in measuring up to her expectations. Evidently these familial and social factors generated in him a submissive tendency to remain alone. His alienation from his wife Sarla and his only child Manu makes him seek refuse in the fantasy world of Urdu poetry.

The novelist brings out Deven's sense of boredom, isolation and alienation through his attitude towards his students and the locale of Mirpore. He is assigned the job of interviewing a renowned Urdu litterateur Nur Shahjehanabadi, but meets failure at every step. He feels utterly helpless. Deven's adventure in the field of poetry and art may be viewed as a search for meaningful existence. The real tragedy of alienation lies in his failure and frustration in reaching his noble goal.

Deven feels alienated. He really feels that he is not being helped by Mr. Siddiqui, Murad, Nur and his wife. He is being hunted down by these people to have their ends meet. Nobody seems to offer him any solace or assistance at this crucial juncture of his life.

> No one was going to come forward with help or with a solution that he would have to correct matters himself or be thrown out of college for false pretences, misappropriation of funds, fraud, cheating and incompetence.

This alienation of a college teacher is from his own roots and culture. The alienation is not complete but Deven feels estranged from his own job, his own family, and his own immediate environment. His vision of life and art drawn from Westernized system of education comes in conflict with the day today life; Anita Desai depicts very beautifully the inner-conflict of Deven who ultimately finds the truth that life is not an ivory tower but a reality.

Deven's alienations is born out of opposite, conflicting tendencies like Western education and cultural roots urbanization and rural way of life, industrial society and placid Indian agrarian society. Deven feels estranged because he is pressurised by growing consumerism where money is all in all. Consequently he becomes utterly sad, helpless and hopeless. The sense of isolation and self-exile often grips Deven's psyche. He feels alienated not only from his immediate environment but also within himself. The very existence becomes a burden for him.

Deven's sense of isolation and loneliness has two significant connotations. He wants to break the imprisonment by taking an interview of the great Urdu poet Nur. He wants to break away from his marginality. At another level he feels ill equipped and incapable of adapting himself to the emerging complexities of life and society. He is discontented and yearns for what is not. He feels trapped in its solidity and stubbornness. He now seeks to review his existence and its problems. He feels, "Then where was freedom to be found? Where was there fresh air to breathe?"

Through the alienated figure of Deven, Anita Desai presents before us in the novel In Custody the realistic picture of the changing socio-economic Indian scene and its impact on educated Indians who feel lonely, bore, alienated marginalized on account of materialism consumerism and industrialism. Deven Sharma, like other protagonists of Desai, is brought up to be diffident, meek and quiet in the face of exploitation. Yet he is highly sensitive and is desperate to find an outlet to his pangs. He finds his peace at last after discovering his identity and work in this alliance. Thus unlike Desai's earlier novels this novel ends on a positive note. "Deven runs to meet the calamities of the day, stopping only to pull a branch of thorn from under his fort."

Thus Desai's fictive world including In Custody in the centrality of self is concentrated in terrifying isolation, finding it hard to reconcile with the world around 'Self'. Her protagonists, like Deven are constantly confronted with the stupendous task of defining their relation to themselves. Acceptable behavioral pattern is alien to them. The root is not far to find. Her central characters, by and large, have strange childhood from which they develop a negative self-image and aversion. The immediate result is their fragmented psyche to view world as a hostile place. For them the domestic life is not their world, rather, it is a trap where their individuality is endangered and thus complete lack of interest and dissonance in their relationship bring solitary confinements and show their reluctance to face reality. Deven is the living example of such alienated characters created by Anita Desai.

19

Thematic Study of Love and Marriage

Anita Desai, in her novel *In Custody* presents the thematic problem of man-woman relationship and theme of love and marriage in a very exquisite manner. The theme of husband-wife alienation and marital disharmony, though not a new theme, gains depth and meaning in this novel by Anita Desai.

"Marriage is the destiny traditionally offered to women by society" says the feminist Simone De Beaurvoir. Desai in her portrayal of man-woman relationship mostly concentrates on the predicament of modern woman in this male-dominated society and her destruction at the alter of marriage. According to Desai most marriages prove to be unions of incompatibility. Her women long for love and communion of the spirit which they perceive as the panacea of the ills of the world. Except for *Voices in the City* Desai's women protagonists are lonely and dissatisfied. In an interview on 16th November 1979 in Jaipur, Jasbir Jain asked Anita Desai, "Do you feel the man-woman relationship doesn't have the capacity to be a satisfying one, is it inadequate in every respect?" Anita Desai replies, "I think all human relationships are inadequate. Basically everyone is solitary. I think involvement in human relationships in this world invariably leads to disaster."

The novel *In Custody* analyses the problem of Deven Sharma an impoverished college lecturer. After his marriage with a sullen and dull lady Deven sees a way to escape from the meanness and hopelessness of daily life. He is a temporary lecturer in a private college but he lives in a fool's paradise. His extreme devotion to art leads him to indifference to his wife. Rather he has cultivated an aversion to and dislike for his wife. Like zola he lets his wife feel widowed.

Here Anita Desai also deals with a purely marital problem of this materialistic civilization in a pent-up city like Delhi, where the relation of husband and wife is always under strain because of the undue indulgence of husband in extra activities and his attachment with other women. Relationship between Sarla and Deven is not satisfactory. Deven refuses to respond to her approaches and bars her entry into his world. Sarla withdraws into silence.

Apart from this the derelict house in the novel reflects on Deven's incongenial and less harmonious conjugal ties. It also reveals the isolation and conjugal chaos leading to insanity. Deven is but they are not able to get along happily as husband and personal relationship has not been going smoothly. Both of them in their own ways but they are unable to do anything, for each feels as if he were in a prison. Marriage his family, his job had a sort of trap, a cage, and there was no way out of it.

Deven Sharma wanders in search of money only. He craves for named dreams of gold bangles of his wife Sarla. He plans a Utopian: Sceme and lives in a dreamy world. However his wife Sarla is puzzled by these dreams of Deven. How can she become satisfied with a husband who, loves others, have ties with them but maintains a distance from his wife and son. Problems of post-martial life are dealt in this novel. In fact Deven often feels as if his marriage has stood behind his imagination like a heavy weight. He also believes that marriage has clogged his progress in life; it has given hostage to his festive, it has placed him in such a cage from where it is impossible to escape. It is a common thinking of the improvised husband. He feels dejected. Had he shown his love and affection to his own family life, his wife and son, he would have led a happy and contended life, full of satisfaction and peace. As a matter of fact the husband of his heart is never true to his wife in the real sense of the terms. In his relation with his wife there is lack of harmony, adjustment, and concordance.

Deven could never understand that as a wife Sarla needs love and affection more than money. She needs only sympathy, consolation, appreciation of her work and sharing of pain and pleasures. In married life of Deven and Sarla what is missing is the real feelings of love and affection. This problem of marriage and love is dealt in detail by Anita Desai in this beautiful novel *In Custody*. Here Desai presents a kind of humour and pathos of married relations that he wants to be more familiar and closer with others, not with his wife and child. Marriage is a means to combine two souls and two bodies into spiritual harmony. But under the complicated situation Deven's married life does not give better and sweeter results. His pessimistic wife presents the picture of an ill-matched wife. While Deven is pained to notice the bad aspect of his married life. Complicated problems of married life settle upon him like a grey monster. He feels aged and haunted. Neither he understands his wife and her motives and intentions nor she can understand him. Deven thinks that she does not care for him and his feelings while Sarla thinks that he neglects her all the time and is engaged with some other girl. Both feel insulted and humiliated living in one room. No one tries to understand the heart of other person. As Desai narrates beautifully in simplest words, "Deven had been more a poet than a professor when he married Sarla—he had only taken on as a temporary lecturer and still had confidence in his verse—and for the wife of a poet she seemed too prosaic."

Only at the end of the novel Deven admits and understands her disappointment "because like her he had been defeated too, like her, he was victim of circumstances" (p. 68). In the common problems of post-marital life, he came to understand her predicament also. It is true that Deven Sharma leads a very cultured life of a college lecturer grooming under the crushing agonies of poverty. But there is another aspect of this marital relationship too. All the time Deven thinks about his wife and son. He wants money but that too for Sarla. He desires to buy gold jewellery for his wife. He says "I have my job to think of, and my wife and Son." Perhaps he "would have...earned a name for himself, a little fame, even gold bangles for Sarla...."

He exclaims in terror, "Oh God, he would be ruined and Sarla and Manu with him".

Sarla also tries to fulfill her duties of a wife and mother when Deven needs support. Sarla gave him some herbal tea to drink and went off to fetch some powders from the homeopath in the bazaar". As a mother she is happy when Deven spends time with Manu and she says, "He has gone to the neighbours to show them his new clothes, Sarla said, not looking up". My parents have given him new clothes. And shoes.

The major reason behind the failure of their marriage is that it was a settled marriage and not a love marriage. Love was no where to be seen in their relationship. No body from Deven's side could understand that Sarla as a girl and as a new bride had aspirations, too. "She had dared to aspire towards a telephone, a refrigerator, even a car...while her mother collected stainless steel cooking pots and her sisters embroidered pillowcases and anti-macassars for her, she dreamt the magazine dream of marriage herself stepping out of a car with a plastic shopping bag full of groceries and filling them into the gleaming refrigerator, then rushing to the telephone placed on a lace doily upon a three-legged table and excitedly ringing up her friends to invite them to see a picture show with her and her husband who was beaming at her from behind a flowered curtain."

But what really happened is completely different. By marrying into the academic profession with a lecturer of Hindi, that too in a small town Mirpore; none of these dreams had materialized. And that made her naturally embittered. "The droop of her thin, straight hair on either side of her head repeated these twin lines of disappointment." Deven was also disappointed as he is depicted as a victim but at least he had his poetry, while Sarla had nothing and so there was an added accusation and bitterness in her look. Sometimes she becomes sarcastic in tone while talking to Deven. The author predicts Deven's problems on both fronts: home as well as job. Deven's miserable life with unsympathetic and sarcastic wife makes him think that he "must look like a caged animal in a zoo to any creature that might be looking down at earth from another planet."

There is another aspect of marriage shown by Nur and his two wives. While his elder wife stands for duty the second one for love. Nur and Imtiaz Begum do care for each-other to the certain extent. Nur, for her treatment wishes to admit her to a hospital but she refuses the hospitalization due to illness because she feels that she will be deprived of the affectionate nursing from her husband. Nur too decides to nurse her. Nur refuses to give interview to Deven due to the illness of Imtiaz Begum. There is a enormous attachment of husband and wife. But wife is the controlling agent in this case unlike Deven and Sarla. Nur's own life is miserable on account of it. We have no details as to how Nur married Imtiaz Begum, but it has been clearly shown how inspite of his infatuation for her, he is not able to derive any happiness or satisfaction from her.

Thus it is clear from the above discussion that Desai's female protagonist points out the 'mad clarity' of all family relationships, the farcical nature of all marriages, the illusory quality of all human relationships, male and female. What she portrays is the deeply felt and suffered rebellion against the entire system of social relationships. The question of real love is always present there in Desai's novels including *In Custody*. In the some way, Desai's presentation of man-woman relationships in a patriarchal society reveals her concern and understanding of different forms of woman's experiences through an effective interplay of motive and the medium. The women in the book seem vicious, specially the enraged young wife of Deven's hero, the poet Nur. Just as the male characters are entrapped in an unsuccessful world, the female characters feel frustrated within a patriarchal society that reduces them to clinging to these men who fail to provide them what they want. Deven's wife Sarla hates him and feels disgusted at his failures. All her dreams of a luxurious life and dashed to the ground because of his meger income. But the way she registers her protest is nothing more than a symbolic dissatisfaction with her lot. "Sarla never lifted her voice in his presence—countless generations of Hindu womanhood behind her stood in her way, preventing her from displaying open rebellion. Deven knew she would scream and abuse only when she was safely out of the way, preferably in the kitchen, her own domain. Her method of defence was to go into the bed room and snivel, refusing to speak at all, inciting their child to wail in sympathy."

Anita Desai has conveyed her women character's fundamental dependence on men through her lexicon and types of mastery, command and domination.

In her previous novels, women protagonists were of poetic temperament and male characters were cold and calculating: Maya-Gautam, Monisha-Jiban, and Sita-Raman, all represent such couples. But here, the situation is reversed. Imtiaz Begum and Sarla mock at the poetic sensibilities of their husbands because they fail to meet their corporeal needs.

20

Desai's Use of Irony

Irony comes as the result of the quest for meaning in the universe, at the result of human experience. Irony is a literary artifice which heightens the artistic effect in art. It is an art of expression. It is a mode of speech. It conveys one's feelings to the reader in a literary way. It suggests the double meaning A.C. Ward has written "Irony is the art of expressing two meanings simultaneously the obvious, surfacing meaning which the majority will regard as the only meaning and matter (under the surface) meaning which may possibly be detected only by those who can read the author's mind as well as the author's words." Anita Desai's sense of irony embraces the whole emotional range of her characters. Unlike the satirist who for ever distances herself from her creatures and describes their actions from outside, Desai probes into the inner recesses of her characters.

Desai's irony is mild, genial, pure and solid and chiefly related to human life. Her outlook towards life is free from all envy, doubts and fears. Her irony is free from bitter satire. It is a delicate perfume. She is against preaching openly. There is no satirical vehemence in her irony. It is no exaggeration to say that irony constitutes the basic fabric of her novels.

In the novel *In Custody* the narrative mode is characterized by irony. The novelist creates an *Irony of situation* by making Deven, a lecturer in Hindi, interview Nur, the great living poet of Urdu. The sense of Irony is further intensified when Nur begins to interview him instead of being interviewed by him. Nur feels that Deven has come to torture him by his insane questions. *The Irony of situation* is always there. The novelist again brings out Deven's disillusionment with his glorious concept of poetry through a highly ironical situation in which he encounters Nur's second wife, Imtiaz Begum, and finds Nur lying in an abject condition on the floor of her room. Deven runs away from the abominable sight of Nur and his world of poetry reeking with liquor and vomit.

Later on also a succession of episodes are marked by irony, Deven is exploited by everyone. In this process he discovers the dichotomy between dreams and reality. The irony lies in the interview and the recording of Nur's poems and memoirs and in a fiasco, leaving Deven's artistic aspirations crushed and his career in a ruin.

Here ironic mode comes to dominate the narrative. It is also evident that a pattern of contrast and contradictions runs through the narrative lending a certain poignancy and artistic effect. "Indeed that is forte of the ironist; he looks at the contradictions in human experience and this perception yields a detachment, and detachment which grants a perception." In fact, the ironist is deeply concerned with both aspects of the contradictions he perceives, and this concern leads to an ambivalence of attitude to one side and to the other—to both at once.

Again, there is *Irony of character* too. Irony lies in the very manner in which Deven's character has been conceived. His is an interesting study in characterization for manifests inherent contradictions. He has an innate poetic sensibility but turns out to be a boring teacher, because he has distanced himself from the profession he has accepted. Deven's irony is that he has always been a timid creature and conscious of his inadequacies, but indulges in a vain enthusiasm. Deven thinks Nur is like a comet to show him light, but very soon he starts having doubts. "The comet was something to be feared he just remembered, it was a bad omen, not lucky."

The element of fantasy as part of the manner in which Deven's character has been delineated, also contributes to the *ironic tone of the narrative.* Fantasy requires a heightened awareness of one's surroundings and once it traces shape, fantasy becomes concrete rather than abstract. There are several instances of fantasy, nightmare, fears and heightened imagination scattered throughout the novel *In Custody*. For Deven, initially Delhi was the city of his dreams of fame and literary achievement. Consequently Delhi is symbolic of fantasy while he saw Mirpore as a trap but ironically, very early in the novel. Deven realizes that his town Mirpore and Nur's Delhi share a common element of decay, decadence and disorder. "He was thinking that the great city was no different from his own small town and that the dissimilarity lay only in scale."

Deven is fully aware of Murad's tricks and his deceptive ways. He knows that Murad can betray him. At one place in the novel he broods that it has been foolish on his part to trust Murad:

> Deven sat bemused upon a wooden stool in the shadows watching Murad pass through one act after another like some chameleon giving a bravura performance. Considering the full range of his moods and shifts in temper, his contradictions and discrepancies, he wondered why he had trusted his world, taken it seriously enough to use his one free day to catch a bus to Delhi.

But the irony is that he is unable to make himself get rid of Nur or Murad and bound to suffer the pangs of ever lasting conflict. Ample examples of *Verbal Irony* are there in the novel. Sarla's comment upon the Deven's visit to Delhi, his meager earning etc. exemplifies it. Anita Desai's irony is more prominent when directs towards Deven's romantic notions about poetry and the poets. He believes in the separateness of art from life and that art belongs to a higher sphere. The extent to which Deven had idolized the poet is evident in the description of his first meeting where the very diction suggests the narrative strategy of felt romanticism and an unmistakable undertone of irony. "It was to him as if God had leaned oven a cloud and called for him to come up, and angels might have been drawing him up these ancient splintered stairs to meet the deity: so jubilantly, so timorously, so gratefully did he rise. This, these empty years, only he had not known it would assume this form. In his mortal myopia and stupidity, he had expected it come from Sarla when he married her, or from the head of the department at his college who alone could promote and demote and alter his situation in life, or even from Murad who, after all, lived in the metropolis and edited a magazine.... He mounted the stars as if sloughing casting meanness dross off and costing away the manners and doss of his past existence and steadily approaching a new and wondrously illuminated era."

But his idealized visions of the poet and his life, receive a rude jolt immediately. In contrast to his expectations Deven had visualized him utterly different. This perceived contrast between his vision and the reality facing him is very ironic. He was nauseated by the way in which he was compelled by Nur's wife to clean up the poet's vomit with pages. The irony of the situation hits him when he realizes later that those papers might have been inscribed with Nur's verse. It is a stroke of irony perceiving how Nur's sly words progressively take on grandiose hues, get enhanced and embroidered in Deven's imagination to satisfy Deven's literary ambition.

The 'wherewithal' referred to is the tape-recorder he buys intending to record the interview and Nur's recitation of poems. The interview lasts not for three days but for three weeks, and it becomes central point of discussion ironically and humorously too. The recording sessions prove to be Mehfils which were attended by Nur's rowdy companions. He allowed himself to be palmed off with a second-rate tape recorder and inept operator. It is ironic that he realizes too late that all that luck and timely help had only dragged him deeper and deeper into a disaster. With his successive meeting with Nur the illusory world of Deven's creation regarding the poet, is shattered. There comes, then a moment of bitter irony, a moment of agonized self-scrutiny and realization of the utter delusion of it all.

The very title of the novel points to this central irony. It means in the novel guardianship and not a physical prison. The epigraph to the novel taken from Wordsworth's "Rob Roy's

Grave" also suggests the ironic perspective that controls the narrative.

"They should take, who have the power and they should keep who can." Thus we can conclude that Desai's whole style is ironical. Her delicate irony is the very essence of her style. Irony of style has been created by Desai deliberately. It sparkles out in every twist of a phase. Desai as an Ironist naturally, deserves fame and praise.

21

The Language Controversy

Language is a tool of society primarily to communicate but now language has become a powerful medium not only for expression of culture in the form of literature but also for expressing the national, the socio-cultural identity of a nation. It is deeply *rooted in our psyche,* exercising powerful influence on our sentiments. Language controversy and its socio-cultural and political implications and effects are peculiar to a country like India which has multilinguistic groups. Language instead of being related to any community in particular, is related to the people who use it irrespective of the community they belong to. In the process it marks a preference of Bakhtinian view of language that treats the language or parole in use as the real language. Another view about language that finds fictional expression in the novel is related to the use of language—its teaching or learning—is not always a matter of communal responsibility, rather it is more related to one's vocation. The novel *In Custody* presents the Hindi/Urdu controversy that involves communal implications and does not allow the languages to become objective mediums of communication.

In the context of the novel—it is presented by the novelist that the question of Urdu is communalized and politicized. But in fact Hindi or Urdu was never exclusive to any community. That's why the lover of Urdu poetry is a Hindu lecturer of Hindi, in the novel *In Custody* by Anita Desai. Although politics does not figure directly yet political views indirectly affect the life of protagonists. The language controversy of

Hindi and Urdu is referred to in the novel. The two camps of Hindi and Urdu are represented respectively by Trevedi, the Head of the Hindi Department in Deven's college, and Nur the Urdu poet. It is ironical that Deven's enthusiasm and love for Urdu literature is misunderstood by Trevedi who is a staunch Hindi walla and on political front who can be a better advocate of Rashtrabhasha than the RSS.

Trevedi dislikes Deven's interest in Urdu and this dislike comes openly when he goes to him for asking for one week's leave to go to Delhi to interview the poet "One week? It would be a relief to me if it were one year.... I'll get you transferred to your beloved Urdu department. I won't have Muslim toadies in my department; you'll ruin my boys with your Muslim ideas, and your Urdu language." Trevedi's reactionary stance encapsulates the culture of fear and paranoia that surround Hindi and Urdu speakers in a national climate where language is ironically both the carrier of religious identity and the mark of national loyality. Trevedi's utterance, long before of destruction of the Babri Mosque in Ayodhya, tells its relation with RSS. Thus, Nur and Trevedi have the similar attitudes towards their language controversy.

The language controversy and the conflict between Hindi and Urdu have received much attention in the novel. Deven is caught between two languages, Hindi, on the one hand, is the source of his livelihood and Urdu which he loves. The Urdu supporters vomit out all their hatred against Hindi, Murad is one of them. He is the editor of an Urdu magazine *Awaaz*. He worries much about the dwindling number of Urdu readers:

> Worries, worries, worries, and where are the reader? Where are the subscriptions? Who reads Urdu any more?

Murad considers himself a patron and a well-wisher of Urdu language and feels great pride in saying that he is trying to keep alive the delicate language. But that is not enough.

In order to establish the superiority of the Urdu language he tries to denigrate Hindi by calling it that vegetarian monster, Hindi, that language of peasants, the language that is raised on radish and potatoes. He compares the two languages also, like the vegetables. Hindi flourishes her, while Urdu the language of the court now languishes in the back lanes and gutters of the city.

Even the great poet like Nur is not free from such comparisons. Nur is as contemptuous of Hindi as Murad. Nur criticises Deven for teaching Hindi in a college. He absurdly alleges that Hindi is being given top priority only to uproot the Urdu language, and that Deven is a party to it. Deven insists his point and says that love for Urdu poetry and his teaching Hindi literature in a college indicates that the reality of life is quite different from the dream of it. Although he loves Urdu poetry, he cannot earn a living by it. After listening to Deven's reply and reasoning of this kind Nur gets very angry. He taunts Deven and asks him to forget about Urdu literature and his poetry and go back to his college and "Teach your student the stories of Premchand, the poems of Pant and Nirala. Save, simple Hindi language, saves comfortable ideas of cow worship and caste and the romance of Krishna". Thus one can see that this language controversy becomes the conflict between two religions and two castes instead of just the literature of two languages Hindi and Urdu. Anita Desai tries to focus this vital social issue in the novel very beautifully. It is so entwined in the fabric of the novel that it becomes the part and parcel of the plot. Deven, Murad and Nur, are all caught in a nostalgic remembering of Urdu, wishing to restore it to its former glory. This novel by Desai is ostensibly a narrative about the death of a language and raises uncomfortable questions about its demise. Desai's overall fictional portrayal of Urdu marks an elegiac farewell to a lost tradition. Nur's character is the great help to present this issue in the novel *In Custody*. According to Nur, Urdu died in 1947 when the country became independent. He says in a gathering of young poets who are reciting their poems in tarannum at Nur's house.

> We need the roar of lions, or the boom of cannon, so that we can march upon these Hindi-wallahs and make them run. Let them see the power of Urdu, he thundered.

A more rational approach comes from another man who may have been a journalist or a mere spectator: Nur Sahib... "To feed the Hindi-wallahs with Urdu poetry is like feeding cows with-hunks of red meat". There are some Hindi supporters also who speak in praise of Hindi, "vegetarian Hindi".

Ismail Merchant in an interview with Ameen Meer said, "I always wanted to do a film about the Urdu language, which is disappearing. It's the most gracious and expressive language and the poetry is so sublime, the thoughts are so great, that it is impossible to supplant it.... It will remain a language of poetry, certainly because all the popular songs are in Urdu, as one sees in Hindi cinema; they're not in Hindi. A pure Hindi song will never become popular, because no one will be able to pronounce it. And if I want to express love, I'll speak to you in Urdu. Or if I want to express tragedy or sadness, I'll speak to you in Urdu. So the Urdu language itself will continue because of its songs, and people will still enjoy it. But the education, people writing or people reading—that will disappear."

Desai's treatment of the questions related to the social role and implications of language forms the central thrust of the novel. Her motives become amply clear when she replies to a question related to the theme of the novel in the following words: "I was trying to portray the world of Urdu poets. Living in Delhi I was always surrounded by the sound of Urdu poetry, which is mostly recited. Nobody reads it, but one goes to recitations. It was very much the voice of North India. But although there is such a reverence for Urdu poetry, the fact that most Muslims left India to go to Pakistan meant that most schools and universities of Urdu were closed. So that it's a language I don't think is going to survive in India.... There are many Muslims and they do write in Urdu, but it has a kind of artificial existence. People are not going to study Urdu in school and college anymore, so who are going to be their readers? Where is the audience?" (Interview with Magda Costa 2001)

Desai's worry about the future of Urdu language reflects not only through her statements but also through her novel and screenplay for the film *Muhafiz*. At the same have Desai also tries to expose the false beliefs of the people who develop a highly romantic attitude towards poetry and language. Nur also expresses his attitude towards poetry and language. Even genuine attempts of persons like Deven are surprised by Nur simply because he fails to understand language freed from established views associating language with certain cultural groups or persons and artists live himself: "Urdu poetry.... How can there be an Urdu poetry when there is no Urdu language left? It is dead, finished.... So, now you see its corpse lying here, waiting to be buried...."

The novelist's artistic achievement here lies in keeping the fictional discourse free from such views about language. The fictional presentation of different perspectives about language also finds extension into existential issues related to broader human experience.

We cannot deny that novelist is aware that since the two languages belong to two different and hostile religions, the language issue is politicized and Deven dislikes and avoids this as he had always kept away from the political angle of languages. Anita Desai observes that language controversy has vitiated minds of the intelligentsia evoking from it stereotype responses and arguments. Language issue and its controversies are described in a very special way by the novelist in novel *In Custody*.

22

Use of Symbolism and Images

In Desai's novels one comes across a symbolic link between different images, which form an interface, a common bond. Imagery is primarily used to capture and crystallize a wide range of experiences. It lends clarity and vividness to the situation she describes, events she documents and characters she delineates. Most of the images used by Desai in her novels are so sharply condensed and chiseled that they resemble a piece of painting.

The experience of fragmentation and disintegration of alienated victims of Desai is conveyed through images. Highly functional, they form an integral part of the fiction. "These images" observes Anita Amin "look contrived and far fetched, a striving after effect for its own sake without relevance to the emotions felt or the situations described."

In the words of Madhusudan Prasad Desai's imagery which is chiefly anticipatory, pre-figurative or demonstrative in nature is always considerably functional. "Lusciously lyrical, her image patterns are singularized by interrelatedness and continuity."

Anita Desai is a symbolist as well as an imagists as in her novels she has generously woven symbols and images. Through symbols and imagery she has tried to crystallize the various complexities of man-woman relationship, a regular theme of her novels. Her symbolism and images also assume an ornamental dimension and create mosaic textural richness.

A characteristic use of symbols and images also helps the novelist to reveal her protagonist's psyche. As Wimsatt and

Brooks suggest, every colour sound, odour, emotion and every visual image has it correspondence in traits of human self whether it is the Cry of Peacock, or The City of Death, Calcutta, or the locale of Manori island or sleepy Mirpore of *In Custody*. Desai has used them symbolically. Her novels also abound in recurrent motifs. Even more distinctive feature of Desai's novels is her use of apt images. The recurrent images are from certain well defined areas. For example, we come across animal imagery frequently. Wild animals according to Freud represent human beings whose senses are excited, and hence, evil impulses or passions. The images of traps, bonds and cages are also there. Deven's journey back to Mirpore is a journey from ignorance of reality to its awareness. He tends to replace nightmare by reality illusion, by facets of life.

The sun-image for Deven is symbol of reality. On the morning on which Deven's last hope of getting the recorded interview is shattered, the sun rises in an especially sharp, clear atmosphere. It also notifies his emergence from a timid man into a personality with dignity and strength. The water-image functions as a symbol of Deven's troubled mind and tormented life. The dreariness and vacuity of his existence are reflected in the water.

"He stopped on the canal bank and stared at the water that stopped and turned concentrically in whirlpool at that point. The whirlpool was an opening into the water, leading into its depths." The city itself in the novel images Deven's place of trap and imprisonment. The city's mosque, a symbol of spiritual life of the people in general and Nabard's act of thanksgiving in particular is submerged. Though people pray in the mosque, yet it defined the misery of the people of the town and Deven's wretchedness as an individual. The city imagery is used by Desai to see Deven's plight. Desai uses the image to concretise the process of his defeat and his awareness of reality.

Desai's use of the house to objectify the psyche of the characters is consistent in the novel. The conditions of the Deven's and Nur's house, are used to define and describe each other. Nur's house with its semi-darkness evokes Nur as an antithetical figure. The stair sumbolizes his moral and material prosperity. The house with its dereliction reflects the failure of

Deven's marriage, as well as the couple's insanity. Siddiqui's dilapidated house symbolizes his imprisoned life. His inner discontent and alienated self are evoked through the house which is blackened. The pink house where the recording of Nur's poems and memoirs goes on is on the top. It represents Deven's illusory world.

The image of dome in the novel symbolizes all artistic creation in its intangible form like a bubble in its distance from the concrete reality of the earth, and in its being as silent as breath and yet maintaining a barely perceptible relationship with the conrete reality of the earth from which it emanates. The serenity of the image of the dome is the serenity of artistic creation. Deven reaches a park after walking aimlessly. There sitting on a bench inside the park, he looks at the dome and the eastern walls of the great Friday Mosque. Deven finds an answer to his questions about the significance of poetic art in the image of the dome which he perceives against the background of the sky and in contrast to the earth. The novelist reveals the nature and significance of poetry and of all creative art through this image of the dome of the mosque:

"The white and black marble facing of the eastern doorway made a graceful calligraphic pattern. The enormous arched doorway soared upwards to the dome which rose like a vast bubble that the flat earth had sent out into dusty yellow grey sky, a silent exhalation of stone."

Imagery of City

City life in India, in all its variety and detail, constitutes a large chunk of her writing. Calcutta, New Delhi and Old Delhi, Bombay and Mirpore are not actualities but are the recreated images of the Indian social scene in her various novels. The novel *In Custody* deals with issues like poetry, language and even monetary problems. Desai has taken a shift in this novel from her obsessive, compulsive predilections for and felicity with inner realms of the feminine. She has concentrated upon different objects like fantasy, imagery, irony, etc. In this connection the most important thing is that Anita Desai pictures the city as a trap from which none of her characters escape. In her earlier novel, *Voices in the City,* city evokes the imprisoned life of Nirode Ray, Monisha and Amla.

The city, with its 'dark' pandemonium, 'brutal noises' and demonic voice, adopts the role of 'living spirit'. It frustrates the aims of the protagonists like a powerful adversary.

Likewise in the novel *In Custody* the city itself is as the much a victim of circumstances as the protagonist. But Mirpore is unidentifiable as particular city on the map of India. Deven cannot find a place for himself in such a city. For Deven initially. Delhi was the city of his dreams, of fame and literary achievement. Consequently Delhi is symbolic of fantasy whereas he visualizes Mirpore as a trap. Ironically he is happy to free himself from it but does not know that he is landing himself into another labyrinth.

"The bus soon left Mirpore behind. It comes as a slight sock to Deven that one could so easily and quickly free oneself from what had come to seem to him not only the entire world since he had no existence outside it, but often a cruel trap, or prison, as well, an indestructible prison which there was no escape."

Consequently, the journey from town to city implies no change from one order of reality to another. It is this impossibility of transposing one level for another that makes Deven function. Thus his attempt to escape the stifling world of the small town makes him repeatedly have the nightmare of no exit.

Mirpore as well as Delhi is used to see Deven's plight. The cities themselves cease to be antagonists and are shown as much blighted by the dirt and squalor as the central character Deven in the novel. The city is not a static objectification of one of Deven's qualities but a dynamic vision of his plight. Desai uses the image to concretize the process of his defeat and his awareness of reality. It is used to measure as much his drab and dry existence as to prove the unnatural disorder and corruption in things and people around him.

Deven realizes that his town Mirpore and Nur's Delhi share a common element of decay, decadence and disorder.

"He was thinking that the great city was no different from his own small town and that the dissimilarity lay only in scale: this was certainly larger, noisier, more crowded and chaotic, but that was all, and it was the scale and not the unfamiliarity that made him feel so small weak and inadequate."

Thus we had seen that the city imagery is not an auxiliary ornament in Anita Desai's fiction. She has used it most effectively in the novel *In Custody*. Through this depiction of the city Desai has systematically fused three thematic motives: craze for freedom, imprisonment and death-life. No one can deny the importance of the city in the novel. It is described in much detail, an oppressive city but all the same exercising a powerful influence on all the major character.

Zoological Imagery or Animal Imagery

Desai's use of zoological imagery in the novel *In Custody* predominantly drawn from circus animals deserves all applause and admiration. In this novel Desai makes a considerable progress in the use of zoological imagery. It is significant in two ways. It explodes the predicament of the characters as imprisoned creatures aspiring desperately for their freedom and secondly men are as much starved and harassed as the animals. Animal imagery is woven artistically in the novel. Nur asked Deven "Are you part of his circus?"

From circus image only springs the image when "Nur's wife screeches" in agony and the fight between both the Begums is as between jealous tigresses. Nur's house is the house of ferocious cats. Nur's young wife has reptile hand and for her Deven is a jackal. Her attendants kept a distance as from a poisonous snake. Deven sees for the first time in Nur's house a tap dripped, a broken cycle and a cat slept. These three images explore Nur's indisciplined life and Nur as a broken and useless man and his wife as ferocious tigress.

Besides the circus animals image of imprisonment there is the figure of a dog to describe Deven's dejected and futile life. When Deven visits Nur for the first time, he witnesses the symbols of death and decadence on his way. A dead body of dog, a floating fly in the cup of tea and a group of crows feasting on the dead dog: "He turned and peered out of window to see if the dog lay on the road, broken, bleeding or dead. He saw a flock of crows alight on the yellow grass that grew beside the ditch, their wings flickering across the view like agitated eyelashes." The dead body of dog stands for the putrefying condition of Urdu language in the hands of its new masters, it also bears a resemblance to Nur and his exploitation by his cronies. He identifies his fate with it. This image comes to his mind through the malice and mockery of his wife over the marriage shirt. Therefore he does in the form of an agonized dog. His miserable life with his wife makes him think that he must look like a caged animal in a zoo to any creative that might be tooling down earth from another planet.

Animal imagery used to describe Nur's various attitudes of nervousness, impatience regret and his imprisoned self. Murad tells Deven, "Please windup your circus, send your star performer home." When the poet looks at Deven the circus animal's image is evoked. Even pigeons we see are hungry for Nur's flesh and blood. He was living a pig like life.

Thus there are ample examples of Desai's use of animal imagery or zoological imagery in the novel. Desai is quite in the tradition of literature by making beasts, insects and birds of prey the thematic focus in *In Custody*. She has depicted in an unique manner the ingratitude unkindness and disruption of traditional human values and relationships through zoological imagery. Deven's and Nur's degradation are communicated through this zoological imagery predominantly drawn from the circus and artistically woven in the texture of the novel.

There are some more important symbols like Nur's ailing body symbolically represents the sickening state of Urdu. Apart from this, the use of different symbols and metaphors marks the way the dynamics of motives and mode functions in her novel. Symbols and metaphors are the beautifying components of the novel. Symbol of Surahi appears twice in the novel and in different contexts. First it appears when Deven is singing to himself the poetry of Nur and is nourishing a lingering hope in his heart to make his life worthwhile with his friendship of Nur. Surahi an earthen jar, container of water becomes a reservoir of nectar of life, in search of which Deven is travelling. It holds the promise, fulfillment of Deven's hopes. At another time, towards the end of the novel, Surahi becomes a signifier of impending summer, like a doom waiting for Deven, slicing his throat.

23

Various Episodes of the Novel

Deven's First Meeting with Nur

Deven Sharma, a temporary college lecturer in the department of Hindi, Lala Ram College, Mirpore, travels from Mirpore to Delhi for the purpose of interviewing Nur, a great Urdu poet. Deven reaches Nur's house at a wrong time and disturbs him in his afternoon sleep. Nur becomes annoyed and shouts at him from his room on the upper storey of the building. But at this juncture Deven is unmindful of the insult. Then Nur asks Deven to come upstairs. Still annoyed Nur grumbles that only fools keep him company. Intoxicated with the joy of meeting the object of his worship, Deven imagines that he has achieved the purpose of his life and risen above banality of his former existence. This first meeting places both Nur and Deven within a corrected perspective—Nur is no God, nor is Deven any fool or a court jester but for a few moments in the drama of their meeting we see the superior being—Nur and the nervous admirer and devotee Deven.

Nur feels that Deven has come to torture him by his insane questions and inadvertently recites a line from his own poem which Deven has remembered since his childhood. To his own amazement, Deven begins to recite this poem of Nur, who is impressed by his memory and his chaste pronunciation of Urdu. A mood of ecstasy prevails over him and as he continues reciting Nur's poems, he is transformed into a different being. Deven's first meeting with Nur leads him through a series of tantalizing experiences. He passes through various phases of emotions like hope and despair, shock and expectation, anguish and elation, alienation and belongingness. Even before Deven is able to begin the intended interview, other people come in and encroach upon the joy and intimacy that Deven has been experiencing in the company of Nur. He is filled with disgust when he finds them indulging in drink, and mediocre poetry. Deven feels repulsion at Nur's gluttony and his clumsy manners. The brief spell of joy and recognition of poetic beauty is shattered when Nur calls Hindi 'a fodder chewed by the peasants'. The novelist brings out Deven's disillusionment with his glorious concept of poetry through a highly ironical situation on which he encounters Nur's second wife, Imtiaz Begum and finds Nur lying in an abject condition on the floor of her room. Deven runs away from the world of liquor and vomit. His first-meeting with Nur leaves an indelible impression of horror and disgust on his mind. His bitter experience of his first meeting with Nur makes him perceive a gap between romance and poetry and reality of existence, though for a very short time. In the interview that Deven hopes to have with Nur, he really aspires to experience the bright promises of poetry as against the grey shades of his own incomplete existence. But Nur is already old and has lost much of his creativity at the time of their first meeting although Deven, blinded by his own adulation of the poet and his need to experience greatness and fame through him, refuses to accept this fact. In this self-deception lies much of Deven's later misery and the seeds of Nur's decision to exploit him. In fact, at the first meeting itself Nur identifies him as a possible future victim. "A wrinkled eyelid moved like a turtle's and a small, quick eye peered out at Deven as if at a tasty fly."

The first time when Deven gets out of Nur's clutches, he is happy and reassured to be back in his world, leaving the failed interview behind. After his first visit to Nur, Deven decides to abandon the ideas of having to continue the interview because the sordid aspect of Nur's personal life is too unpalatable for him. In his imagination Deven has pictured Nur living either surrounded by elderly, sage and dignified literary men or else entirely alone in divine isolation. Contrary to this he meets a senile and debilitated old man presiding over a court of clowns and jokers and jugglers. He has lost much of his creatively at the time of meeting. Nur comes to him with all the sordidness of his personal life—his poverty, his age, parasitical companions and his vulturish family. Deven gets disappointed at Nur's house as his all hopes are shattered. He cannot reconcile the impurity of Nur's personal life with the purity of his poetry. Moreover forsaking the project is a face-saving device which suits his temperament and simplifies his existence.

"He had made a timely escape from complexities with which he would not have known how to contend. Compared to the horror of that threat, this grey anonymity was sweet."

He grows apprehensive that his interview with Nur may also turn to dust, spilled blood and laments. In fact Deven had no faith in himself. He is cutely conscious of his lack of courage and the banality of his existence. That's why Deven decides to abandon the idea of interviewing Nur after his first visit to Nur.

Deven's Second Visit to Nur

Anita Desai reveals the subtle nature of the relationship between art and the pecuniary aspect of life through the incident of Deven's second visit to Nur. This subtle relationship between art and money suggests the dependence of art for its survival on money. His second visit to Nur's home also gives him a view of another unpleasant facet of the poet's personal life. A letter from Nur inviting him to be his secretary breaks the spell of his satisfaction with his sweet anonymity. He arrives at Nur's house on the occasion of Imtiaz Begum's Birthday celebrations. The sight of a large gathering at Nur's house relieves him of his fear of being drawn into the vulgarity of the poet's personal life. His hope of listening to Nur is shattered when he finds Imtiaz Begum to be the central figure of the celebration. As he looks at the audience swaying their heads, he looks at them with disgust at their low tastes and is distressed to find Nur alone and abandoned.

Deven finds that Imtiaz Begum has stolen not only Nur's verses but has robbed him also of his wealth and audience. Nur confides this fact of his life to Deven in a moment of sudden intimacy after they have escaped from the boredom of Imtiaz Begum's theatricality to the privacy of Nur's room.

Deven tells Murad that the poet is interested in reading his old poems to him. Murad asks him to get a tape-recorder to tape that treasure of Urdu poetry. Murad leads Deven into the dream of recording Nur's poems and memoirs on the tape and presenting to the world of Urdu literature, not only Nur's words but also his voice. But Deven is dismayed to realize that he cannot afford to buy a tape-recorder. The solution to this problem comes in the form of Abid Siddiqui, the Head of Urdu Department in his college. Deven manages to get him interested in his project of taping the poet's reminiscences and poems, and Mr. Siddiqui manages to persuade the college authorities to sanction funds to buy audio-visual equipments for use in the Department of languages, Deven intends to buy the best equipment. He says, "We must be very careful—Murad—don't let them swindle you." Murad replies that he knows only one thing about tape-recorder and that is their price. He taunts Deven about the meager amount sanctioned by the college.

The dealer seems to know Murad too well. And laughs at Deven by saying "No fancy price? Then how will you get your fancy goods hah?"

But Deven's felicity receives a setback when Murad again deceives him by making him purchase a defective secondhand tape-recorder without consulting him. Deven's ignorance of the use of a tape-recorder burdens him with the liability of engaging a person who may operate it for him. Mr. Jain offers him the help of his imbecile nephew, Chiku, who has the pretensions of skilled technician in electronics. Deven, as he knows nothing about electronics cannot contribute to the conversation regarding the purchase of tape-recorder. Murad too seems ignorant about it but he shouts, "very good. As good as new, Jain sahib, and Japanese also. Deven this is the machine that is going to help you in your project, it is better than a secretary or a type writer or even both together."

Thus the dream of purchase of tape-recorder is proved a fiasco as a second-hand tape-recorder and Deven's ignorance to use it and his dependency on Chiku creates quite a humorous situation.

Incident of Recording the Interview

Encouraged by his friend Murad and a grant from his college authorities, Deven arranges to buy a second-hand tape-recorder to record the interview of great Urdu poet, Nur Shahjehanabadi. But the whole episode assistant Chiku was not knowledgeable enough to record the interview properly. Deven spends the money given by the college authorities not only to produce the recorder but also to feed Nur and gratify the lady who arranges the whole show. Everyone abandons the project. Murad gives an advice and goes away. Mr. Jain just offers him his nephew to help him and Siddiqui simply watches quizzically. Deven apprehends that he would be thrown out of the college for false pretences, misappropriation of funds, and incompetence. The ostensible aim of the entire enterprise is to keep the tapes on which Nur's voice is recorded in the college library for the pleasure and benefit of all lovers of Urdu poetry. But during the interview Chiku misses the genuine portion of the interview and records the nonsense talks about eatables drink and recitation of other poets, work by Nur. Further when the tapes are played they produce neither a coherent dialogue nor the recitation of poems but a nonsensical jumble of voice. Cheated by his friends and suffering from the pangs of failure, Deven feels:

> He could lead the rest of his life in this near-unconscious state. He hoped his former life of non-events, non-happenings, would be resumed, empty and hopeless, safe and endurable.

After the failure of the entire project Deven is under tremendous social pressure. When after taking all kinds of pains Deven reaches Delhi for recording an interview with Nur, he feels, hazardous euphoria trickling through him. But the recording of Nur's reminiscences and poems does not prove to an easy job for him. The poet is not as keen to recite his poems to him as to talk and take rich food and wine. However, whenever the poet is in a good mood and recites without much prompting. Chiku, the technical assistant, is unable to switch on the machine in time for recording. Nur's talks are usually not about poetic inspiration and creation, but about food, wine and women. His students who help him to restore a semblance of coherence in the tapes demand first division marks. Nur writes to him for medical allowance and an endowment for his child from the college authorities. Murad wants him to complete his article on Nur. Reading under various kinds of pressures and demands Deven feels himself trapped under unavoidable circumstances. "He had imagined he was taking Nur's poetry into safe custody, and not realized that if he was to be custodian of Nur's genius, then Nur would become his custodian and place him in custody too."

However Murad again tries to take advantage of Deven's helplessness. He asks him to give him the sole rights of the recorded cassette of Nur so that he may make money out of it. But Deven refuses to do so. From all sides Deven gets only accusations, defeats and threats. The only different and positive thing symbolically depicted by the novelist is his inner turmoil marked by the desire to fight such stale. He becomes restless to come out of this.

Imtiaz Begum, who writes in her own defense, stands out as the most outrageous of these women. In fact, she radically redefines her experience by insisting on telling her story. This character's self-justification has continued in recent years as women writers tell their own stories and that of other women. When women make the lives of real women the centre of their books, they go beyond creating sympathetic female characters. The illicit, self-interested qualities so condemned in earlier fiction become liberating, positive and creative forces.

Desai near the end of her novel presents Nur's young wife's point of view in a letter to Deven, in which she claims that Nur married her because of her 'gifts and abilities', not because of sexual entrapment as had been assumed throughout the novel. She challenges him to read her enclosed Urdu poems and tells him:

> Let me see if you are strong enough to face them and admit to their merit. Or if they fill you with fear and insecurity because they threaten you with danger—danger that your superiority to women may become questionable.... Are you not guilty of assuming that because you are a male, you have a right to brains, talent, reputation, and achievement, while I, because I was born a female, am condemned to find what satisfaction I can have in being maligned, mocked,

> ignored and neglected? Is it not you who has made me play the role of the loose woman in gaudy garments by refusing to take my work seriously and giving me just that much regard that you would extent to even a failure in the arts as long as the artist was male? (p. 196)

Deven's timidity presents her defiant letter from gaining her acceptance in the world of Urdu poetry. Frightened of having to 'enter that world on a mission of mercy or rescue', he tears up her poems. But her angry statements make the reader reevaluate what they previously had only seen through the eyes of a male character. By making women's frustration understandable, Desai subverts her book's primarily unsympathetic portrayals of women which turn out to have been Deven's not the author's perceptions.

Now we see that Imtiaz Begum gains respect as a character by asserting her rights and abilities. Ismail Merchant in an interview with Ameena Meer commented upon the character. "Imtiaz Begum is a very strong, ambitious, and forceful character who writes her own poetry. But she's not as good a poet as Nur. That's why Deven doesn't pay any attention to her. He's totally enamoured of Nur and his work. He knows Imtiaz Begum steals Nur's work, and that is totally unforgivable to him.... I thought she was very sympathetic, particularly when she tells Deven, "You will become a rich man, if only you will give me a chance". The way that scene was done, your heart goes out to Imtiaz. But for me, the story is about Nur and Deven. The rest are all figures on a canvas.

Towards the end of the novel the hour of day break symbolizes the dawn of existentialist awareness in Deven. "The strength of his inner convictions gives him the courage and confidence to make his choice. As he rushes back to his home, he stops only to pull a branch of thorns from under his foot." It is though the symbol of thorns that Anita Desai crystallizes the change is Deven's attitude to the assaults of existence. His present misfortune is no more than a prick of throns to him and the novel ends at this juncture with a positive note showing the courage of Deven to face it. Indeed *In Custody* offers an image of India that is full of hope.

Multiple Choice Questions

(1) Anita Desai published her first novel in the year

(a) 1993 (b) 1963

(c) 1966 (d) 1996

(2) How many novels (till 2003) are written by Anita Desai?

(a) 10 (b) 11

(c) 12 (d) None of the above

(3) On which of her novels did Anita Desai win the Sahitya Academic Award?

(a) *Fire On the Mountain* (b) *In Custody*

(c) *Cry, The Peacock* (d) None of the above

(4) Who is the contemporary of Anita Desai?

(a) Shashi Deshpande

(b) Raja Rao

(c) Lal Behari Dey

(d) Bankim Chandra Chatterjee

(5) Anita Desai is born in the year

(a) 1973 (b) 1935

(c) 1937 (d) 1975

(6) Anita Desai has

(a) German mother and Bengali father

(b) Bengali mother and German father

(c) Hindu mother and German father

(d) None of the above

(7) Which of the Desai's novels was serialized in the *Illustrated Weekly of India* during 1965?

(a) *Cry, The Peacock* (b) *Voices in the City*
(c) *In Custody* (d) None of the above

(8) The latest novel of Anita Desai is
(a) *Fasting Feasting* (b) *Diamond Dust*
(c) *Fire on the Mountain* (d) None of the above

(9) Anita Desai started writing since she was
(a) Three (b) Seventeen
(c) Seven (d) Thirteen

(10) Desai's favorite authors are
(a) Wordsworth and Keats
(b) Chekhov, Henry James and Dostoevsky
(c) Raja Rao and Kamla Das
(d) None of the above

(11) Anita Desai was educated in
(a) Mumbai (b) Boston
(c) Delhi (d) London

(12) Anita Desai has been awarded the Neil Gunn International fellowship in the year
(a) 1994 (b) 1992
(c) 1949 (d) 1984

(13) *In Custody* was short listed for the
(a) National Academy (b) Nobel Prize
(c) Booker Prize (d) Holt by Memorial Prize

(14) *In Custody* was published in the year
(a) 1987 (b) 1988
(c) 1984 (d) None of the above

(15) How many chapters are there in the novel *In Custody*?
(a) Seven (b) Twelve
(c) Eleven (d) Twenty-one

(16) A film was made on this novel by
(a) Shashi Kapoor (b) Mahesh Bhatt
(c) Ismail Merchant (d) None of the above

(17) As a novelist Desai excels in writing
(a) Realistic novel (b) Gothic novel
(c) Adventurous novel (d) Psychological novel

(18) Desai's central preoccupation as a novelist is with the
(a) Existentialist outlook (b) Religious outlook
(c) Social outlook (d) None of the above

(19) The name of the heroine of *In Custody* is
(a) Sarla (b) Maya
(c) Imtiaz Begum (d) None of the above

(20) Deven Sharma is lecturer in
(a) Hindi Department (b) Urdu Department
(c) Delhi College (d) None of the above

(21) Deven and Sarla's marriage was
(a) Love marriage (b) Arrange marriage
(c) Based on mutual understanding (d) All the above

(22) Murad is Deven's
(a) Collegue (b) College friend
(c) Childhood friend (d) Neighbour

(23) Deven's journey from Mirpore to Delhi commences to attain
(a) Money (b) Respect
(c) Job security (d) All of them

(24) The name of the elder wife of Nur is
(a) Sarla (b) Sofia Begum
(c) Imtiaz Begum (d) Mrs. Siddiqui

(25) Deven finds the atmosphere at Nur's residence
(a) Warm (b) Stuffy but comfortable
(c) Quite suffocating (d) Pleasant and entertaining

(26) The name of the little son of Deven is
(a) Manu (b) Chiku
(c) Dhanu (d) Pinkoo

(27) Dhanu is Deven's
(a) Son (b) Servant
(c) Student (d) Friend

(28) Nur had
(a) No son (b) One son
(c) Two daughters (d) No issue

(29) The fund for tape-recorder was given to Deven by
(a) Sarla (b) Jaydev
(c) Nur (d) College

(30) Imtiaz Begum was suffering from
(a) Temperature (b) Asthma
(c) Tuberculosis (d) Malaria

(31) The room for interview was arranged by
(a) Sarla (b) Imtiaz Begum
(c) Safia Begum (d) Unknown lady

(32) Who belongs to family of Nawabs?
(a) Imtiaz Begum (b) Jaydev
(c) Mr. Siddiqui (d) Nur

(33) Desai's irony is
(a) Bitter (b) Satirical
(c) Genial and pure (d) None of the above

(34) Nur quotes from the works of
(a) Premchand (b) Keats
(c) Shelley (d) Keats, Shelley and Byron

(35) Tape-recorder purchased by Deven was
(a) Indian (b) Chinese
(c) Japanese (d) None of the above

(36) "I am surrounded by fools, fools will follow me" who said this?
(a) Mr. Siddiqui (b) Nur
(c) Murad (d) Imtiaz Begum

(37) What was the name of Nur's servant

(a) Dhanu (b) Manu

(c) Ali (d) Chintoo

(38) Nur was fond of

(a) Red meat (b) Soft drinks

(c) Rum and biryani (d) Vegetables

(39) The name of Deven's college is

(a) Mofussil College (b) Mirpore

(c) Lala Ram Lal College (d) None of the above

(40) "I am a beggar myself now, all my jewels stolen away", who is the speaker of this line

(a) Murad (b) Deven

(c) Nur (d) Sarla

(41) "He is a whale in a pail of water" who said this and about whom?

(a) Nur about Murad (b) Murad about Deven

(c) Siddiqui about Nur (d) Deven about Nur

(42) Who was Mr. Jain?

(a) A fruit seller (b) A shopkeeper

(c) A teacher (d) Deven's friend

(43) Who was the resourceful little bird with the black, bright eye?

(a) An eagle (b) Mr. Siddiqui

(c) Register (d) Manu

(44) Who knows all the dancer's tricks?

(a) Imtiaz Begum (b) Sarla

(c) Safia Begum (d) Mrs. Jain

(45) 'Chotu' is the name of

(a) Deven's student (b) Siddiqui's servant

(c) Deven's son (d) Nur's son

(46) The name of the journal edited by Murad is

(a) *Delhi Times* (b) *Urdu Magazine*

(c) *Awaaz* (d) *Nur's Awaaz*

(47) Who accompanied Deven to Mirpore?

(a) Pinto (b) Murad

(c) Chiku (d) A dog

(48) Who was in the custody?

(a) Murad (b) Nur

(c) Deven (d) Deven and Nur both

(49) 'He ran stopping only to pull a branch of thorn under his foot' indicates

(a) Deven was in a hurry

(b) Deven's foot was wounded

(c) The place was full of thorns

(d) Deven's present misfortune is no more than a prick of thorns to him

(50) When Deven first visit Nur's house he sees three things, what are they?

(a) Cat, pigeons and dog

(b) A tap dripped, a broken cycle and a cat slept

(c) Louts, lasagnas and beggars

(d) A broken cycle, two tigresses and a cat

(51) The shortest novel of Desai is

(a) *Where Shall We Go This Summer?*

(b) *Fire On the Mountain*

(c) *In Custody*

(d) *Cry, The Peacock*

(52) How many times Anita Desai was nominated for 'Booker Prize'?

(a) Four (b) Three

(c) Two (d) One

(53) Has Anita Desai written beautiful poetry?
(a) Yes (b) No
(c) Sometimes (d) None of the above

(54) Who is the shopkeeper?
(a) Chiku (b) Murad
(c) Pintoo (d) Mr. Jain

(55) Novel *In Custody* has
(a) Positive ending (b) Negative ending
(c) Melodramatic ending (d) None of the above

(56) Deven wanted to buy
(a) Gold bangles for Sarla (b) A house for himself
(c) Toys for his son
(d) Gold necklace for his mother

(57) Deven comes from
(a) Higher class
(b) Upper-middle class background
(c) Lower-middle class background
(d) Poor class

(58) The name of Urdu teacher in Deven's college is
(a) Mr. Jain (b) Mr. Trevedi
(c) Mr. Srivastava (d) Mr. Siddiqui

(59) The address of Deven is
(a) 11D/96 (b) 68 P. House
(c) D11/69 (d) 12/24

(60) Deven's colony was named after a leader of
(a) Harijans (b) Brahman
(c) Dalit (d) None of the above

(61) Deven is by nature
(a) An introvert (b) An extrovert
(c) An philanderer (d) None of the above

(62) Nur lived in

(a) Hawa Mahal (b) Chandni Chowk

(c) Qutub Minar (d) Cannaught Place

(63) Who is known as small vicious ferret of a man?

(a) Mr. Siddiqui (b) Murad

(c) Mr. Trevedi (d) Nur

(64) What was the day when Murad came to Deven first of all?

(a) Wednesday (b) Monday

(c) Thursday (d) Sunday

(65) Who is called 'two-cigarette man'?

(a) Nur (b) Murad

(c) Deven (d) Mr. Siddiqui

(66) Murad was the son of a

(a) Poor widow

(b) Wealthy service man

(c) Wealthy Kashmiri carpet dealer

(d) Cloth merchant

(67) Deven's father was

(a) A school teacher (b) A rich manager

(c) A poor rickshaw puller (d) None of the above

(68) In the first scene Deven as a Hindi teacher was teaching the poetry of

(a) Sumitranandan Pant

(b) Subhadra Kumari Chauhan

(c) Jaishankar Prasad

(d) Mahadevi Verma

(69) Who called Hindi, 'that vegetarian monster'?

(a) Nur (b) Murad

(c) Deven (d) Pintoo

(70) 'He is like a comet into the dark' who said this and about whom?

(a) Nur about Murad (b) Murad about Nur

(c) Deven about Nur (d) Siddiqui about Nur

(71) Deven has written a monograph about Nur, what is a monograph?

(a) A long poem

(b) A fiction work

(c) A detailed written study of a single particular subject

(d) None of the above

(72) Mirpore was

(a) A hill station near Delhi

(b) A formless/shapeless town without any

(c) River or hill

(d) None of the above

(73) What was a trap for Deven

(a) City of Mirpore (b) His family

(c) His Marriage (d) All of the above

(74) The educational qualification of Deven was

(a) He was a graduate

(b) He was a post-graduate

(c) He had a Ph.D. degree in Hindi

(d) None of the above

(75) Murad's office was there in

(a) Kashmiri Gate, Delhi (b) Chandni Chowk, Delhi

(c) Mirpore Cantt (d) None of the above

(76) When Deven had drunk tea to the bottom of the glass he saw a

(a) Small coin

(b) Dead fly floating in the dregs of his tea

(c) A mosquito

(d) None of the above

(77) The signboard outside the Murad's office was

(a) Awaaz

(b) K.K. Sahay Sons Printers and Publishers since 1935

(c) Murad's office

(d) The Urdu Magazine

(78) At the time of his first meeting with Nur Deven finds him

(a) Entirely dressed in black

(b) Entirely dressed in white

(c) Entirely dressed in black and white

(d) Entirely dressed in multi-coloured clothes

(79) The full name of Murad is

(a) Murad Beg (b) Murad Ali

(c) Murad Sharma (d) Murad Shahjehanabadi

(80) Nur called Hindi as

(a) Peasant language

(b) Fodder chewed by peasants

(c) Language of fools

(d) Royal language

(81) Name the Hindi picture whose songs Nur considered to be better than Urdu poetry

(a) Don (b) Sholay

(c) Kalia (d) None of these

(82) "You are like a star fallen into the well of the courtyard" who said this and about whom?

(a) Nur about Deven

(b) Deven about Nur

(c) Audience about Imtiaz Begum

(d) Imtiaz Begum about Nur

(83) Who called Deven 'A Village Pumpkin'

(a) A student (b) Murad

(c) Nur (d) All the above

(84) Sarla regularly performed puja before a tinted oleograph of the

(a) Goddess Lakshmi (b) Goddess Saraswati

(c) Lord Rama (d) Lord Krishana

(85) Chiku wanted to leave the work of recording because

(a) Of his sister's marriage (b) His marriage

(c) He was getting bore (d) None of these

(86) Where was the Nur's flat in Delhi?

(a) Cannaught Place (b) Darya Ganj

(c) Chandni Chowk (d) None of these

(87) The epigraph prefixed to the novel *In Custody* has been taken from

(a) Wordsworth's *Rao Roy's Grave*

(b) Wordsworth's lyrical Ballads

(c) Greay's Elegy

(d) None of the above

(88) What happens with Deven in the end?

(a) Deven dies peacefully

(b) He leaves his job

(c) Mr. Siddiqui gives him money

(d) None of the above

(89) *In Custody* was short listed for the Booker prize in the year

(a) 1984 (b) 2002

(c) 1986 (d) 1988

(90) Who was Raj?

(a) Deven's cousin

(b) Sarla's childhood friend

(c) Deven's old school friend born with one leg

(d) Murad's employee

(91) Where was Raj's house?

(a) A flat in New Delhi (b) Mirpore

(c) London (d) None of the above

(92) What was the news about Raj, received by Deven?

(a) Raj was a rich man

(b) Raj was teaching in a school in Cairo

(c) Raj was coming to Mirpore

(d) None of the above

(93) Who was handicapped?

(a) Tailor (b) Raj

(c) Imtiaz Begum (d) Raj's aunt

(94) Who accompanied Raj's aunt in her house?

(a) Deven (b) Murad

(c) A tailor who worked in a small shop under the staircase

(d) None of these

(95) The tailor played part of

(a) Devotional singer (b) A cook

(c) A priest (d) None of the above

(96) "Let more such fish fall into my net and I will be able to move out of Darya Ganj" who is the speaker of this line?

(a) Nur (b) Deven

(c) Murad (d) Tailor

(97) Who threatened Deven to pay the bills for the room taken on rent?

(a) Murad (b) Policeman

(c) Nur (d) Bulu clad in a lungi

(98) Name the title of the recently released Hindi film printed on the shirt of the Pintu

(a) Love Story (b) Chachi 420

(c) Yadeyn (d) Ashiqui

(99) What was the demand of the Pintu while going back to Delhi?

(a) Five hundred rupees (b) A pair of shoes
(c) Bus fare to Delhi (d) None of the above

(100) What was the subject of Jayadev's colleague Vijay Sud who got job in America?

(a) English (b) History
(c) Bio-Chemistry (d) Hindi

ANSWERS

(1) B	(2) B	(3) A	(4) A	(5) C
(6) A	(7) B	(8) A	(9) C	(10) B
(11) C	(12) A	(13) C	(14) C	(15) C
(16) C	(17) D	(18) A	(19) A	(20) A
(21) B	(22) C	(23) C	(24) B	(25) C
(26) A	(27) C	(28) B	(29) D	(30) A
(31) C	(32) C	(33) C	(34) D	(35) C
(36) B	(37) C	(38) C	(39) C	(40) C
(41) C	(42) B	(43) B	(44) A	(45) B
(46) C	(47) A	(48) D	(49) D	(50) B
(51) A	(52) C	(53) B	(54) D	(55) A
(56) A	(57) C	(58) D	(59) A	(60) A
(61) A	(62) B	(63) C	(64) B	(65) C
(66) C	(67) A	(68) A	(69) B	(70) B
(71) C	(72) B	(73) D	(74) A	(75) A
(76) B	(77) B	(78) B	(79) A	(80) B
(81) B	(82) C	(83) B	(84) A	(85) A
(86) B	(87) A	(88) D	(89) A	(90) C
(91) A	(92) B	(93) B	(94) C	(95) A
(96) D	(97) D	(98) A	(99) C	(100) C

True or False

(1) Anita Desai's father was Bengali and her mother German.

(2) The person with betel-stained teeth and bristling moustache is the hero of the novel—Deven.

(3) When Murad came to Mirpore to see Deven it was Friday.

(4) *In Custody* was shortlisted for the 1984 Booker Prize.

(5) Mirpore is a hill-station in the novel *In Custody.*

(6) Anita Desai explores the inner psyche of human beings.

(7) Marriage, his family and his job had placed Deven in a sort of trap, a cage.

(8) Murad was the son of a wealthy fruit merchant.

(9) The novel *In Custody* is a departure in the sense that it deals mainly with the male characters.

(10) Deven was an unsuccessful teacher.

(11) The relationship between Sarla and Deven was a satisfactory relationship.

(12) Sarla was a pessimistic wife.

(13) Towards the end of the novel, the hour of day break symbol sizes the down of existentialist awareness in Deven.

(14) Deven's marriage was a love marriage.

(15) Nur's elder wife stands for duty and the second one for love.

(16) Nur refuses to give interview to Deven due to the illness of Imtiaz Begum.

(17) Anita Desai's irony is mild, genial, pure and solid and chiefly related to human life.

(18) The very title of the novel points to the central irony that means guardianship and not a physical prison.

(19) The language controversy of Hindi and Urdu is one of the major themes of the novel *In Custody*.

(20) Deven always wants to take Nur into his custody.

(21) Mr. Siddiqui arranges money to buy the tape-recorder from his own pocket.

(22) Desai's irony is nowhere mild.

(23) In the novel *In Custody* the narrative mode is characterised by Satvi.

(24) The novel *In Custody* revolves around Trevedi's effort to interview the great poet Nur.

(25) Deven is an Urdu teacher.

(26) In *In Custody* there is the figure of a tiger to describe Deven's dejected and futile life.

(27) Anita Desai's characters are generally neurotic females.

(28) Anita Desai has made extensive use of stream of consciousness technique in her novels.

(29) Desai also makes use of poetry to convey the meaning more effectively.

(30) The plot of the novel *In Custody* is intricately connected with the character of Deven and Nur.

(31) Desai never makes use of certain Hindi words in her dialogues.

(32) Mr. V.K. Sahay is the owner of the journal *Awaaz*.

(33) Mr. Jain is a Shopkeeper. Who sold second-hand tape-recorder to Deven.

(34) Chintu and Pintu are Deven's students.

(35) Dhanu wanted to get good marks from Deven.

(36) Tailor lives near the house of Raj in Delhi. He was ladies-specialist tailor by profession.

(37) Raj is the colleague of Deven in Hindi Department.

(38) Murad is the editor of an Urdu magazine *Awaaz*.

(39) According to Nur, Urdu died long ago in 1947 and only its ghost exists in India.

(40) During the journey the dog crushed by the bus signals an ill omen.

ANSWERS

(1) T	(2) F	(3) F	(4) T
(5) F	(6) T	(7) T	(8) F
(9) T	(10) T	(11) T	(12) T
(13) T	(14) F	(15) T	(16) T
(17) T	(18) T	(19) T	(20) F
(21) F	(22) F	(23) F	(24) F
(25) F	(26) F	(27) T	(28) T
(29) T	(30) T	(31) F	(32) F
(33) T	(34) F	(35) T	(36) T
(37) F	(38) T	(39) T	(40) T

Bibliography

Acharya, Shanta, "Problems of the Self in the Novels of Anita Desai". *Exploration in Modern Indo-English Fiction.* (Ed.) R.K. Dhawan, New Delhi: Bahari Publications, 1982.

Asnanai, Shyam Mohan, "Anita Desai's Fiction: A New Dimension". *Indian Literature XXIV.* March-April, 1981.

——, "Contribution of Women in Indo-English Novel". *Treveni.* July-Sept., 1975.

Bala, Suman and Pabby, D.K. (Eds.), *The Fiction of Anita Desai,* Vol. I & II. New Delhi: Khosla Publishing House, 2002.

Bande, Usha, *The Novels of Anita Desai.* New Delhi: Prestige Books, 1988.

Beauroir, Simon De and Freedom, Betty, "Sex, Society and the Female Dilemma: A Dialogue". London: *Saturday Review.*

Belliappa, Meena, *Anita Desai: A Study of Her Fiction.* Calcutta: Writers Workshop, 1971.

Bhatnagar, Parvati, "The Theme of Man-Woman Relationship in the Novels of Anita Desai". *The Fiction of Anita Desai,* Vol. I. New Delhi: Khosla Publishing House, 2002.

Budholia, O.P., *Anita Desai: Vision and Techniques in Her Novels.* Delhi: B.R. Publications, 2001.

Chaddah, R.P., "Symbols and Cities of Anita Desai". *The Tribune,* June 13, 1992.

Chaudhary, Indranath, "Indianness in Indian Literature". *Comparative Indian Literature.* New Delhi: Sterling Publishers, 1992.

Chttopadhaya, Kamla, *The Awakening of Indian Women.* 1939.

Dalmiya, Yasodhara, "An Interview with Anita Desai". *The Times of India.* Sunday Edition, April 19, 1979.

Desai, Anita, "The Indian Writers Problems". *Exploration in Modern Indo-English Fiction.* New Delhi: Bahari Publication Pvt. Ltd., 1982.

——, *In Custody,* New Delhi: Penguin Books India (P) Ltd., 1984.

——, "Contemporary English Literature in India". *Literary Criterion.* Jan., 1982.

——, "Replies to the Questionnaire". *Kakatiya Journal in English Studies.* Vol. 3, No. 1, 1978.

Dwevedi, A.N., *Papers on Indian Writings in English.* Vol. II, Delhi: Amar Prakashan, 1991.

——, *Studies in Contemporary Indian Fiction.* Allahabad: Kitab Mahal, 1987.

Gupta, Santosh, "Bridging the Polarities of Imagination and Reason in Clear Light of the Day". *The Fiction of Anita Desai* (Ed.) R.K. Dhawan.

Jain, Jasbir, "Anita Desai Interviewed". *Rajasthan University Studies in English,* XII, 1979.

——, "Anita Desai". *Indo-English Novelist.* (Ed.) Madhusudan Prasad. New Delhi: Prestige Books, 1989.

——, "The Use of Fantasy in the Novels of Anita Desai". *Exploration in Modern Indo English Fiction.* (Ed.) R.K. Dhawan. New Delhi: Bahari Publisher, 1982.

Kripal, Viney, "The Perfect Bubble: A Study of Anita Desai's *In Custody*". *Image of India in the Indian Novel in English,* 1993.

Krishna, Swamy Shanta, "Anita Desai: The Sexist Nature of Sanity". *The Woman in Indian Fiction in English.* New Delhi: Ashish Publishing House, 1984.

Lal, Malashri, "Literary Feminism in India: In Search of Theory". The Tribune News Services, *The Tribune.* June 16, 2001.

Lawrence, D.H., "Morality and the Novel". *20th Century Literary Criticism.* (Ed.) David Lodge. London: Longman, 1972.

Maini, Darshan Singh, "The Achievement of Desai". *Indo English Literature.* (Ed.) K.K. Sharma, Ghaziabad: Vimal Prakashan, 1970.

Pathak, R.S. (Ed.), *Indian Fiction in English: Problems and Promises.* New Delhi: Northern Books Centre, 1990.

Pathak, R.S., "Alienated Self in the Novel of the Anita Desai". *The Fiction of Anita Desai.* (Ed.) R.K. Dhawan, New Delhi: Bahari Publication, 1989.

Prasad, Madhusudan, *Anita Desai: The Novelist.* Allahabad: New Horizon, 1981.

Raizada, Harish, *Indian English Novelists: Some Points of View.* Delhi: K.K. Publishers, 1996.

Ram, Atma, "An Interview with Anita Desai". *World Literature Written in English.* Nov., 1977.

Rao, B. Ramachandra, *The Novels of Anita Desai: A Study.* New Delhi: Kalyani Publishers, 1972.

Sharma, K.K. (Ed.), *Indo English Literature: A Collection of Critical Essays.* Ghaziabad: Vimal Prakashan.

Sharred, Paul, "Tradition and Tragedy: Anita Desai and R.K. Narayan". *Australian and Indian Literature: Studies in Mutual Response.*

Srivastava, Romesh K. (Ed.), *Perspectives on Anita Desai.* Ghaziabad: Vimal Prakashan, 1984.

Tripathi, J.P., *The Mind and Art of Anita Desai.* Bareilly: Prakash Book Depot, 1987.